A SWEET, SOFT GLOW

JOSH MAGNOTTA

Copyright © 2020 by Josh Magnotta

All rights reserved.

No part of this book may be reproduced in any form or by any electronic or mechanical means, including information storage and retrieval systems, without written permission from the author, except for the use of brief quotations in a book review.

Although inspired from historical events and including actual historical figures, all characters within this book are fiction. Any resemblance to persons living or dead is pure coincidence.

Cover design by Emily's World of Design

Published by Fyresyde Publishing

ISBN: 9798694505451 (kindle edition)

I would like to dedicate this book to my wife Victoria without whom none of this would be possible. My parents for believing in me and encouraging me. Sierra for being my first audience. Alex, Anna, Jorge and Becky for all your support along the way. And also to FyreSyde for guiding me through this process.

Foreword

To know when the world will end is a desire that permeates society. From fear or fascination, those yearnings have led to many failed prophecies and misplaced assumptions. But, will anyone recognize the apocalypse?

Prologue

ASHES SWIRLED amid the smoke and floated into the night sky as John Malley tossed more paper onto the flames. The notes blackened and burned quickly. As each page ignited, a part of the past was erased.

It's easier this way.

It was hard to focus on creating when everything he loved was gone. Any passion John had for the bracelets died with Abigail and Helena. Even if Harry had lived, John couldn't work with him again. Not after that night. The man that killed John's family was not the friend he spent years working with.

He was always nervous about selling the bracelets. He worried that they would be too expensive. I guess he wasn't wrong.

John watched the fire flicker and dance within the barrel. The blueprints disintegrated into black dust. He threw more pages onto the fire. Nothing could remain.

It wasn't as cathartic as he had hoped, but it was the closest thing to closure. Now if he could just forget everything, maybe he could be happy.

He tossed the last few papers into the barrel. His medical degree burned blue as the ink melted down the paper. He wasn't a doctor. He couldn't help himself, let alone anyone else. Part of that was stubbornness, but the other part was knowing the truth of that night.

Yes, Harry had killed Abby and Elly, but it may as well have been John himself. That wasn't something that could be solved with a therapist. It was something he would have to live with for the rest of his life.

Chapter One

Harry

I WILL FIND HIM. I must. He is the only one who knows. These thoughts and many others ran circles through Harry Davis's mind.

From his perch atop an old evergreen, he glanced at the group of three gathered below. They were the first wrist watchers. The black armband along their left arms shone in the sun's rays. It was different from the bracelets they had created years ago, but John would recognize their work if he looked for it.

Soon, Harry would activate the other armbands and set his plan in motion. For now, he needed to find John Malley.

It should never have taken this long. The rage inside him climbed.

Harry knew that John didn't want to be found. Nonetheless, after years of searching, he believed he had finally tracked down his old friend.

Determined to go through with his plan, Harry decided tomorrow would be the final day he'd spend searching for John. He couldn't wait any longer. Suspicions concerning the armbands proved too great a risk. It had to be now.

He dropped from the branch and felt the wind beneath his

wings as he gently came to rest by his three assistants waiting for him. He said nothing but looked each one in the eye. His thoughts alone would be enough to guide them. And there was only one thought on Harry's mind. Find John and kill him.

The group departed, and Harry watched them leave in silence.

Chapter Two

John

ANOTHER LONG NIGHT FINISHED, John Malley was exhausted and ready for sleep, but a cold beer and a shot or two of whiskey sounded perfect right about now.

The coffee brewing in Ted's Dead Rose Tavern was a welcome scent as John opened the door. Depending on who you were, you could get in before the bar opened and talk with Ted over coffee. If you were on really good terms, he might even fry up a couple of eggs for you.

John happened to be one of the lucky few. Only he wasn't looking for coffee. The heavy wood door slammed shut as his mud-splattered, and glass encrusted boots shuffled toward the empty bar.

"Bushmills and a Coors," he told Ted as he took his seat at his usual stool, where Ted already had the drinks waiting.

"Another long one?" he asked, already knowing the answer.

John looked at the shot and smiled. His gaze drifted up to Ted; his light blue eyes rested easily on the friendly face behind the counter. He took a deep breath and exhaled long and slow before he raised the shot glass. He downed the shot and savored the flavor as well as the kick.

"You cut yourself last night?" Ted asked, pointing to John's hand.

"Damn it, I didn't even notice," he muttered, looking down at his hand.

"You got a towel back there?"

"Yea, no problem. That glass sneaks up on ya, don't it?" Ted remarked as he grabbed a towel from behind the bar and lobbed it at John.

"Keep it," he said.

John wiped the blood from a cut on the back of his hand and pulled the culprit out of the wound; a glass shard about half an inch long.

John laughed, then sighed. "I guess so. It wouldn't be Friday unless I cut myself, would it?" He pulled out a pack of Marlboro's from the front pocket of his red flannel jacket and lit a cigarette. Tilting the pack over the bar, he offered one to Ted, who grudgingly took one.

"I really shouldn't," Ted said with a hint of regret in his voice.

"Well, then give it back ya bastard! You know these aren't cheap," John laughed as he lit Ted's cigarette.

Ted laughed and shook his head as he relished the camaraderie and tolerated the cigarette.

They had been friends for a few years now after John did some work on Ted's old truck. Since then, John stopped by in the mornings when he got off work from the glass plant down the road.

Vanceload Industries was nearly a hundred years old and the only factory left in Watsonfield. There was always talk they were going to close the doors, but so far, that was still only talk.

The work was hard and often went unappreciated. More often than not, John walked out with more than one cut and multiple burns for his night of work. Not to mention the heat; which was brutal even on the night shift.

John remembered his first night in the basement, making cullet, which is the broken-down glass used for remelting. There had been a thunderstorm that night. Water poured through cracks in the cinderblock walls. When the water met the heat from the machines transporting the broken glass, it steamed immediately. The basement had been like walking through a miserable haze.

John had grown accustomed to the work, but it was management that got under his skin. He didn't mind busting his ass day in and day out. It was actually the reason he liked the job. But, the foreman constantly looking over his shoulder made the work drudgery.

"Another double-shift?" Ted asked.

"Yeah. That new fucker they hired isn't working out worth a damn. He called off again yesterday, and I had to cover for his ass," John answered as he set his cigarette in the ashtray next to him.

"Seems like they can't get any good help," Ted said.

John took a swallow of the Coors and closed his eyes, relishing the taste. Ted walked into the kitchen, leaving John to enjoy his beer for a few minutes while he fried up some eggs and sausage.

Even with the TV on in the background, the bar was a haven of quiet solitude compared to the incessant cacophony of machinery at the factory. This had become his favorite spot, soaking in the silence in the early dawn hours as the world just started to wake up.

He was already finished with his eight-hour shift as much of the world started theirs. That sense of accomplishment almost made him forget the nightly struggle.

The TV droned on, talking about some new legislation that had just passed.

Uninterested in something he didn't understand, John got up and walked around the bar and changed the channel to the sports network so he could watch something hopefully without politics.

The ESPN logo popped up, and the anchors were saying they would be right back after a commercial break.

A young woman with a black band on her arm appeared on screen. She flowed effortlessly between different sports, showing off the armband. Just another commercial. John sighed and walked back around the other side of the bar.

He returned to his stool to take another sip of the beer. Outside it was still dark; the street lamps were the only light in the falling rain.

Sleep will come easily today.

He looked down at his hand where he had cut it last night. The blood had congealed and closed up the wound. Soon, it would be just another scar.

Ted yelled something unintelligible from the kitchen, and John pretended not to hear him. He sighed and took a long drag on his cigarette, slowly exhaling the blue-grey smoke and gazing blearily eyed through the fog at the liquors behind the counter.

Ted set two plates of steaming hot sausage and eggs down on the bar, then returned to the kitchen for coffee.

"You are too kind." John picked up his fork and tore a chunk off the sausage.

"It's the least I can do. Life ain't been too kind to neither of us," Ted remarked and started eating the eggs.

They talked about sports for the next hour while they ate. Ted took the plates to the kitchen, and John watched the commercials through half-closed eyes. He noticed the armband in a different commercial and thought of the marketing that must go into such an ugly accessory.

A yawn emanated from some deep pit within, and he knew it was time to get some sleep. He got up lazily and strolled to the kitchen door.

Ted had his back to the entrance as he cleaned the plates from their breakfast. John leaned against the doorframe and watched the older man clean the dishes. The chore probably could have waited, but John admired the bartender's diligence. Slowly, his gaze drifted across the small kitchen. Skillets and steel mixing bowls were stacked on shelves to the right above the flat top. At first, the kitchen equipment seemed disorganized and shoved out of the way, but as John looked at the shelves, he realized everything had its place.

"I'm gonna head out, man," he called.

"You're coming back tonight, yea?" Ted asked.

"Assume so, why?"

"Just making sure. I'll hide the rest of that bottle of Bushmills if it gets too low."

"You're always looking out for my best interest," John replied.

"Keep them happy, and they'll keep coming back."

"I'll remember that," John said, "Later."

He walked back across the barroom, his boots echoing louder than usual on the hardwood floor in the early morning stillness.

He stepped outside and smelled the clean rain pouring down. It made a mud pit of the dirt parking lot. The water splashed onto his already filthy boots as he crossed the potholed lot toward his old single cab pickup.

He glanced back at Ted's tavern. From the outside, the bar wasn't much to look at, but it was one of his favorite views in this dirty old town.

The drive home was short, just ten miles on Route 17, then east down a dirt road heading out of Watsonfield. That was where John's single-story house waited for him. It was a shabby house, and John loathed the place. On more than one occasion, he had considered burning it to the ground. But it worked for what he needed.

The rain was still pouring down as he pulled into his dirt driveway. He hoped it would last a little longer so he could get to sleep easily.

As he got out of the truck and walked to the house, the only thing on his mind was a hot shower and some sleep.

He climbed the steps to his dilapidated house and pushed open the front door.

The joys of small-town life, John thought, one needn't lock their doors.

John strode across the small living room to the couch where he kicked off his boots. He sank into the soft cushion and could have fallen asleep. But caked with sweat and glass dust as he was, he wanted a shower. So, he forced himself up.

Grabbing a Coors from the refrigerator, John made his way down the narrow hall to the bathroom. He set the beer on the top shelf in the shower, turned the water on, undressed, and stepped in. The water was warm and felt good on his back. He turned around and let it rain over his head and down his face. Nothing felt so good as a hot shower after a long night of work.

After a minute of just absorbing the warm comfort of the water, he reached for his beer and cracked it open. He took a long sip and set what remained back on the shelf before he began washing.

Sometimes it's the little things that are the most rewarding; he thought as he enjoyed the water. He turned the faucet to cold and relished the chill on his skin as goosebumps rose along his arms and thighs. The cold water shocked the body, but it felt good. He took a slow deep breath, and he turned the water off.

As water dripped from him, he grabbed the Coors and drained the last few sips. Then he dried off and walked naked out of the bathroom to his left, away from the kitchen and living room, to his bedroom on the backside of the house. Water still dripped from his dark hair, which was streaked with grey and needed cut, long waves fell back from his forehead to the nape of his neck like a lion's mane.

He had aged remarkably well and only had slight pains in his joints now and again. His muscular chest and shoulders could have easily been mistaken for a man half his age. His stomach was flat, lacking the characteristic paunch of an alcoholic. The long muscles of his back and shoulders showed prominently beneath the skin.

John entered the room and finished drying his feet on the carpet. The bedroom was small, with only space enough for a mattress and dresser with a small closet in the corner. The ceiling was low, leaving only a couple inches above John's head.

On the dresser, sat a bottle of Evan Williams half gone.

Winnowing the amber liquid within, he hesitated for just a second, then he twisted the cap off and took a long swallow.

As he set the bottle down, his brow furrowed, and he sighed as he glanced miserably at the diminished supply. He would need to buy more.

He lay down on the bed. His mind was a haze. When he moved, the world around him lagged some. Exhaustion and booze had taken their toll, exactly as he had planned. He didn't like to stay sober long.

The last thing he saw was the alarm clock on the dresser which read 10:43 a.m. Where did the day go? Where did the time go?

THE MUSIC WAS HAPPY, *filled with the joy that only summer brought. John looked into the rearview mirror at his only daughter, Helena, Elly for short, fast approaching eleven.*

It seemed like only yesterday he and Abby were saying their vows, running down the church steps as friends and family peppered them with rice laughing like fools.

In the back seat, John could see Elly smile whenever his eyes met hers in the mirror's reflection. Her eyes were just like his, light blue. Her hair was her mother's, though, golden brown waves with strawberry blonde highlights shining in the summer sun.

The day offered the perfect weather for a party to celebrate the culmination of years of work completed by John and his friend Harry. It all began back in college when Harry's mother developed dementia. Following the diagnosis, the men worked tirelessly to find a cure. Now, their research and trials were finished, and it was time to celebrate.

John reached over and touched his wife's thigh as she gazed out the window.

At thirty-five, she was more beautiful than ever. There was a glow about her all the time. He could not describe it, but wherever she was, it was a little brighter because of her presence. She had a huge smile and a contagious laugh that started as a giggle but soon had the whole room in bouts of laughter. She had a way of making the darkest rooms warm and light.

Abby averted her gaze, their eyes met. Behind her sunglasses, John could see the love in his wife's eyes. She reached up and cupped his chin in her hand then drew him close for a brief kiss.

As their lips parted, her hand left John's jaw. His eyes were still closed, living in a moment that would never end. Abby lightly pushed his head forward so he was looking at the road once again.

"Pay attention," she said with a flirting smile.

Their vehicle was only just starting to pass over the white line now; John straightened the wheel. Her hand was on his thigh; the day was beautiful.

He smiled broadly. Life with his two favorite women was perfect.

Then the scene shifted; they were on the patio behind Harry's house. Elly was lying limp in John's arms. Behind them, Abby was already dead.

Elly's dress was soaked with blood where the bullet had entered her body. A dark pool formed beneath her. Her eyes flickered open.

"Daddy?" she cried weakly, tears streaming down her cheeks.

Everything had happened so fast.

"Daddy, what happened? Where's mommy?" she moaned.

John fought a losing battle against his tears.

"It's okay, honey. She'll be right back. Daddy's right here, baby, I got you."

"Is she okay?" Elly stuttered through ragged breaths. "Daddy, I'm dizzy."

John tried to ease his daughter's worry as he brushed the hair from her forehead.

"Mommy's ok. You are going to be fine."

Elly lifted her head slightly to look for her mother. In doing so, she saw the dark stain upon her dress. Then her eyes grew big as she realized what was happening.

"Daddy! Daddy, I don't want to die, I-I don't want to d-d-d-die," Elly jerked and sputtered. Her voice was raspy as she tried to speak and squirm away from the blood.

John pulled her close. He buried his face in her wavy locks of hair and kissed her head. He raised his gaze and searched nearby for anyone who could help. But there was no one.

He turned his eyes back to his daughter. The bloodstain was growing larger. She would die from blood loss before they even made it to a hospital. All he could do was comfort her.

"Daddy, I'm scared," she cried.

"It's okay, El," he said before placing a gentle kiss on her forehead. Then soft and low, like every night, he sang to her. "You're my pretty little girl, so don't you cry cause daddy's gonna sing a lullaby."

Elly's eyes were filled with tears, but a smile formed at the corner of her lips.

"Golden slumbers kiss your eyes, smiles await you when you rise. Sleep, pretty baby. Don't you cry, Daddy's gonna be here when you rise."

Elly reached up and wiped a tear from John's face.

"Daddy, I don't want to die," Elly breathed to her father.

"I know, baby. Try not to think about it. Just close your eyes like you're going to sleep. It's just a dream."

"It's just a dream," she muttered as her eyes slid closed.

"Sleep, pretty baby. Don't you cry, Daddy's gonna be here when you rise," John sang once more. He ran his fingers through her soft hair and kissed her forehead while tears rolled down his face. Elly died peacefully in her father's arms.

"Elly," he cried.

THE FOGGY HAZE of his dreams faded slowly, giving way to the bedroom. He felt the tears roll down his cheeks and dried them away.

His alarm clock read 11:27 a.m. *Not even an hour.* There would be no more rest.

John rolled out of bed. It was useless to try to sleep more. He was now stuck between the agony of exhaustion and the fear of sleep. If he could control his dream, perhaps he would have, but his dreams were only memories, and he couldn't change what happened.

Instead of staying in bed, he went to the bathroom, washed his face, and after a glance in the mirror, decided he needed a haircut. It was time. While dressing, he glanced out the window and noticed the rain had lessened to barely a drizzle. It would have been a nice day to sleep hard, he thought.

John grabbed a book from his shelf on the way out the door, knowing he would have time to kill at the barbershop. He picked at random and came away with *For Whom the Bell Tolls*. Kind of dense for sitting in a barbershop, he thought, but he brought it anyway.

Spring was in full bloom. The smell of lilacs and wet grass permeated the drive to Watsonfield; their scents made stronger by the storm.

Watsonfield sprang up around a particularly sharp corner on the road. If you didn't know better, you would think the town was trying to hide within the forest. Indistinguishable from most other small towns you find in rural Pennsylvania, Watsonfield boasted the usual repertoire of businesses along its Main Street.

He pulled into an empty spot and saw Mick through the window. The old man was asleep in front of the television. This wasn't the first time Mick had been woken from a midday nap.

The door to the dusty barbershop squeaked when John walked in. The old man greeted John and sat him down. Mick asked the same questions which John entertained every time he went, tiresome as that was. There were only so many ways a man could tell someone he was no longer married.

Mick got to work cutting his hair and informed John of the latest town gossip. At some point between the snips of the scissors, John drifted back to sleep.

He woke to Mick's gentle prodding. Elly's voice dissolved into memory as he slowly climbed out of the barber chair. He was still blinking the sleep from his weary eyes when he saw his reflection in the mirror. The grey hair was more noticeable now.

He paid Mick and thanked him and left the old man to his daytime television. John was sure Mick would fall back asleep in a few minutes. The thought brought a smile to his face and helped him forget his dream for a moment.

Outside, he jumped in his waiting Dodge. He put the keys in the ignition and started the truck. Unsure where to go, John listened to the rumbling in his stomach and decided to go back to Ted's.

Dark clouds were gathering on the horizon, and it looked like it was going to storm any minute.

A few minutes later, John rolled into Ted's and could tell from the parking lot the bar was packed. He walked in and sat down at his stool. Everyone at the bar, including Ted, were talking about a robbery that was the top story on the local news. Small town living indeed, John thought.

"Weird shit, isn't it?" Ted asked him as he came over with a can of Coors and a shot of Bushmills.

"Huh?"

"The robbery, it doesn't make much sense," Ted informed John.

"Oh."

"I've been watching this all day. Tom Bradbury's wife and kids were all shot, and Tom is on the run. They've been saying all morning it was a robbery, but from the sounds of it looks more like murder, doesn't it?" Ted explained.

"I don't know."

"He lives over your way, doesn't he?"

"I couldn't tell ya," John answered.

"You haven't been watching the news?"

"No, I haven't," John said, not really interested in the town gossip. He caught a slight moment of disappointment in Ted's face. The old man loved this sort of thing. However, the frown was quickly gone, replaced by a friendly smile.

"Let me know if you need anything."

"I always do."

The robbery was definitely big news for Watsonfield, but John's mind was elsewhere. He was still thinking about his dream. Why couldn't he get the thoughts out? It had been ten years since he lost his daughter and wife. It was the reason he came here to Watsonfield in the first place. To get away from the life they had created, away from the memories.

Ted was back down at the other end of the bar talking to the old guys again. John looked at the shot and a can of beer in front of him. He picked up the shot glass and downed the Bushmills. He lit a cigarette and sipped on his Coors, uninterested in the conversation at the other end of the bar.

Ted waltzed back over to John's end of the bar and cleaned a couple of glasses in the sink.

"Ya got any fries back there?" John asked him.

Ted looked up and smiled. He went to the kitchen and returned with a full plate of fries which John smothered in vinegar. The greasy bar food was exactly what he had been craving.

John quietly ate the fries and drank his beer alone. He watched the ebb and flow of the patrons over the next few hours, drinking all the while. As the afternoon shifted to evening, the bar reached maximum capacity.

John stood up and stretched. On the bar, he left a half-empty can of beer to let Ted know he was just going out for a smoke.

Outside there were cement steps leading into the bar; John stood to the side of the steps and leaned against the wall. While he smoked, he noticed the heavy dark clouds above still threatening rain. But it was the light, low against the horizon, that captured his full attention. The last fleeting rays of sun cast their burnt orange glow. John rested in the beauty of that timeless moment.

His peace was broken when a group of college kids shuffled past. The girls were laughing and giggling, the guy stoic, too cool to show any emotion. They sauntered in, and John cracked a smile.

Another man followed close behind. He arrived in the parking lot almost out of nowhere. He was tall with pale skin and a shaved head. His walking was erratic; his lanky body jerked awkwardly with each step. He wore a plain t-shirt and jeans and on his left arm was one of the familiar armbands John had seen on TV. The man took the steps, his hips and legs jerking haphazardly, and he swayed side to side. John watched, thinking the guy must have already had something to drink.

Then he saw his eyes. They were completely black, even where the whites of his eyes should have been, like two dark beads of coal dropped into the man's face. The veins on the man's neck and temples stood out and slithered beneath his pale skin. The longer John stared, the less sure he became of what he saw. His heart hammered behind his ribs. A sense of relief fell over John when the strange man finally went inside.

From outside, John heard the sound of a chair screech as it dragged across the floor. The voice and laughter from within were muffled behind the door.

He closed his eyes and enjoyed the feel of the warm spring night. There was a wet earthy smell to the air, the smell of spring. Mingled with that, was the faint smell of rain to come, more of a feeling than an actual scent.

The moment of peace disappeared in an instant with the shrill cry from a woman inside the bar, "No! Please!"

Then, the unmistakable sound of gunfire. John's heart was in his throat.

More shots rang out. He froze for a second, then jumped up the stairs and pulled open the door, casting the last bit of daylight across the floor. From the outside looking in, the scene was pure terror. People ran toward the door, falling out of their stools and chairs and scrambling in a crazed rush to be out of this madness. The tall, pale, skinny man John had just watched walk-in had a Glock in his hand and was indiscriminately shooting anyone he could. John held the door open with one arm and yelled, "Come on! Get outta there!"

The two women, who had only entered a few seconds ahead of the bald man, were almost at the door when they were hit. Their friend was shot in the back of the head. Pieces of skull with blood and ooze exploded over the two women. Their faces were covered with the man's blood. Frozen with the shock of death, the shooter focused his aim on each of them. The woman closest to John was shot through the spine; the bullet protruding from the middle of her chest. Her eyes rolled back, and she fell to the floor.

The other woman made a break for John. He caught her arm

and started to pull her outside only to feel her go limp as a shot pierced her. John let go of her as she fell to the concrete and died. His heart pounded, and the scream of gunfire sounded in his ears.

Think, THINK!

John turned his back to the tavern and searched the parking lot, but as far as he could tell, he was the only one outside. There wasn't time to wait for anyone else. John would have to do something. That being said, he wasn't about to walk in unarmed. He needed something, anything.

His shotgun! It was in the truck! He jumped down the steps and ran for his truck. He threw open the driver's door and pulled the gun off the rack. He threw the seat forward and found the box of shells on the floor. He kicked the barrel forward and loaded the shells then slammed it shut. He took off for the bar, knowing every second counted.

John raced across the parking lot and threw open the entrance again. Inside, he saw the bald man aiming and firing without hesitation. His movements were smooth and effortless like he wasn't even thinking. Without even looking, the man replaced an empty clip with a full one and kept firing.

Smoke filled the room; bodies were scattered all over the floor. John raised the shotgun, stock pressed firmly into his shoulder and took aim.

The bald man spun to face him. Frozen, with his finger on the trigger, John barely had time to take aim before the bald man fired. The shot hit the wall to the right of John's head. Dust and smoke fell over his shoulder, clouding his vision. He pulled the trigger, knowing there wouldn't be a second opportunity. He saw the bald man stagger. Quickly, John readied and fired again. This time, the man dropped to the floor. To be sure he was dead, John reloaded the shotgun as he approached and put another shot through the man's head.

Once John finished the gunman, he surveyed the remaining patrons to see if anyone was alive. From behind the bar, a slight moan reached John's ear. Ted lay on the floor, bleeding profusely from a wound in his stomach.

"John," he said weakly. "What happened?"

"You were shot," John answered. "I got him though."

Ted half laughed and coughed out a gob of blood. He reached up to try and wipe it away. John took his hand and set it down. He pulled a towel down from the bar and wiped the blood from Ted's mouth for him.

"Thank you, John," Ted struggled. His breath was coming in short raspy spasms, "You gotta go, don't let them find you in this mess."

John looked at the pain in Ted's eyes. Tears began to well-up in the corner of his own, a lump formed in his throat. He didn't understand why anyone would want to hurt his friend.

Ted's head slipped backward; John's hand kept it steady.

"Go John," Ted whispered with his dying breath.

John laid Ted to rest on the floor, covering his friend's face with a towel. When he rose, he could see the full extent of the devastation caused by the gunman. Nothing, not even the tables and chairs, had escaped the destruction. Not one soul remained alive, save his own.

Ted's words sounded in John's head. It was a disturbing reality, but he knew if he were the only survivor, it would be difficult to prove he hadn't been responsible for the massacre. To avoid being caught in an even worse scenario, John ran for his truck, tucked the shotgun back into the rack, threw the truck in gear and took off for home.

Driving along the dirt road, John was distracted by the leaves above. In his headlights, the leaves cast strange silhouettes that danced before his eyes. They were like little demons in the trees beckoning him to join them.

"Murderer," they said.

He shook his head, trying to shake the words out. The road ahead started to blur.

The events from the bar felt surreal. Ted couldn't be dead. John couldn't have killed a man. It all had to have been some kind of delusion of a sleep-deprived mind.

Above, the threatening clouds John saw earlier finally gave way. It started raining hard and the wind grew stronger.

"Turn John, turn John, turn!"

The voices screamed in his ears. Without knowing why John obeyed, he turned sharply and slammed into the trunk of a tree. The impact jarred him awake. His face smashed into the steering wheel and crushed the bones in his nose, causing blood to pour into his eyes and mouth. John lay limp against the crumpled door until he fell to the soft wet earth below.

Chapter Three

Maggie

MAGGIE SAT SILENTLY in her Buick Regal, watching the raindrops splash on the parking lot, pooling here and there where the paving was uneven. She remained still, her eyes scanning the distance intensely for any sign of movement. So far, she had seen neither the black truck or the man, John Malley.

She was thin with the same black eyes like the man who terrorized Ted's bar. All three of Davis's assistants had those black, doll's eyes, indicating the armband was in control.

Maggie had no memory of how she came to the parking lot or why she was there. She couldn't explain the knife that sat in her lap. Everything she did was under Harry's control.

"It's time to go, Maggie," Harry's voice whispered in her head. She left the parking lot and sped through Watsonfield without knowing where she was going. Harry was driving. He was always in control. She could not remember a time before this moment.

She pulled into a small-town bar. Music droned from inside, but there were no voices. Maggie climbed the steps and went inside.

Bodies lined the floor. She walked through the devastation and saw the remains of the bald man who had started the day with her. He was dead like everyone else. However, a quick scan of the bodies told her that John Malley wasn't here. He was still alive, somewhere.

She left the bar. Waiting in the parking lot next to her vehicle was a white car. As Maggie put her hand on the door handle of her car, she heard someone exit the vehicle beside her. She looked over her shoulder and saw the familiar face of Harry's third assistant.

Over the roof of the white coupe, he stared at Maggie, and she stared back. Their dark eyes remained locked for a moment, but neither spoke. An understanding was reached. John was not here. They both entered their cars and left in opposite directions.

Though Harry had narrowed John's whereabouts to Watsonfield, he had not actually found the house John called home. So, as Maggie left the bar, there was no guiding voice to tell her where to go.

She cruised the small town and looked for any black truck that might be John's. Although there were many vehicles that fit the description, Maggie did not find John.

Then, turning down a small dirt road, her fortunes changed. It was pouring rain now, but she clearly saw the tire tracks ahead of her as she drove. Just a couple miles down the road, she came upon her quarry.

Maggie saw his body splayed alongside the black truck covered in mud and blood.

She parked the Buick and left the headlights on. As she neared John, she saw his chest rise and fall, which let her know he was still alive. She readied the knife in her right hand and knelt beside his body.

Maggie held the tip of the knife just below John's sternum. Just one good push, and it would be over. But, at that moment, she saw something.

A face, a memory from some long-forgotten past. It wasn't John that waited under her knife, but her father. The soft loving features of the man that raised her rushed through Maggie's mind.

Glancing down at her hands, Maggie saw the knife and was suddenly horrified. It was like she was seeing the scene for the first time. She dropped the knife and let it disappear in the mud beside her.

As she sat there, confused and scared, Maggie realized she couldn't remember the last time she saw her father. His lighthearted smile and warm laugh were but fleeting memories, nothing concrete. The more she tried to remember, the more puzzled she became. Questions swirled through her head.

What happened to her?

Then a deep, calm voice sounded in her ear.

"Maggie, what's wrong?"

She dared not answer.

"Tell me, what are you thinking?"

Maggie glanced at the car behind her. The headlights were two bright suns in the dark road. She didn't remember driving here, but she assumed she must have.

She turned her attention to the man beside her. His name was John. Somehow, she was sure of this, but she couldn't say why. In the pit of her stomach, she felt the urge to leave, to just run from this place. Yet, something forced her to stay.

Her head slowly turned to the knife in the mud. She wanted to look away, she wanted to run, but she couldn't.

Then, as Maggie grappled with the sudden realization of this lack of control, her hand reached for the knife. In her mind, she screamed. She wanted to turn away and leave the knife behind. Whatever was happening, she wanted to leave, but she couldn't. Something, or someone, made her pick up the blade.

With every movement, Maggie fought for control of her limbs. She was failing desperately. The knife was raised above her head, and she was ready to deliver the killing blow when deep inside she momentarily won the battle for command.

She slammed the knife into the dirt beside John, splattering mud over both of them. The man remained motionless, but Maggie quickly scampered to her feet. She couldn't wait to see what happened next, she needed to run as fast as she could away from this place. She didn't know how or why she came here, but she was sure that she needed to leave before things got worse.

Soaked from the rain and the mud, Maggie flung herself into the car, threw it in gear, and sped away from John.

Chapter Four

Harry

HARRY COULDN'T UNDERSTAND what he saw. The armband on Maggie was activated. She shouldn't have been able to refuse an order. It went against all his programming. The algorithms he created long ago had safeguarded against this very phenomenon. Yet, here was something that should not be, a ghost in the machine.

He slammed his fist against the desktop, from where he watched. One and three were working fine. Well, one was dead. That didn't matter now. But, Maggie, his favorite, had been able to refuse his commands, and that did matter. It was especially important concerning his plans for tomorrow. One-third of the armbands not working could ruin everything.

What was different about her? What had changed with her armband that hadn't affected the others?

Harry needed to find out. This was not the sort of mistake he could ignore. If there was something fundamentally wrong with the armbands, he had to know now before he tried to do anything more.

But before Harry could leave, he had to do one last thing. He closed his eyes and let his mind drift back to the images he had seen from Maggie's eyes. There in the mud, she had seen him. After all these years, he had finally found his best friend and his greatest enemy. For the moment, a smile crossed Harry Davis' lips. No, their friendship was in the past. Those days were gone. The smile was gone as fleetingly as it appeared.

There was a voice in Harry's head that told him to go and kill John himself. But he couldn't. John had to die, but even through all his hatred, Harry couldn't be the one to do it. Not after the deaths of John's wife and daughter. He never meant for that. Despite all the evil he planned, killing the man who helped create the armbands was the line that Harry Davis could not cross. He needed someone else to do this. Once finished, that would be the last time he asked anyone to do anything for him.

For now, there was still one more hunter tracking down John. Hopefully, that would be enough. In the meantime, Harry needed to get to Maggie and figure out just what was happening with her armband. This couldn't wait.

Chapter Five

John

JOHN'S BODY lay in a heap under the open driver's side door of his truck. Rain-soaked his battered body. His face was a bloody mess. Physically he hadn't broken anything other than his nose, but the blood that covered his face and shirt made it look so much worse. A thin trickle of blood ran from the corner of his mouth where his teeth had gouged a chunk of flesh from the inside of his cheek. His eyes were still closed. He could have passed for dead were it not for the slow rising and falling of his chest.

The clouds above rumbled with thunder as the wind picked up and the downpour began. The heavy drops descended upon John. The mud beneath his body started to pool with the onslaught. He opened his eyes slightly. Everything was cloudy. He tried to blink away the water only to realize the blur persisted. The force of the impact had given him a concussion.

Though his body ached, the rain felt good. It was cold and real. In his head, John struggled to wrap his mind around all that had happened.

"Don't worry about it, enjoy the rain," a voice whispered.

But why am I here, what have I done?

John, you killed them. Don't you remember?

No. That wasn't me. I only killed the shooter. The bald man. I was trying to help. As he tried to reason through what just happened, his thoughts circled back to the gunman. *What was he doing in Ted's?*

He was looking for you, John! You are the only one who knows where he came from.

I don't, John wanted to say, but something about the man seemed familiar. Then he remembered the armband. So much like the one, he and Harry worked on all those years ago.

There it is! Now, you are on the right track. How long has it been Johnny, ten years?

All the alcohol over the years had not numbed the memory of that one night. It was a bloodstain on a white shirt; a memory that would never completely fade away.

I want to forget. Please. Please! John cried inside.

Johnny boy, you know that's not how this works. You can't forget. It's who you are. You can never outrun that memory. Never. Until the day you die, that night will haunt you forever.

Tears streamed from his eyes. He wanted this to end. The insomnia, the flashbacks, even the happy memories, were too much to take anymore. He just wanted to forget everything. He had lost his life ten years ago and had been living in a daze ever since.

You know how easy it would be to end it all, John.

It was then that Elly's voice rang in his ears, *"Daddy, don't. Please, Daddy, don't!"*

His chest heaved with the sobs. He couldn't take this any longer. He wanted to hold his daughter again. He wanted to watch Elly grow up, with Abby right there by his side. He had been robbed of that opportunity.

"I can't live without you and mommy anymore. I miss you too much," he said.

"Daddy, please don't. You can't die yet."

John raised his head despite the double vision and the nausea it induced. He pulled himself out of the mud and groped for the truck door to steady himself. With some struggle, he was able to raise himself completely and stand. He saw the shotgun along the back window like it always was.

"*No! Daddy, no!*" Elly screamed.

"It's okay, baby. I'll see you soon."

He pulled the gun out of the rack and loaded a shell into the double barrel chamber. His hands shook as he dropped the plastic cartridge into place. The muzzle clicked closed. He leaned the butt against the edge of the driver's seat. With his head leaned back, John uttered an almost silent prayer to the dark sky above, "Lord forgive me." He opened his mouth against the cold metal barrel and closed his eyes. Arms outstretched, his index finger rested against the trigger.

Tears leaked from the corners of his closed eyes. He just wanted to see Abby and Elly again. They had been his world. It was hard to believe ten years had gone by already. They had passed in a daze.

Just a little push of the finger, and he could be with them. It would all be over.

But, Elly's voice rang in his ears.

"*Daddy, please! Don't do it, Daddy.*"

She broke his heart. Her sweet and tiny voice begged him not to do this, but how could he live another day without her? She had been his weakness in life. He would have done anything for her. He would do anything now just to see that smile again.

He felt a soft, cool touch on his arm. He opened his eyes, and to his right, standing next to him in the rain was Elly. Tears streamed down her cheeks, her hands outstretched toward her father. John let go of the gun and rushed to her. He swept her off her feet and held her close. Her small arms squeezed him around his neck like they always had. She was here; he could feel her heart beating against his chest as he held her tight to him.

"Elly," he cried, his tears fell into her locks of golden-brown hair.

"*Daddy,*" she said.

Her arms still tightly around his neck, Elly leaned back so John could see her face. Her bright blue eyes shone back at him. And there it was, that smile he missed so much. Her face was bright, ebullient as always.

Then she was gone. John's arms were still locked in her embrace, but she was no longer there. When he blinked, he could see her like the image on a polaroid coming into focus except in reverse. Each time he blinked, she became a little less. His head was numb, and he suddenly felt lightheaded.

John went limp and collapsed back into the mud. He cried into his palms, his body shaking with each breath.

"God, why?" he moaned into his hands. "Why did you take them from me?"

The rain fell in torrents on him now. He was drenched and shivering against the cold. But minutes passed, and he didn't move. This was all a cruel joke. For the first time in ten years, he had been able to hug his daughter. Then she was gone.

Eventually, the tears stopped, and John had no choice but to pull himself up. The rain had started to relent. He picked the gun out of the mud and threw it on the floor of the passenger side. He fell into the driver's seat and shut the door behind him. John slumped over and laid along the bench seat. *For Whom the Bell Tolls* was still in the seat where he put it earlier. He used this for a pillow and slept for a little while.

Chapter Six

Maggie

MAGGIE SPED through Watsonfield and followed road signs to the highway. She didn't recognize this place. How had she arrived here?

Her head was swimming. Memories came back in waves, overwhelming her. Birthdays, school, college, parties, all at once, with little time to focus on any one specifically. Then another memory, stronger and much more intense than the others, flashed through her mind. It was summer, and she and her father were fishing. She couldn't remember where, but that didn't matter because it wasn't the details of the memory that she remembered most, it was the feeling the memory evoked. It was love. The kind of unconditional love that can only exist between a parent and child.

As the memory faded, another replaced it. This memory wasn't hers in the same way that the fishing trip was. This one was hazy and unclear, like trying to see through a foggy mirror. People screamed all around her, but she couldn't understand why. Something was wrong, terribly wrong.

She shook her head, and the memory vanished.

The headlights from the Buick cast two narrow beams of light on the dark road ahead. For as far as the headlights shone, the highway was empty. A sign ahead showed the distance to the nearest city. Seventy miles. Maggie's head was still reeling, but she decided to follow the highway until she reached the city. Maybe by then, her thoughts would have settled, and she could think straight. For now, just having a simple goal was enough.

The clouds above blocked out any light from the stars and moon. So, there was no light to reflect against the metallic band on Maggie's arm. She, like so many others, was completely unaware of the armband's effect on her life. It was only when she knocked her arm against the inside of the driver's door and heard the clang of metal that Maggie noticed anything.

For Maggie, seeing the armband was like trying to decipher an optical illusion for the first time. Confused, she grasped the steering wheel with her left hand and with her right hand, inspected the band. It was cool to the touch. As her fingers gently investigated, a chill ran up her spine.

She could not remember when or why she had put on this strange device. It was ugly and cumbersome, but Maggie knew there must have been a reason. Yet, as her fingers searched for some clue as to the band's purpose, she found nothing but smooth black metal.

At the edge of the band near her wrist, Maggie tried to wriggle her finger underneath, but it was tight to her skin. She pulled at it. There was no give. It wouldn't budge. A cold sweat formed along her brow. She knew there was something dangerous about it. She felt it in the pit of her stomach.

How had she not noticed it until now?

As she plucked at the edge of the band with no avail, Maggie's heart rate climbed. She needed to get this thing off. Then, from a distance, she heard him.

"Maggie, where are you going?" His voice was calm and deep.

It soothed her nerves, and she felt safe.

"What is this?" she asked out loud.

"Nothing with which you need be concerned," he said.

"But..." Maggie began, not knowing what she would say next.

"Why don't we turn around, Maggie? There is nothing for you this way," he said.

Maggie saw the wheel turning in her hand. She felt herself being pulled under. Dark clouds formed at the edge of her vision. She was losing the fight. As she desperately fought for control, the thought of her parents ran through her head again. The thought of their love grounded her. That connection was enough for Maggie to fight off Harry's attempt at control, at least for the moment.

She stepped on the gas, and the Buick lurched forward. She glanced at the black band around her left arm; its true purpose suddenly dawned on her. As long as that was there, she would never have complete control again. She sped into the early morning dark, knowing what she had to do.

Chapter Seven

Harry

THE AIR WAS thin this high up. The wind against his face was freezing, and his eyes were watering. But he didn't feel the cold. Inside his rage burned hot like a red coal, driving him forward.

The silver rays of moonlight reflected off his metallic body as he scanned the earth below. This high above the freeway, he was nothing more than a glistening speck in the sky. No one would notice him, and no one could stop him.

She was close. He could feel it. The fact that he could still feel her, even faintly, meant the armband was still attached. Thus, there was still a connection between the two of them.

He had connected with her briefly, just long enough to utter a few sentences. But that wasn't enough. He needed more. He needed control.

Harry closed his eyes and focused on Maggie.

At first, he couldn't see anything. His anger distracted him. He needed to let go. He inhaled slowly and held the cold air in his chest before gently exhaling. Again, he breathed in the thin air and drifted further from his feelings. Deeper and deeper, he dove into this trance. The more distant he was from his own thoughts, the more acutely he was able to identify Maggie's.

Slowly, he began to see through her eyes. The steering wheel, her hands, the road, everything was coming into focus. As Maggie's vision gradually became his own, Harry began to feel that sense of control that the armband yielded. He flexed her left hand and felt the steering wheel beneath his fingers. They were still most definitely connected. Now, she would feel his wrath.

"Hello, darling," he whispered in her ear. *"How I missed you."*

He felt her shudder at his voice. But he had her now. Her hands squeezed the wheel with new life, strong and capable. Harry forced her to crank the vehicle sharply to the left.

The Buick whipped across the two lanes of traffic. Maggie's car careened into a vehicle in the left lane and pinned it to the guardrail. Through Maggie's eyes, Harry saw the terror on the driver's face. From far away, his lips parted in a toothy grin. A truck following close behind Maggie stomped on its brakes, but there was no time. It smashed into the back of her car, spinning the Buick back into traffic and blocking the road behind her.

Maggie now faced the oncoming vehicles. Harry stepped on the accelerator. The engine whined, and the tires screamed as the vehicle jettisoned into oncoming traffic. There was nowhere to go. An SUV came barreling toward Maggie. Like watching in slow-motion, Harry saw the SUV dodge a head-on collision. Unfortunately for the driver, the back-passenger tire clipped the nose of Maggie's car. The back half of the automobile launched into the air, and the car rolled. The woman was thrown from the vehicle. She landed on her back and skidded across the pavement. Her ensuing screams of agony were short, for no sooner had she stopped sliding than a sedan rolled over her limp frame, killing her immediately.

Traffic plowed into the wreckage behind her. The crunch of glass and scrapping metal filled the air. Screams from trapped drivers rang in Maggie's ears. Their pain was an affirmation to Harry.

"Here it comes, Maggie, the big one," he whispered.

An 18-wheeler was barreling toward the blockade Harry had created. There was no time for it to stop.

"*Let's see you work,*" he said, as he relinquished control. Now that he knew he could still control her, he wanted to see what would happen when she wasn't completely under his thumb. Would she once again try to tear off the armband? If so, there was work to be done.

Chapter Eight

Maggie

A RED SPORTS car slammed into the driver's side door of her Buick. Maggie was thrown across the seat to the other side. Instinctively she put her hands out to cover her face, and in doing so, realized she could move once again. She flailed for the door handle. Through the window, she saw a truck whizz past; then she heard it collide with the pile-up behind her. She flung the door open and tumbled onto the wet pavement.

She heard the squeal of the semi's tires as the driver tried to bring the truck to a stop. Maggie saw a grassy embankment beyond the guardrail. She scrambled to her feet and rushed toward safety. Behind her, she heard the crumbling of steel as another vehicle plowed into the Buick. She dove over the rail to the soft dewy grass. Then her focus returned to the semi. It had slowed down but not nearly enough.

Maggie saw, amidst the mangled pile of debris, flames leaping skyward. The truck weaved as the driver tried to slow it down, but she knew it was too late. Screams erupted from the flaming pile of metal. From the semi, Maggie heard a low muffled *moo*. It was a cattle trailer. Her heart raced, and she couldn't think straight as she witnessed the chaos unfold before her.

"Watch this," he whispered.

No. I can't. I won't.

"You will!"

Harry Davis once more took control of her body. Maggie felt the slow release of control, like the numbing effects of Novocain, course through her body once more.

The semi plowed into the wreckage and came to a screeching halt. The trailer jack-knifed and crashed into the carnage, further blocking the road. The trailer doors creaked open once the truck ground to a halt. The Holstein cattle within thundered out the door clambering over one and other, some sliding and falling on the pavement and being trampled beneath the onslaught of rushing hooves.

Diesel fuel leaking from the semi only added to the already abundant supply of fuel on the pavement. Flames danced in the wreckage, leaping to and fro, in eager anticipation. The fire jumped from the pile of mangled cars and kissed the gasoline. *Whoosh!*

The Holsteins had nowhere to run. The fire erupted in one all-consuming blast igniting everything it touched. The cattle were lit ablaze; their fur smoked black and eyes bulged from their skulls. Their cries of pain sounded almost human.

The cattle hurtled toward the oncoming traffic, their burning bodies looking for any escape.

Maggie's eyes were glued to the devastation. She lay motionless in the grass while people and cows roared in anguish. Then, she rose. Traffic across the median and slowed to a halt. People were rushing from their vehicles to come and help. Maggie waited. A man ran toward her.

"Are you okay?" he yelled.

She stumbled and fell.

"Stay right there!" he yelled again.

She waited. He was closer now.

"What happened?" he asked. Maggie was leaned over on her hands and knees. He put his hand on her back and bent closer to her. Close enough. With a closed fist, she threw a quick hard uppercut that caught the man in his Adam's apple. He collapsed to his knees on the ground next to her, groping at his throat. He gasped for air. Her punch had been perfect, crushing his windpipe. Maggie placed her foot on his chest and pushed him to the ground. Hooked to a belt-loop, Maggie spied a knife. She grabbed it.

Chapter Nine

John

WHEN JOHN WOKE, a haze of bright sunlight flickered through his windshield, and the chirping of birds outside told him it was morning. He sat up and rubbed his face. He still had a headache, but he could see clearly.

He stretched his arms over the dashboard and felt the ache in his lower back. As he stretched further, a deep pop released the pressure between his joints, and the hurt disappeared. It felt good.

John almost forgot the night before, but as the sun's rays warmed his face, he closed his eyes and watched scenes like a movie play out in his mind. There was so much blood. The screams echoed in his ears. He felt the pain in his shoulder as he pulled the trigger. He opened his eyes again and saw the blood caked to his shirt. This wasn't just a bad dream.

John saw the keys were still in the ignition as he looked over the cabin. The inside was no worse than usual. It was the outside and the engine that worried him. If there was major damage, he wasn't sure what he would do.

He stepped outside and inspected his truck. The steel bumper along the front had absorbed most of the damage. The front quarter panels were dented from the force of the impact. The engine was the big question. But when John lifted the hood, he didn't see any major damage.

He climbed back in the cab and turned the key. The engine stuttered. John's heart sank. He tried again. This time the truck showed signs of life but still failed to start. John turned the key again and jockeyed the gas pedal. The engine roared to life. John fell back in his seat and listened to the motor hum, like sweet music to his ears. He went back outside and looked over the front of the truck once more before closing the hood and taking off for home.

Once there, he grabbed a bag from the closet in the living room and started packing everything he could think to take. Clothes, primarily jeans, and tee-shirts, were thrown helter-skelter within. In the top drawer of his dresser was a Ruger .357. He wrapped it in a towel and placed it in the bag as well as two boxes of hollow point shells. There was half a pack of Marlboro's on top of the same dresser. He stuck one in his mouth and lit it before putting the pack in his breast pocket.

John knelt beside the bed and pulled a small plastic box from underneath. Inside was a Taurus .44 revolver. He flipped the latches on the box and admired the stainless-steel finish of the pistol. A black leather holster lay next to the gun as well as a box of bullets and a couple of speed-loaders. John stood and placed the box on the bed.

Next, he made his way to the bathroom. In the mirror, he saw his face was covered with blood and dirt.

John flaked a piece of mud from his cheek and watched it fall into the sink, where it broke apart in a cloud of dust. *From the dust and to the dust all return,* John thought as the cloud dissipated. Here one second gone the next.

"Shit," he muttered as he contemplated the enormity of last night. Just like that, everyone was gone. *Except me,* John thought. *I'm still here.* How thin was that line between the living and dead?

He took another puff on the Marlboro before balancing the cigarette on the edge of the sink. He peeled his shirt off. It clung to him where the blood had dried. Then he washed his face. Leaning on the sink, he looked at his reflection. He had aged overnight, the wrinkles on his forehead and around his eyes were more prominent. He wanted to say it was from getting his haircut, that now all the tell-tale signs of his age would show more, but he knew that wasn't true. He knew, although he still felt good most days, he was getting older. He wasn't one to bemoan the effects of aging; it was simply a matter of fact, he was indeed older. He grabbed the Marlboro and took a long drag, relishing the feeling as the smoke wisped down his throat into his lungs.

Back in the bedroom, he slid the holster on top of a white tank top. He locked the .44 into place and covered the gun and holster with a plain white shirt. He filled the speed-loaders and dropped them in a side pocket on the bag. The rest of the bullets he left in the box and tossed in the main part of the bag.

In the kitchen, he opened the cupboard above the countertop and was dismayed to see how bare the shelves had gotten. A nearly empty jar of peanut butter and a couple cans of tuna. The thought of tuna right now made him gag.

The smiling fish on the side of the can wasn't an accurate representation. Tuna always tasted like cat food, and worse yet, it reeked. John pulled a can out of the cupboard and looked at the recipes on the side. Tuna salad, tuna alfredo, tuna tacos. *What the can doesn't tell you is they all taste the same, like shit in a can,* he thought. He tossed the can back in the cupboard.

I'll have to find food on the road he decided.

John strode across the living room to the television stand where he kept the house phone. He hadn't talked to his brother Rich in at least two years. Rich lived up in the Northwestern corner of Connecticut on the border of Massachusetts and New York. John planned to lay-low up there for a little bit. If all went well, he would look to settle down and disappear from society like he had here.

John knew it wasn't ideal, though. If he was a suspect in last night's shooting, the first place the police would search after his own home would be any family. So, he wasn't really buying himself much time, maybe a day at the most. But, this was all just precautionary. He might not even be a suspect. Beneath the phone was his address book. He pulled it out and dropped it in his bag. The first chance he got, he would give his brother a call. Not here. No, never use the home phone. He would look for a payphone when he stopped for food.

He took one last look over the living room. He would miss this place. This house had been home for longer than any other stop since Abby and Elly had been killed. Part of him had hoped to stay here till the end.

Back outside, he threw the bag behind the seat. He scraped the shotgun off the floor on the passenger side and placed it behind the bench seat on the floor. He sat, his hands resting on the warm wheel, soaking in the bright gold rays lighting up the dashboard through the pine trees. It was a five-hour trip to Rich's. He would be there before nightfall. If he got a couple of hours under his belt now, he could stop and get some breakfast somewhere and hopefully give his brother a call. John turned the key, the eight-cylinder engine hummed. *Here we go.* He put the truck in first and took off out of the dirt driveway.

Chapter Ten

Walter

JUST OUTSIDE OF New York City, where, in less than 24 hours, a murderous hoard would flood the streets, Walter Makichinski awoke with a start. Mr. Whiskers was purring loudly as he gazed longingly into Walter's eyes. Walter felt the prickle of Mr. Whiskers' claws gently kneading his chest.

"Go," Walter mumbled, as he brushed the cat away. Mr. Whiskers rolled onto his back beside Walter's leg and begged for a belly rub. Walter scratched the tufts of fur along Mr. Whiskers chest as the cat closed its eyes and started to doze.

Walter glanced up at the television, hanging on the wall and felt a dull ache between his shoulder blades. He stretched his neck and moved his head in circles, trying to work out the knot. He felt his muscles tighten, then release as his neck popped. The relief trickled down his spine and radiated throughout. Walter sunk into the cushions and turned his attention to what was on the screen.

Some people were testing out a vacuum. Not a connoisseur of

household cleaning products, the impressive suction power of the product was lost on Walter. This wasn't the same channel as last night, he thought. Well, it was, but the content had changed remarkably while he slept. He reached for the remote to change the channel.

He wouldn't have thought anymore of last night were it not for the early morning sun reflecting through the window. The light bounced off the metallic band on Walter's arm, creating a blinding glare that caught his attention.

Deus lux mea est.

Walter remembered the Latin phrase from Pastor Perry's recent sermon. *Deus lux mea est,* God is my light. Then, from the bright armband, his eyes were drawn to a dark stain on his sweatpants. Residue from Walter's film experience last night. His stomach turned. A wave of guilt coursed through him. He felt dirty, disgusting.

He sighed and turned the TV off.

He remembered the movies, the women he would never know, and scenes he would never see. This guilt would only grow if he stayed on the couch any longer. So, Walter made his way to the bathroom and turned on the shower.

As he undressed, he saw his reflection in the mirror. The man he saw made him feel even worse. The hairless torso perched atop his hips seemed too big. The rolls of fat that gathered at his waistline were stacked one on top of the other. Walter quickly turned from his reflection to avoid having to look on his hideous body for a second longer.

The warm water didn't bring Walter any solace. He still felt filthy when he got out of the shower. He knew there was only one way to mitigate his sin. After putting on clean clothes, Walter knelt beside his bed and prayed.

It was some while later that he rose with a renewed sense of being. Prayer worked. He felt better; he felt forgiven.

As he made eggs in the kitchen, Walter noticed how the black armband glistened in the light from the LED bulbs above the stove. For the first time since putting on the armband, Walter finally understood why Pastor Perry gave the armbands to the congregation. They were the perfect reminder.

Deus lux mea est, God is my light.

Chapter Eleven

Isaac

ISAAC PARKER OPENED the fridge and found the carton of eggs and package of bacon he wanted. He had been looking forward to this day all week. It was the first weekend in a long time that he didn't have to work. More than anything, he just wanted a day with his wife and daughter. He whistled happily as he bounced around the kitchen, preparing breakfast.

Melanie would be down first. She was like him, she didn't sleep in late. Already, the maple smell rising from the pan of bacon made his mouth water. Isaac knew that aroma would slowly make its way upstairs and wake the sleepers.

There were no plans for today. It wasn't a vacation. It was just Saturday, the first full day of Memorial Day weekend. There would be plenty to do if they wanted. There was always something to do in New York City. As yet, Isaac hadn't made any arrangements. His thoughts pertained to the here and now, frying bacon, flipping the eggs at the right time, and listening for the sound of footsteps coming down the stairs.

The window above the stove was cracked open, and Isaac could hear the monotonous drone from outside. It was always there, like a nagging bug bite that never heals. It was just a part of life. He couldn't remember a time when there weren't the sounds of the city echoing in his ears. Somedays, Isaac thought of leaving, going somewhere quiet for a change. But, that was just a dream he would never experience.

From upstairs, Isaac heard the soft thump of Melanie's feet as she crawled out of bed. A few seconds later, he heard her slowly make her way down the steps. She was still half-asleep. She shuffled into the doorway and waved as she rubbed her eyes.

"Why you up so early?" she mumbled.

"It's not that early," Isaac said.

"It's six o'clock on a Saturday," Melanie replied. "It's early."

Isaac laughed. Six o'clock seemed late to him.

Melanie rubbed her face and then groaned as she stretched her arms wide.

"That smells really good."

Isaac just smiled. He could tell her it was a unique brand of bacon that is difficult to find, but that didn't really matter, not to Isaac anyway. He just wanted time with Melanie and Delana. The time away from his family, that was the most difficult part of being a police officer.

Melanie slumped into a chair. She laid her head on her arms, her long dark hair covered face and spilled over onto the table.

Isaac heard Delana moving around upstairs. The bacon must have woken her as well. That was good, everyone was up, and the bacon was almost ready.

Soon the three of them were seated at the table, enjoying breakfast. There was laughter and love. The day started just as Isaac had hoped it would. If only that joy could have lasted. If only Isaac could have shielded his family from the tragedy to come. But he couldn't stop what was coming. No one could.

Chapter Twelve

John

AS THE SUN ROSE HIGHER, it warmed the inside of John's truck. He continued to make his way north. Two hours on the highway had passed in near silence with just the sound of traffic on the highway. John enjoyed the quiet. It was relaxing. But now, the fuel needle was flirting with empty, and he needed to stop for gas. John had just passed a sign for the next turnoff, Exit 54. Another sign whizzed by with the names of restaurants off the same exit. Included were the usual fast food stops, and below them, the sign listed another place which John assumed was local by the name: Mama Patti's, Home of the Best Waffles in New York State.

John's stomach growled. Waffles sounded good.

Mama Patti's sat kitty-corner to a Sunoco, where John filled up, on a hill just on the outskirts of a town called Blisse. As he walked in, John noticed a table to his left overflowing with tie-dyed shirts emblazoned with corny sayings: *New York is Blissful. Blisse: the joy of New York. When you're in Blisse, you don't give a p*ss.* John smiled, then turned his attention from the table to the restaurant before him.

Old license plates from across the country adorned the walls, adding country charm to the quaint greasy spoon. Large booths with red cushions sat along the wall, and to the right was a bar behind which waitresses scurried. A cooler with sliding glass doors sat behind the register at one end of the bar. Inside the cooler, John saw all sorts of homemade pies and cans of whip cream. He wondered if the pies were the best pies in New York too. He took a seat at the bar.

"Be right with you," a girl no older than twenty said without looking at him. She turned and headed toward the back of the restaurant with two coffees. As she turned, John saw her protruding belly and realized she was very much pregnant.

She returned quickly and slapped a menu on the counter. "Coffee?" she asked.

"Yes, ma'am," he replied. The menu was a sheet of laminated paper. On the front was breakfast and the back lunch and dinner.

"First time here?" she asked as she set a steaming mug before him.

"Yea," he replied.

"Specials are on the board over there," she pointed over his shoulder to a whiteboard with meals listed 1, 2, and 3 in blue marker. "I'll give ya a minute."

Before John could even say thanks, she was gone in a flurry heading back to the kitchen. He looked over the specials and decided on Number 1: two eggs, two waffles, and breakfast sausage. He had to try the waffles.

"Decide on what cha want, hunny?" she asked when she had returned.

"I'll try the Number 1 special, eggs over easy," he said.

"No problem, that'll be right out," she took the note with his order back to the kitchen and left John alone with his coffee.

Behind him, John heard the distinct breaking news alert from a television hanging on the wall. With a sinking feeling in his stomach, he turned to see what the news was. He saw the familiar front of Ted's Tavern, blocked off with caution tape. The hot, acidic taste of vomit rose to the back of his mouth. He took a sip of coffee to bury the putrid flavor.

"Twenty-four people killed in a shootout that can only be described as terrorism," the news anchor reported. "Mark is on the scene with a local resident."

"Thanks, Lisa, I'm here with Tina Brown, who was the first person to walk in after the shooting. Tina, what was it like?" Mark asked the disheveled woman.

John recognized her face. She was a regular at Ted's, but they had never really been introduced.

"Oh my God, I was just walking in, and I saw all them bodies. I never been so scared in my life. I never seen a dead body, and I thought the guy that done it might still be there. So, I ran out the doors and called 9-1-1 right then. I felt sick, ya know? Like I was gonna throw up. There was so much blood," Tina said.

"Yes, thank you, Tina. Terrible tragedy here in Watsonfield. The local police are saying this is the biggest crime to ever happen in the rural Pennsylvania community. Back to you, Lisa."

"Thank you, Mark. We will keep you updated on this story as we learn more. Now to sports with Brett."

John turned back to the bar. Behind the counter was the waitress, her name tag read Lita. He opened his mouth to say something, but just as he did, he saw her eyes were vacant and dark like she was lost in thought. Her mouth hung open slightly, and he was sure if he waved his hand in front of her face, she wouldn't move. Not wanting to be rude, he turned to look back at the television, but just then, her hand shot out from behind the counter and caught his arm, stopping him. The sudden movement startled him, and he was just about to say something when Lita shook her head as a cold chill broke her stupor.

"Terrible, isn't it?" she asked. John looked her in the eyes, not sure what had just happened. Her eyes were normal now. The odd blank stare was gone, and she was waiting for an answer.

"Yea. . ." he said, watching her expression. She raised her eyebrows slightly; she was listening to him. "I've been there a couple times."

"Really, you been there?" she asked, her eyes were wide with intrigue. They were a beautiful shade of green, John noticed. He continued on.

"Yea, a couple times, passing through. It's a small town. Not much happens there."

"I know what ya mean. This town ain't got more than a thousand people, but lately, we been havin' a rash a break-ins. No one can explain it, and the cops sure as hell ain't catchin' anybody. Scares the shit outta me, I got a two-year-old at home and another on the way," she said. patting her belly.

"What are they taking?"

"Guns," she said. "It don't make much sense to me, I know you can sell guns for decent price up in Bishop, bout an hour North of here. But hell, so many old folks in this town you'd think they'd be after their meds more than anythin'. These old folks got oxy and percs just laying around waitin' to be took, but no one's missing any. Least not that I know of, and I would be able to tell ya. Lot a them old folks is regulars here. I know way more than I want to about 'em. Like Rosie over there," Lita leaned on the counter, her belly looked like it might burst should she put too much weight on it, her voice got quiet so only John could hear her.

"She's been giving Judge Walter head for the last three months! Can you believe that? At her age? Her hubby doesn't know yet, but I don't think he cares much. Guess he plays golf more than he sees ole Rosie."

Lita snickered. He tried to smile, but his stomach turned at the thought.

"That's strange," John said. "About the guns, I mean. I don't know Rosie well enough to comment on her hobbies."

Lita's jaw dropped open. Then she burst into a laughing fit. Her face shone red as the blood rushed to her cheeks. After a moment, she got control of herself and slapped John on the arm.

"Yea, you're right," was all she could say with a straight face before she went back to the kitchen. John watched her walk away and saw her shake her head a couple times, still laughing to herself. He thought about what she had said concerning the guns.

"You tell me how those waffles are alright, hun?" Lita asked when she returned with his plate.

John saw she had recovered from her bout of hysteria, her face only slightly blushed now. It was weird being called hun by someone who could be his daughter. He drowned the waffles in syrup, then took a bite. It was sweet and soft, melting in his mouth.

"Wow," he said with his mouth still full.

Lita's eyes lit up at the praise, and a big smile spread across her face, little dimples poked out at the corners of her mouth.

"We call 'em the best in New York for a reason!" she said.

John laughed and nodded his head as he took another bite.

"I'll let ya eat in peace," she said. "Let me know if ya need anything."

"Alright, thank ya, ma'am," John said through a full mouth.

Lita was gone in a flash. She moved effortlessly through the diner as she waited on table after table. Despite being at least seven months pregnant, she seemed to match her coworker's attentiveness, step for step.

John marveled at her work ethic. She would have run circles around half the people he used to work with in the factory.

Once done with the pancakes, he slid the plate to the side and pulled the pack of cigarettes from his jacket. He was just about ready to take one from the pack when he saw the front page of the newspaper.

"Armbands to blame for recent break-ins?" the title read.

John slipped the cigarettes back into his pocket, picked up the paper, and began reading the article.

Local police are still searching for the culprit in the recent streak of break-ins throughout Blisse and North Hampton townships. Numerous items have been reported stolen, not least of which has been guns. Shotguns, pistols, rifles, and even some assault rifles have been reported stolen, leaving residents fearful of what the culprit or culprits may be planning. While police are still searching for evidence to point them in the right direction, some residents already claim to know the true cause of the break-in.

We spoke with one local resident who believes she has the answer. "It's those armbands," she said. "I see the kids wearing them all the time. Don't seem to pay attention to anything."

While there has been speculation about the use and supposed benefits of Imperium Armbands, there has not been any evidence linking their usage to the recent break-ins. Imperium Products refused to respond to requests for comment from this newspaper. . ."

The story jumped to the last page of the paper; John was just about to flip to the back when he saw Lita at the counter again. She smiled as he set the paper down.

"Enjoying the local rag?"

"I've read worse," John said.

"That's probably true. I don't know, just seems like they make stories out of anything," she stated.

"Guess so," John mumbled.

"I'll leave this here," Lita said as she set the check in front of John. "Let me know when you are ready to check out."

Then, as she pulled her hand away, John noticed the armband on her left forearm. Instinctively he reached out and grabbed her hand. Not hard or forcefully, but lightly. Lita quickly drew her arm back. Her eyes were intense, locked onto John's.

"I'm sorry," he said.

Her defenses were on alert as she waited for him to say something more.

"Your armband?"

She sighed and relaxed.

"Oh, this?" she raised her arm on the counter. "Don't believe the paper. This here's just a monitor device like you can get on a cell phone. This is just more accurate is all. The paper just likes to get people riled up."

"So, you don't actually need it?" he asked.

"Not really, but they say it makes it easier to monitor what you put in your body ya know? There is an app that connects to your phone and what not," she answered.

"Do you feel any different?" he asked.

"No, I don't think so. I mean maybe a little, but nothing crazy."

"That's interesting. Was it expensive?" he asked.

"Only like twenty bucks. Costs more to get a couple packs of smokes than to get this," she said.

John knew how expensive cigarettes were, but he was surprised that something like that would be so cheap. "I got mine just down the road. I can give ya directions."

"Thanks, but I have to think about it," he replied.

He pulled out his wallet and placed a twenty on the counter.

"You keep the change."

"Thank you," Lita said with a smile. She was very beautiful, John realized. Although he didn't even really know her, he felt a pang of worry for her. He remembered the man from last night; it seemed like forever ago. He remembered the way the man's eyes seemed completely dark, how his movements were mechanical and how he opened fire so easily. It was only luck that John was alive this morning, luck that led him here to this restaurant with a waitress wearing the same armband. Luck, or perhaps something more.

"I enjoyed meeting you. You keep safe now," John said as he got up from his stool.

"You too," Lita waved as he headed out the front door. He reached the door and remembered he still needed to call Rich. He turned back, Lita was still at the counter.

"Do you have a phone by any chance?" he asked.

"Sure. It's old. Still got the cord on it. You ever seen one of them before?" Lita asked.

John just smiled.

"Once or twice," he said. She handed him the receiver. With his little address book in his left hand, he dialed Rich's number and put the receiver to his ear. He waited. No one answered. He hung up and tried again. Still nothing. He would have to try again later.

"Thanks," he said, handing the receiver back to Lita. Her eyes were glued to the TV while she munched on an English muffin.

"You take care now," she said absently.

As John walked across the parking lot, he couldn't stop thinking about the armband. It was so similar but different from the bracelet he and Harry worked on. Lita said it only cost twenty bucks.

That was what Harry wanted.

It was just a coincidence. Harry was dead, and John's mind was still reeling from last night.

John took a cigarette from his breast pocket and lit it. The cool morning air had given way, and it was starting to get warm. The sun felt nice on his cheeks. It was going to be a hot one.

He leaned against the driver's side door of his truck and enjoyed the view while he smoked. He realized this town was similar to Watsonfield. It certainly wasn't any bigger. In fact, it may be a bit smaller. He could see the street on which the Sunoco and Mama Patti's were located met up with Main Street a little further on. The town opened up to his east. Mama Patti's overlooked the town. From the dirt lot, John could see the houses neatly aligned along the roads jutting off Main Street.

I could settle right here. Find another job in a factory and get a little place to call home. It could work. It had for the last ten years. Gazing across his surroundings, his eyes settled on a set of fresh tire tracks in the dirt lot. They came to a stop right next to his truck. There were footsteps going from the tracks to where John stood now. Slowly, John stepped away from the truck. There, beside the spot where he was just leaning, was the imprint of a hand. Someone was following him. He had to get moving.

He pinched off his cigarette at the filter and dropped the butt into the dirt. He scuffed the cigarette remnants with his book and climbed into the truck. He looked in his mirrors and waited to spot his stalker. But he didn't see anything. He would feel better once he got back on the road, he decided.

Chapter Thirteen

Maggie

MAGGIE WAS COVERED IN BLOOD. Behind her, bright flames licked the sky. The wailing sirens from police and emergency vehicles drew closer. It was time to leave.

"Maggie, run," Harry's voice sounded in her head.

In the southbound lanes across the median, cars had pulled to the side to offer aid. There among the organized chaos of volunteer EMS personnel, Maggie saw a truck idling. It's driver door hung open, almost inviting her to take it.

She sprinted for the vehicle.

From behind her, the shrill cry of a child caught her attention. The scream made the hair on the nape of her neck stand on end, and her skin broke out in goosebumps. Maggie stopped dead and turned toward the yell.

Harry was telling her not to go back, but his words were muffled. Overpowering the voice in her head were the screams from the child. She had to help.

Maggie scanned the scene and found a scared little girl clutching a unicorn and sucking her thumb. She couldn't be any older than four. Her face was black from the smoke; her tears left streaks down her cheeks.

The voice in her head was gone. For the moment, she was free from influence. At that moment, Maggie sprinted across the grassy median and came to a stop right in front of the girl. She knelt down, so they were at eye level.

"Are you okay?"

The little girl didn't answer but stared at Maggie with huge, watery eyes. Then, she slowly started to back away.

"It's okay, honey, you can trust me," Maggie said as she reached out to take the girl's arm.

The girl stumbled away from Maggie, tripped over her own feet and tumbled to the grass. Instantly, she began to wail.

"It's okay, it's okay," Maggie tried to soothe her, but it was no use. The girl was inconsolable.

"No! No!" the girl cried.

"I won't hurt you," Maggie said. She tried to offer her hand to the girl again, but this time the girl pointed at Maggie as she backed away screaming.

Maggie was confused. She thought the girl would welcome the help of an adult. The girl was still pointing at Maggie as she scooched away. Maggie glanced down and was horrified at what she saw.

The front of her shirt was completely soaked with blood. Her arms, up to her elbows, were nearly black with the sticky substance. In her right hand, a knife was still clenched tightly. She recoiled as she dropped the knife and fell away from the girl.

"What have I done?" she whispered.

She glanced over her shoulder and saw bodies strewn across the grassy median. How many people had died by her hand? How long had this been going on?

"What have I done?" she repeated.

"You have done what I told you," a voice answered through the cloud of smoke. Maggie quickly turned toward the voice. It had come from somewhere behind the girl. After a moment, a towering silhouette began to emerge through the haze.

"Who are you?" Maggie asked. The figure drew closer, its shadowy outline becoming more concrete with each step.

"Who are you!?"

The figure was near, the gleam from the metallic suit shining through the heavy, dark cloud. He was right behind the little girl. Maggie watched as he knelt next to the girl, and his face, no longer hidden in smoke, became visible.

"Maggie, you are scaring our little friend," he said.

His voice was smooth and deep. Maggie recognized his voice. They had talked before, but where?

"Come closer, darling. Show her you mean no harm," he said while he placed one hand on the little girl's shoulder. She recoiled at first, but he quickly assuaged her fear with a gentle smile.

"It's okay, I won't let her hurt you," he whispered. Then he lightly brushed a few stray hairs from her face before returning his gaze to Maggie.

"What do you want?" she asked.

"Just you, Maggie. Come with me, and I'll help you get that armband off."

"How do you know my name?" Maggie asked.

"I know many things."

"Tell me, how do you know who I am?"

"You won't like the story, Maggie," he said. He turned his attention back to the little girl. "Where are your parents, little one?"

The girl pointed toward the pile of mangled cars.

"Oh, dear," he said. "Would you like to see them again?"

She nodded her head eagerly.

"I thought so. Let me see something here," he said, turning the child's head to the side. He rested his hand along her throat and turned to Maggie with a smile.

"She just wants to see her parents, Maggie. Who am I to refuse the wishes of a child?"

"No!" Maggie screamed.

She dove forward, but he was too fast. He stood, wrapped the girl in his arms, and leapt out of Maggie's reach.

Just as Maggie realized she had fallen into his trap, she felt the swift sting of his steel boot against the side of her head. The ringing in her ears drowned out all other sounds. Frantically she tried to find him, but she couldn't see straight. Everything was spinning.

She rolled onto her back in time to feel Harry Davis slide an arm beneath her midsection, lifting her from the pavement and squeezing her tight. The last thing Maggie saw was the billowing clouds of black smoke and people running every which way beneath as she jettisoned toward the sky. She soon succumbed to the urge to close her eyes. As she drifted into unconsciousness, she wondered if the people could see her through the smoke. Would they even know she was there?

Chapter Fourteen

Walter

WALTER CLIMBED the steps to the old brick church. He knew Pastor Perry would be inside preparing for Sunday's service. Walter wanted to help, even if that meant just folding the bulletins.

He felt rejuvenated and energized after this morning. He bounced up the cement steps and found the door unlocked, just as he knew it would be. The door opened in on a narrow hallway that led straight to the sanctuary. Pastor Perry's office was to his right.

For a moment, Walter stood in the hallway and tried to decide whether or not to knock on Pastor Perry's office door. He decided to wait in the sanctuary, at least for a little bit. Pastor Perry would come out of his office eventually, and when he did, Walter would be here to lend a hand.

Walter sat in a pew toward the back of the sanctuary and pulled a hymnal out from beneath his seat. Although he didn't sing with the choir, Walter enjoyed listening to the hymns. He opened the old book to his favorite song, "Be Thou My Vision," written by Saint

Dallán Forgaill in the sixth century. He started humming the tune as he read over the words.

> *Be thou my vision*
> *O Lord of my heart*
> *Naught be all else to me*
> *Save that Thou art*
> *Thou my best thought*
> *By day or by night*
> *Waking or sleeping*
> *Thy presence, my light*

BY THE TIME Walter began reading the second verse, he was no longer satisfied to just hum and began to sing the words lightly under his breath. The lyrics flowed from his lips. As he sang, he felt the hot sting of tears at the corner of his eyes. By the time he got to the final verse, the tears streamed down his cheeks, and a knot had formed in the back of his throat, making it difficult to sing. The last line tumbled from his mouth, jagged and broken. Walter set the hymnal to the side and wiped the tears from his face.

Just then, he felt the gentle touch of Pastor Perry's hand on his shoulder.

"You really should join the choir Walter," Pastor Perry said. Walter hurriedly tried to wipe his runny nose. "There's a box of Kleenex next to you," Pastor Perry said, taking a seat in the pew in front of Walter.

"Thanks," Walter said, taking one of the tissues and cleaning his nose. "That hymn always hits me hard."

"It's definitely powerful."

"Yea. It's my favorite," Walter said as he set the used tissue aside.

"Got bored again?"

"Just thought you might need some help."

"Oh, I think we got it today, Walter. But, I appreciate the offer."

"Oh. You already folded the bulletins?" Walter asked.

"Yes, first thing this morning," Pastor Perry replied. "I was just finishing up a few things for tonight's service."

"Tonight?"

"The midnight taizé service, I mentioned last week. Did you forget?"

"Oh, jeez! That's tonight? Yea, I did, I completely forgot!"

"Well, it's good you stopped in when you did. You might have missed a really special service," Pastor Perry said with a smile.

"No, no. I'll definitely be here," Walter said.

"Good. I'm looking forward to it. Is everything okay, Walt?"

Walter looked away quickly. For a moment, he thought of telling the pastor about last night and how he had prayed this morning. How the phrase, *deus lux mea est*, God is my light, had come to him by almost divine intervention. But Pastor Perry had given the congregation the armbands. He already knew they would be a catalyst for change. He lifted his head to meet Pastor Perry's eyes and smiled.

"Yea, everything is good. Really good," he said.

"I'm glad to hear that. Now, I'm sorry I can't visit longer, Walt, but I should finish up the last few things for tonight. You are welcome to stay and sing all you would like. I'll be in my office," Pastor Perry said as he stood up and brushed off the front of his shirt.

"I'll let you work in peace," Walter said as he worked his way out of the narrow pew. "I will be here tonight, though. I can't wait."

"Good! It's going to be special."

Chapter Fifteen

John

THE OPEN ROAD hadn't cleared John's mind like he had hoped. He was still thinking about the handprint left on his door at Mama Patti's. What if someone was following him? He couldn't shake the feeling. For the next hour, he continued to glance in his mirrors, but nothing seemed odd.

Eventually, the coffee hit, and he had to make a stop. John found a rest area right off the highway. The early morning rush had already come and gone, so when John stopped, it was the quiet time before lunch. He pulled into an empty space with no cars nearby.

The inside of the building was beautiful. Wooden beams across the ceiling added a rustic feel while skylights offered abundant sunshine. Along the far wall, a floor to ceiling window looked out over an idyllic valley.

After using the restroom, John took a minute to appreciate the view. The country around here was gorgeous. The trees along the hillside, bordering the valley, were in bloom. Their spring foliage decorated the green hills with shades of pink and white.

From John's right, someone said hello. John turned, thinking they were talking to him, only to find a man on his cell phone. John chuckled to himself as he walked past the gentleman. That reminded him, he still had to get ahold of his brother.

There was a solitary payphone on the wall just inside the entryway. The austere contraption seemed out of place in the rest area. Everything else was natural, the wooden beams and the view from the window, making the payphone like some relic that didn't belong.

John pulled some change from his pocket and deposited it in the machine. He dialed his brother's number and waited. The phone rang and rang, and just when John was ready to hang up, someone answered.

"Hello?" The voice was too high to be his brother.

"Hey, this is John, Rich's brother."

"John? Jeez, I can't remember the last time I heard your voice," she said. It was Rich's wife. What was her name? Tracy? Trixie? Trish? Shit, he couldn't remember, it was something like that.

"I know, it's been a while. Listen, could you do me a favor? I'm on my way up from PA, and I could really use a place to crash for the night."

"Oh, John. I'm sorry, we are actually heading out tonight. Rich took vacation all next week. We are heading to the beach down in Maryland."

Fuck.

"John, Rich is just outside, getting the boat ready. Let me get him for you."

"No, no. It's alright. I was actually just passing through, thought I would stop and say hi. It's alright, though," he lied.

"Are you sure? You weren't making a surprise trip up just to visit, were you?"

"No, nothing like that. Just thought I'd stop by and see how everyone was doing. I'm heading up to Maine."

"Maine? You will love it! It's beautiful. As for everyone here, we are doing well. The boys are growing so fast; you wouldn't believe it. Anyway, if you want to stop by on your way back through, we will be back next weekend."

"Alright. Yea, I'll do that."

"Good. We miss you."

"I'll see you guys soon."

"Alright. We will be waiting for you."

John hung up the phone and slumped onto the bench nearby. He massaged his forehead with his calloused fingers as he closed his eyes. A headache was coming on quickly, the blood pulsing in his temples.

"Damn it," he muttered. What was he going to do now? He sat for a few minutes and thought about everything. The years since Abby and Elly died. The time he lost. The events of last night. And now where he would go?

He couldn't go back. Going any further north was pointless if he couldn't stop by Rich's. He would have to figure it out on the road.

As he left the rest stop and approached his truck, he turned his gaze to the ground below to avoid the blinding rays of sunlight that would only aggravate his headache further. Thus, he didn't see the car parked next to his. Only when he had reached his truck did he notice the vehicle. Immediately, his thoughts went back to this morning, and the handprint on the door.

John noticed the shadow at the back of his truck first. He was sure it belonged to whoever was stalking him. The .44 was still tucked under John's left arm. With his eye on the shadow, he reached under his shirt until he felt the holster. He wrapped his fingers around the grip before turning to the back of the truck. He didn't pull the revolver from the holster yet.

"Hey!"

The shadow remained still.

"Hey," he called again. This time the shadow dropped to a crouch. John took a step forward. He heard a click followed by the snap of a magazine as it was set in place. John took another cautious step forward.

Then, the figure dove from behind the truck and rolled to his knees, not far from John. The man had a 9mm pistol pointed directly at John's chest. John yanked the Taurus from its holster and leveled the revolver at his assailant. He was a second too late; the attacker fired three quick shots.

The first bullet grazed John's shoulder. The pain was instant, like fire against his skin. He collapsed against the truck, his eyes squeezed shut against the pain. The next two shots missed. There was a scream from somewhere in the distance. For a brief moment, the memory of last night replayed in John's head. He wouldn't let that happen again. He opened his eyes and raised the revolver. It took all his concentration to focus the split sight on the man.

John squeezed the trigger and watched his target stumble backward as a pool of blood formed in the middle of his shirt. John clicked the hammer back and squeezed the trigger again. The man collapsed in a heap on the pavement. John snapped the hammer back once more, not wanting to take any chances, as he approached the body.

He knelt next to the man and set the barrel of the revolver against his temple.

"Who are you?"

The man stared back at John but didn't say anything.

"Tell me."

John watched his assailant struggle to speak, his dark eyes were focused solely on him. Then, his pupils grayed over, and his head lolled to the side. He was dead.

John slid the revolver back in its holster.

There was a small group of people gathered at the rest area. They were looking in his direction. The police would be on their way any minute. He had to leave. He just killed a man in New York with an out of state pistol. He was screwed.

He ran to his truck and was just about to enter when he had an idea. He took off his flannel shirt and ran to the back bumper. There was just a little gap behind the license plate, which he used to hold the shirt in place. So long as it stayed put, no one could give the police his license plate number.

He jumped back in the cabin and turned the key. From his right, he heard a soft voice.

"Daddy."

In the passenger seat, John saw his daughter. Her strawberry blonde highlights glistened in the sun.

"Yea, sweety?" he said.

"Be careful, Daddy. You can't die yet," she said.

Before John could reply, she was gone. Her seat, once again, empty. How he wished she was still there, just for another second. But, she was gone, a memory. John turned his attention to the task at hand. He had to get as far away from here as he could.

Chapter Sixteen

Melanie

STILL FULL FROM BREAKFAST, Melanie was sprawled across the recliner, scrolling through the images on Ego, a photo-sharing app on her phone. She was still in her pajamas, cozy, and comfortable. Why couldn't everyday be like this? Nothing to do and nowhere to be a perfect Saturday. She loved nothing as much as having nothing to do.

She was in the middle, reading a particularly long post when her phone vibrated as she received a message.

"Have you checked out f_stop39's page?" It was from Bridgette.

"No, why?" she replied.

"Go check it out."

Melanie copied the name from the first message and pasted it in the search bar. Multiple accounts popped up.

"Which one?" she messaged Bridgette.

"B&W gorilla," Bridgette replied.

The account with the gorilla image was the first one. She clicked on it and was taken to f_stop39's page. There were a lot of posts. She wasn't sure what she was supposed to be looking for, so she scrolled through the page.

Then she saw it. There was a photo of an armband with f_stop39's caption below it- "What's the price of privacy?"

Melanie scrolled through the comments:

"You didn't buy that, did you?!"

"@f_stop39, what are you doing?"

"Price of privacy ≤ $20."

The comments continued on, but Melanie got the gist of it. She went back to the page and looked through other photos. Posts disparaging Imperium Armbands were the most prevalent.

"Ok, so?" she messaged Bridgette.

"This is what we were talking about the other night, remember?"

"Sort of. I just meant that people were gullible when I said that. F_stop39 is talking about conspiracy theory stuff. That's different from what I was talking about."

"Mel, this isn't a conspiracy. It's legit. Just look around."

"I don't know."

"F_stop39 isn't the only person talking about it. Check out some of the followers."

Melanie went back to f_stop39's page and clicked on numerous followers. Each page was similar to f_stop39's. But even still, it felt like a conspiracy, like faking the moon landing or the man on the grassy knoll.

"I don't know; it just doesn't seem real," she messaged her friend.

"I believe it," Bridgette replied.

"Mel, I am going to get my nails done. You coming?" her mother called from upstairs. There were a number of things she would rather do, but she decided she may as well go. It wasn't like she was doing anything here.

"Sure," she replied.

"Well, get a move on, you aren't going in your pajamas."

"Why not?"

"Melanie, go get changed!"
"I'm good."
"Mel!"
Melanie was laughing as she climbed the stairs to get changed.
"You aren't funny," her mother called from the bathroom.
"You love me."

Chapter Seventeen

Harry

NARROW RAYS of gold peeked through the overcast sky. Oaks, now bright green in the throes of an uncharacteristically warm spring, tinted the bright rays from above with a natural soft glow. Vines twisted their way from the forest floor upwards around the trunk of the trees with the initial beckoning of spring written on newborn leaves, freshly sprung. The ground was an emerald carpet that gently rolled between oak and hemlock trees in slight waves and dipped low to support dense shrubbery before descending gradually to a slow-moving creek at the edge of the forest. Mist rising from the dewy grass speckled like diamonds in the fragile rays that cascaded through the branches above.

Light whisperings of life were heard in the creak of the crickets, the sudden whoosh of wings as two sparrows took to the air to rest on a low hung branch, the brush of grass while a chipmunk scurried past an opening between bushes. Life was abundant.

Harry Davis stood in this secluded Eden that was his escape. It served as a reminder of the beauty of nature. The air was fresh in his nostrils, smelling of the new life in the dirt and grass beneath his feet as well as the leaves peeping their tiny heads into the world from the mighty oak.

Before him was the stone Harry had set after the death of his mother, Julianna. It wasn't a grave marker, at least not in the normal sense. Julianna was not buried beneath the stone. No, this makeshift memorial was a personal reminder for Harry. It was the reason for the armbands. He needed to remember that. They deserved what was coming. If the forest surrounding Harry's reclusive home was any indication, the world was better without humanity.

From behind him, Harry heard Maggie scream again. He wondered if she would ever stop. So far, the answer was no.

He would silence her soon enough. Time was ticking away. He had to get back to work.

Chapter Eighteen

John

JOHN SPED down the highway looking for the nearest exit. He needed to get off the road quickly. His heart was racing, and sweat trickled down his brow. The adrenaline high he felt masked some, but not all, of the ache in his shoulder. The pain burned along his skin. He fought the urge to scratch the incessant itch; he knew that would only irritate the injury further. He would figure out what to do with it once he was away from the highway.

Up ahead, he saw an exit sign. He turned right as soon as he got to the exit. There was a slight hill that led to an overpass with a traffic light at the end of the exit. The light flashed red as John came to a halt.

On the highway below, a police cruiser raced past. John watched, all the while waiting for the vehicle to spot his truck. But the lights disappeared around a bend in the road, and the traffic light turned to green.

There was a gas station ahead on John's right. He pulled into the lot and backed into a spot near a tree that provided shade.

There weren't many people around to see, but nonetheless, John was cautious as he removed the flannel shirt from the license plate. He was sure he attracted attention on the highway, but at least none of the people at the rest stop had a license number to identify his truck. Still, word would get out. Soon enough, they would be looking for a black truck. He would have to take back roads and try to put some miles between himself and the rest area.

John dusted off the flannel shirt and threw it overtop of his blood-stained one. He buttoned the over shirt despite the heat outside. The fabric was singed, where the bullet had nicked John's shoulder. He moved the flannel, so the hole wasn't as noticeable. It provided a little cover. Not much, but some.

In the gas station, John found rubbing alcohol and bandages. That would have to do.

"These free?" he asked the cashier, pointing to a stack of roadmaps on the counter.

"Two bucks," she answered.

"Alright, I'll take one of those too then," he said as he set the dollar bills on the counter.

"You could just pull the map up on your phone," she said, stuffing the map in a plastic bag with the bandages. "Save ya a couple bucks."

"I don't have a cell phone," John said. He glanced at the door.

"Yea, I'm afraid they spyin' on me too."

"What?"

"You know all them phones has chips in 'em."

"Yea, guess it's good we don't have phones then," he replied. He needed to get out of here.

"Same thing with them armbands," the cashier said as she handed John the bag. His mind was elsewhere, but thoughts of last night resurfaced at the mention of armbands. What about the man he just shot? Had he been wearing one? He hadn't taken the time to look.

"What's that?" he asked.

"Armbands. Those black band things people been wearin' lately. It's the same thing. Government control."

"That so?"

"I'm just saying, why else would they sell them so cheap? They want everyone wearing one, so they can tell where everybody is."

"Well, I don't have one of those either," John said as he turned to leave.

"Good, don't let them track you. Have a good day!"

"You too," he called over his shoulder.

As John left, the parking lot was still pretty quiet, for which he was grateful. He already felt like he was being watched. The less people around the better.

He waited until he was back on the road before he opened the bottle of rubbing alcohol. As he drove, John ripped his shirt open and took his first look at the injury. The bullet left a line of bloody flesh almost an inch wide across his shoulder. The skin around the wound was bright red and slightly puffed. With quick glances between his shoulder and the road, John managed to tilt the bottle just above the gash and pour the stinging liquid over the wound. He winced at the sharp pain but managed to douse the area with another round of alcohol before calling it good.

John drove for two hours along back roads, through forests and podunk burghs. Then, when he felt he had traveled far enough, he stopped at a motel in a rinky-dink town. It was run down, but he was too exhausted to care. Besides, he didn't plan on staying long. Not even for the night, if he could help it. He just needed a place to lay down for a bit and hopefully clean the bullet wound better.

Chapter Nineteen

Melanie

THE NAIL SALON always smelled like dead skin and feet, but Melanie enjoyed the opportunity to be with her mom. These moments were becoming few and far between as she Melanie navigated high school and drifted further from her parents. Unlike many teenagers her age, she found herself wanting to spend as much time with them as she could. Even though she was only fourteen, she realized time was precious.

She leaned back in her chair. Her mother was in the chair next to her getting blue acrylic nails. Melanie didn't care for the feel of the acrylic ones, so she was just getting a new coating of yellow polish. It was bright and summery, perfect for this weekend.

"It's been over a month since we came here, hasn't it?" Delana asked.

"Um, I think," Melanie replied. "We came in March for sure. Did we come in April?"

"No, maybe we didn't," her mother replied.

"I can't remember."

"It couldn't have been that long," Delana pondered. "Oh well, it doesn't matter."

Melanie watched her mother lean back in her chair and close her eyes. This was her comfort zone. She was happy.

There was a sudden prick along Melanie's cuticle, sharp and stinging. She turned to her nail technician, who was apologetically dabbing her nail with an alcohol pad.

"It's alright," Melanie said.

It hadn't really hurt that bad anyway. She was more startled than anything. But as she watched the woman massage the end of her finger, Melanie was struck by how dark the woman's eyes were. It seemed like there was no white to her eye whatsoever. Then, for the first time, Melanie noticed the woman was wearing an armband.

Her conversation with Bridgette drifted up from her subconscious. What was the actual purpose of that band? She wanted to ask the woman, but she decided against it.

Instead, she ruminated on her conversation with Bridgette earlier. Was there something sinister about the bands, or was this just another wild internet theory?

When their nails were done, Melanie and her mother took a stroll through Central Park before heading back home.

Melanie was grateful for the time together. Moments like this were special. All thought of the armbands disappeared.

Chapter Twenty

Maggie

"STOP! MOTHERFUCKER!" Maggie screamed. Her arm was on fire, literally on fire. She felt the flames lick and burn her skin where the band had been on her arm. Since being swept from the highway, Maggie had undergone countless procedures. Was it hours or days since she had tried to break the band off her arm? She had lost all sense of time.

In the midst of excruciating pain, every second seemed like an hour. And from the second Maggie had been pinned to the table with leather straps around her ankles, arms, and neck, she had been in agony. Harry had never said so much as a word to her after she was strapped to the table. Once he had tied her down, he left for a while, and when he returned, he went straight to work on her arm poking and prodding with all manner of devices. Now he was actually burning skin below where the band had been.

Copper prongs were deeply embedded into the flesh and connected to nerves. So, when Harry pulled the band off Maggie, pain rapidly spread up her arm and through her neck to the rest of her body. The pain was blinding; Maggie passed out before the band was fully off. All along, Harry had worked diligently, treating Maggie more like a computer that needed fixing than a person. Her cries and pleadings fell upon deaf ears.

Maggie wasn't sure why she still screamed. Nothing she said had actually eased her pain. Her throat was dry and raspy. She was surprised to find that she had any voice left at all. She had tried to think of other ways to get out. None seemed feasible, though. She was too tightly strapped to think of sliding an arm free. Early on, she had fought to glimpse her surroundings, but with her neck strapped to the table, all she had managed to do was strain a muscle. She was completely and utterly trapped.

Harry cleared his throat. Maggie held her breath. Was he actually going to say something to her? She imagined him consulting her, *So Maggie, my darling. This armband seems to have malfunctioned. I was thinking of putting a new one on, but you seem a little hesitant. What is your expert analysis?*

No. After two hours of silence and agony wrought by this man, his voice was the last thing she wanted to hear.

"What does it feel like?" Harry said, breaking the quiet as though he has been listening to her thoughts.

Maggie didn't want to answer. She didn't want to acknowledge him. Another harsh pain shot through her arm and into her neck again.

"Ahhg!" Maggie gritted her teeth, not wanting to say a word.

She would take the pain as long as it lasted.

"Maggie, answer me, and I will make it stop," Harry said.

The pain suddenly ceased.

"I don't believe you. I'm getting used to it anyway. Give me more."

The strap on her neck became slack. She could move her head.

"Go ahead. Have a look around," Harry said. Maggie closed her eyes and kept her head on the table.

"Nope. I'm good."

"Maggie."

"That's me!" she said, a broad smile spread across her face, but she refused to open her eyes.

"Alright. I'll leave you be for now. I'll check on you in a bit."

What was he, a fucking doctor, or something? She heard his heavy metallic footsteps clink away. She waited. He didn't leave. *He wouldn't leave, would he?* This was some kind of trick. She would open her eyes, and he would be there right above her head, smiling down. Nonetheless, she decided to hazard a peek.

Nothing but ceiling and dim light. She opened both eyes. She didn't see or hear him. Maggie raised her head to look around at the room. This would be her most comprehensive view yet of the area. The room was empty. Just the table she lay on. From the way the shadow of her head fell across her chest, it looked like there was light coming from behind her. She couldn't be sure.

Maybe she could escape. He had freed her neck. Maybe she could wiggle enough now to free one of her arms. She rotated her right arm against the strap. It was too tight. She felt the hairs on her arm pull out as she turned it. She pushed against the strap, but it refused to give an inch. Maybe her left arm, she thought. Yet, when she went to move that arm, something was wrong. She couldn't feel anything below her elbow. It was like her arm wasn't there at all. Maggie sat up as far as she could and looked down to where her arm should be, but she didn't see an arm at all. What she did see was a bloody stump. Her entire forearm from her elbow down had been severed.

"Oh, my God! What did you do to me?!" Maggie screamed.

She threw her head back against the table. Tears poured from her eyes and streamed down her face.

"You asshole! Come back here!" she cried.

"Yes?" his voice was right behind her. Right behind her head.

"Let me see your face, you piece of shit!" she demanded.

"Maggie, calm down. I know you must be upset. Trust me. It's not that bad."

"It's not that bad?" she screamed. "You took my fucking arm!"

"What?"

"Oh, you're probably laughing, aren't you? You sick fuck! You cut off my arm!"

"I would never," Harry said calmly.

He stepped around the table where she lay. He placed a hand on her thigh, just above her knee.

"Look at it!" Maggie yelled.

He was standing next to her left side. He should see the mutilated stump. She wanted him to really look at it, though. So she raised what was left of her arm. But as she did so, she saw her hand was again where it should be. She squeezed it. She could feel her fingers. It felt normal like nothing had ever changed.

"What did you do to me?" she asked. She was still angry inside, but a great relief washed over her at the sight of her arm.

"Maggie, my name is Dr. Davis. I am trying to help you. You came to me because you were seeing things. Things that weren't real," the man beside her said.

"No, that is not true. You brought me here. I don't even know where I am!"

"I apologize for that. Unfortunately, when you came here, you were in such a state of frenzy, I couldn't let you be with the other patients. We had to bring you to a solitary room where you could get the rest you needed. We anesthetized you upon your arrival, and some of the unease you feel now may be related to that. It is an unfortunate side effect that some of our patients report. We just didn't want to take any chances. You seemed like you might hurt the members of our staff or yourself. You actually bit me," he laughed and pulled up the sleeve of his white medical jacket. Sure enough, there were teeth marks on his forearm. "Don't worry, I was able to get away before any real damage was done."

"You are lying. Where is your metal suit thing? Huh? And the wings? Bet ya didn't think I would remember that. Or the accident on the highway? Or how I wanted to tear off the armband, and you were pissed. Remember that Dr. Davis?" Maggie said.

"You always have the most fascinating visions, Maggie. Come, why don't you take a walk with me?" he extended his hand.

"What about the straps?" Maggie asked.

Before Dr. Davis could answer, she looked down. Where the straps had held her down, she saw her arms and legs lying on a hospital bed. She was wearing a hospital gown.

"What was that, Maggie?" Dr. Davis said.

He leaned a little closer like he hadn't heard her. His hand was still extended.

"I . . . uh, nothing," she stammered.

"Come," he said to her.

She took his hand, and he helped her sit up. A pair of slippers sat next to the bed. Dr. Davis knelt and slid them onto her feet. He took her hand again and helped her off the bed. Then they walked out a door behind where Maggie had been lying. They emerged in a bright white hallway. It had the sterile antiseptic smell of a hospital. The floor was alternating blue and cream-colored tiles. Dr. Davis led her left down the hallway, past a nurse's station. A heavyset woman behind the counter smiled at her and waved. Maggie's mouth hung open. None of this was real she wanted to say, but how could she argue with the woman at the counter.

They continued on. The hallway stretched on for quite a distance. They passed wooden doors that Maggie assumed must be other patient's rooms. At the end of the hall, Dr. Davis turned right. Maggie could see a green light at the end of this hall. Suddenly she wanted to stop. Whatever that green light was, she didn't want to find out.

"Are you okay Maggie?" Dr. Davis asked.

"I don't want to go there," she replied. "This isn't real. You wanted to hurt me."

"Maggie, we have had this conversation before. I certainly do not want to hurt you. I'm trying to help. Please, come with me. You love the atrium," Dr. Davis said.

"Atrium?" she asked.

"At the end of the hall, you can see the light from here. Remember, you love to sit on the bench beside the stream and the weeping willow?" he said.

"You can't have a stream and a whole weeping willow in an atrium that's ridiculous," Maggie replied.

Dr. Davis just smiled. "Come and see."

Maggie sighed, "Okay."

Before they even got to the atrium, Maggie could smell the fresh cool air from the plants. She heard the trickle of water over rocks.

She could even hear the soft calling of swallows. This was impossible. The atrium would have to be huge.

Then at the end of the hall, they turned left, and the green light that had glistened from the end of the hall opened into a whole world of majestic plant life. Her eyes were overwhelmed by the world that opened before her. Tall oak trees cast long shadows on the ground. A smooth dirt path was bordered with a myriad of flowers. Pansies and poppies of all colors sprang up from the luscious grass. Maggie stood in awe. There, beyond the flowers and path, she saw the stream and next to it a giant weeping willow. Its leaves hung so low they touched the surface of the water. She felt light, weightless.

"Can we go?" she asked. All her doubts were forgotten.

"Maggie, we are always welcome in the atrium, you know this. Go," Dr. Davis said to her.

She studied his face. He had soft eyes, a warm smile. He was a little older, she guessed from the wrinkles. He couldn't be too old, though. His beard and hair were still a deep black.

He would have been handsome when he was younger. She supposed he still was, but there was a sort of tired look about him. It was only natural. Being a doctor has to be a trying career.

"Will you come with me?"

He looked down at his watch.

"I have a little bit," he muttered to himself. "Yea, I can sit with you."

They walked down the path to the bench beneath the tree. The air was warm with a light breeze. The wind blew her hair back over her shoulders; she felt like an angel walking on clouds. Maggie could not remember having seen a more beautiful place in all her life; this was heaven, she thought.

She sat down on the bench. Dr. Davis made sure she was comfortable before he sat next to her.

"Do I come here a lot?" she asked. Dr. Davis studied her as though he was waiting for her to say more. She was gazing at the stream. Then she added, "I do, don't I?"

"I wouldn't say a lot," he replied. "You come here . . . when you need to, that's all."

"But why am I here now?" she asked. "I don't remember coming here. Where are we exactly?"

"You often don't remember coming here. Usually, you are in such a state of unrest you can't recall anything but your name. But we are very familiar with you at this point. We know exactly what is needed when you walk through the doors."

"And what is that?" Maggie asked.

"We need to get you out of your head. Sometimes you think too much. It drives you insane," Dr. Davis said. They sat in silence for a few minutes. The breeze rolling over the water was calming. Maggie was almost reluctant to ask anything more. Blissful ignorance might be the perfect remedy for what was ailing her. But somewhere deep in her subconscious, she was thirsty for more information.

"How do you get me out of my head?" she asked.

Their eyes met.

"But don't you know?" he asked.

Maggie felt herself falling. The beautiful garden around her collapsed in on itself. Dr. Davis was smiling at her. All the world around them became a blur. It twisted and shifted, so it was no longer a garden. Maggie felt like she was being sucked through a straw away from the atrium and into another dimension. Dr. Davis just smiled all the while, but he was different now. He wasn't wearing his medical jacket anymore. No. It was now the beast that had taken her on the highway. He was still smiling, only; it wasn't a happy smile. It was evil. Like he knew everything about her. Like he could see her naked before him, and they both knew it, but there was nothing she could do to stop him from looking. She knew she was not in control. She knew that she was being controlled. Even if she didn't want to, she knew there was nothing she could do now. She had fought once, and she could try to keep fighting, but it would never end. And she would always lose.

Chapter Twenty-One

Harry

MAGGIE WAS WRITHING on the table before him. Her screams hadn't abated. In fact, after the little stunt he just pulled, they may have gotten louder than ever. Despite her wailing, he was pretty certain he had fixed her armband. It shouldn't give him anymore trouble.

Harry strode across the room just beyond Maggie's field of vision. There on the other side of the room was a table. On it was a decanter half-filled with one of Harry's favorite single-malt scotches. He poured a glass and relished the aroma before taking a sip. The single malt was smokey and smooth with a long finish. Harry closed his eyes and slipped into a memory.

HE AND JOHN stood in the parlor, each holding a glass of amber liquid.

"Here's to the future and the prosperous days that lie ahead," John said with a smile.

John wore a navy-blue suit with a blood orange tie. His hair was combed back neatly. He was ready for the presentation. Harry raised his glass and met John's eyes, "To the future and all that that entails."

Their glasses clinked together. The scotch was warm as it trickled down Harry's throat, warm but smooth.

"I'm sorry Juliana wasn't able to make it," John said. "How is she?"

"It was just a minor episode this morning, but I didn't trust that she would be ok with all the people here tonight," Harry remarked. "I already have her lined up to get the first bracelet, John. Everything is going to change for her."

"I couldn't think of a more deserving woman," John said. He raised his glass again and took another long sip. "Everything's already set?"

"Yea. All set. Mark should be here any minute."

"Have you had a chance to talk to him?"

"Not for a couple days, why?" Harry asked.

"No reason," John said. "Just some thoughts on marketing. I'm sure he will explain it all when he gets here."

"John, it's not about the money," Harry sighed as he took another sip of scotch. "That will only distract us from what we are trying to do. The bracelets are revolutionary. How many years have people like Juliana waited for something like this? We can't lose sight of that."

"No, of course not," John said. "Speak of the devil, here he comes now."

John strode across the room and greeted Mark with an outstretched hand and a big smile. The short, stocky man from Taylor Pharmaceuticals excitedly met John with a toothy grin and a laugh. Harry watched as the men exchanged greetings, and then there was a moment of hesitation as they whispered something he couldn't hear. For a second, there was fear in Mark's eyes. Then it passed, and that grin returned.

"Harry!" Mark bellowed as he strode across the room. "How are you?"

Harry smiled and pulled Mark in for a friendly embrace after shaking hands.

"I can't thank you enough," Harry said. "Here, let me pour you a drink."

"Please only a little."

Harry pulled another glass from the stand nearby and poured Mark a scotch.

"Here's to you, Mark. This wouldn't be possible without you," Harry said as he handed Mark his glass.

"Well, I have to say this was one of the easiest investment decisions I've ever made," Mark said. He took a sip of the scotch and smiled. "This is excellent. I imagine there will be plenty more of this in the future."

"It's good, expensive, but good," Harry replied.

"Well, money won't be an issue much longer, will it now?" Mark laughed. His cheeks shone red above his enormous smile.

"How so?" Harry asked.

"Let's see what's going on outside. Shall we?" John said as he motioned toward the hallway.

Harry's eyes were focused singularly on Mark.

"Mark, for how much are you planning to sell the bracelets?" Harry asked.

There was silence as the businessman surveyed Harry's demeanor. His forehead shined with a thin layer of sweat.

"They are reasonably priced like we agreed," he replied.

"And how much is that?"

"Harry, you don't need to worry about details like that tonight. Enjoy yourself," Mark said.

"Mark, if I may, I think Harry and I will take a little walk outside," John stepped in to alleviate the situation. But even as he stepped between the men, Harry's eyes remained fixated on Mark.

"Answer the question, Mark," Harry said.

"Okay. We did change the price a little. Nothing drastic, just a minor adjustment," Mark said.

"How much?"

"It really isn't a big deal, Harry," Mark said.

"I will decide that. Now, answer the fucking question. How much?" Harry spat.

"Thirty-five hundred."

The glass in Harry's hand slipped from his grasp and shattered on the floor. He stumbled backward, then braced himself with an arm against the wall.

"Thirty-five hundred," he muttered under his breath.

"Harry, they will sell. That's a bargain for what we are providing. People will pay anything for one of your bracelets. You have provided a cure for dementia," Mark said.

"You don't understand anything, do you?" Harry asked. "How can anyone afford that?"

"Harry, this is still dirt cheap. Other drugs and products with the same accolades sell for upwards of fifty-thousand."

"I don't care what other people sell their shit for. This was supposed to be for everyone."

"Harry, it will be," Mark assured him.

"Not at that price," Harry argued.

"The price will come down, eventually."

"After how many people die, Mark?" Harry said. *"No. You don't care about that. As long as you get what you want."*

His eyes drifted to the bottle of scotch. He grabbed it and threw it. The glass smashed against the wall. The smell of smoke and peat enveloped the men.

"You greedy bastard!" Harry roared.

"Harry, calm down. I'm trying to help," Mark pleaded.

"If you want to help, then change the price. Change it now. Call whoever you need to, just get it changed," Harry ordered.

"I can't," Mark said.

"You will," Harry said.

"It's finalized, Harry. It's too late to change anything."

Harry turned his attention to John.

"And you knew?"

"The price will eventually come down, Harry. This is just the beginning phase," he answered.

"Beginning phase," Harry laughed. *"I trusted you, John. I trusted you!"*

Harry's eyes grew dark and deep creases formed along his brow. Inside something snapped. Rage boiled beneath the surface. His racing heart echoed in his ears as the flames of anger grew within.

"The deal is off," he growled through gritted teeth.

"Harry come on, it will be alright," Mark said.

"No. Fuck you. Get out of my house," Harry said. *"Get out!"*

Harry turned his eyes from the men as they left. When he was sure they were gone, and the room was empty, he leaned against the wall and wept. Everything was ruined. Years of research and experimentation destroyed by greed. His body quivered as he cried. His shoulders relaxed as he took a deep breath and exhaled slowly. Then his despair turned back to anger.

Harry slammed his fist against the wall and stormed from the room. As he raced upstairs, the thoughts of betrayal fanned the flames of his anger. There was no quelling the tempest within. In a blind fury, Harry raced through the house to his bedroom. There buried in the top drawer of his dresser, he found his pistol packed away in a box. He opened the lid and grabbed the weapon. The gun was heavy in his hand.

There on the top of the dresser was a photo of Julianna. Anymore she was a shadow of the woman in the frame. Frail and confused, she was wasting away by the day. How many children would have to watch their parents fade into death, weak and afraid? Lost within their mind.

Yet there was an option for men like Mark Bishop. He would never know that pain. It wasn't right. There was a moment as Harry considered the weapon. This wasn't the way to handle the problem, but he also couldn't let this injustice go unpunished.

People were leaving, and the crowd had thinned considerably by the time Harry reached the patio. He easily spotted Mark and John. They were near John's wife and daughter, walking with some of the remaining guests. Mark turned around just in time to see Harry raise the pistol.

"No!" Mark screamed.

Harry aimed the gun at Mark, but just as he squeezed the trigger, the man dove to the right, and the bullet missed. Someone screamed.

Mark slipped as he scurried out of the way and Harry took advantage of the opportunity, and fired another shot at the businessman. The bullet nicked Mark's shoulder and came to rest buried in the chest of John's daughter. There was a moment of disbelief. The girl was confused by the sudden pain in her chest. Harry watched the stain on Ellie's dress grow as she stumbled backward. Then she wavered and fell in a heap. Behind her, Harry saw John was knelt next to his wife.

No. This isn't happening. This can't be real, he cried in his mind.

The pistol fell from his hand and clattered next to his feet. A cold wave crashed over him as his rage was suddenly replaced by fear.

"What have I done?"

Then, Mark came crashing into him. Harry felt the air leave his lungs as Mark's shoulder was buried beneath his ribs, and the two crashed to the ground. The back of Harry's head hit something hard, and there was a sharp pang at the base of his skull. Then the pain disappeared, and he didn't feel anything.

He closed his eyes. This wasn't real. This wasn't happening.

"Call 9-1-1! Hurry!" Mark yelled next to Harry. His voice was distant. He could have been miles away.

When Harry opened his eyes again, John was standing over him. His eyes were red, and his face was smeared with blood.

Harry choked. He tried to say something, anything, but the words stuck in his throat. Their eyes met for one last fleeting second before John turned away. Harry tried to call out. Only a weak raspy breath escaped his lips.

"John," he moaned, but it was too late, he was gone. The sky above was dark, and more than anything, Harry wanted to drift away to nothing.

WHEN HARRY next opened his eyes, a woman was standing over him, yelling. He couldn't make out the words on her lips, and his ears were ringing. Where was he? He tried to stand up, but his body refused.

"Help me," he moaned. The woman knelt next to him. He saw her place her hand on his chest, but he didn't feel the pressure of it. "What happened?" he asked.

"We believe you suffered a spinal contusion, but it might be worse."

"What do you mean?" Harry asked.

"We will find out," she said. Ambulance personnel loaded him onto a transfer board, then to a gurney and an awaiting ambulance.

As they carted him away, Harry saw Mark and John talking, their faces alternating shades of red and blue in the flashing lights.

AFTER THAT, the memories ran together. He was in a white room. A hospital? He wasn't sure. Blurred faces appeared and disappeared too quickly to recognize. The room changed; it was no longer white but dark with brick walls. A laboratory maybe. A fierce sting shot through his neck and traveled down his spine. He could feel again. Then Mark was talking to him in the laboratory. The words sped together like a recording on fast forward. Harry could only make out part of what Mark told him. Murder. Hiding. Death. John. Bracelets. Blueprints. It was all hazy, and he didn't understand what it all meant.

Then the stinging in his neck intensified, and he saw a metal exoskeleton around his entire body. It was hot, too hot, and the heat continued to increase. He was burning from the inside out. He fought against the pain until he passed out from exhaustion. When he woke and was walking in the mechanical suit. It was thick and cumbersome, his movements slow and jerky. But he was moving on his own. That body casing was not as powerful or as nimble as the one he would wear later.

Again he was in the brick room alone with Mark.

"We had your funeral a couple weeks ago," Mark said. "Everyone thinks you are dead, Harry. Everyone, but myself and the limited staff needed to keep you alive."

"John?" Harry whispered. His voice was weak from lack of use.

"Gone. He left after Abigail and Helena's funerals. He didn't come to yours. He signed off on the bracelets and left. You broke him."

"And you broke me," Harry said. His raspy voice was barely audible.

"Yes," Mark sighed. "But I won't let you die. Not yet."

THEN DARKNESS.

FOLLOWED BY A SEVERED HEAD. It was Mark. Harry held the head by the hair.

"Now, you are broken, my friend," he whispered into Mark's ear before entering the conference room.

People at the table scattered before him. He was a little disappointed. He had hoped at least one of the men would start for him, but alas, they had run in a frenzy only to realize they were trapped. Harry stood in front of the only door in or out. When they realized their doom, they collapsed in the far corner and pleaded for mercy. His lips curled in a smile.

"Please, don't kill us! Please. Oh, God! Please have mercy," a young blonde woman yelled as Harry strode toward them. The hydraulic exoskeleton hissed with the pressure exchanges that allowed him to move.

"I'm sorry, my dear, but I don't know what that means. Mercy? Can you tell me what that is?" he asked. The woman stared up into his gleaming eyes, then she broke down in tears.

"Awe, my dear. Do you not know what it means, either? You really shouldn't use words you don't understand," Harry said while Mark's head still hung from his hand. "Can any of you tell me what mercy is? Please tell me you can. This poor woman is distraught all because she doesn't know the meaning of this one word. I would help, but unfortunately, I don't know what the word means either. Please, someone, help us!"

"You're a piece of shit! Leave her alone!" a short chubby man with thick glasses said.

"Finally, someone found their balls! Good for you! Now that you have spoken up is that all you are going to say? Because me and Miss Blondie here are in a serious dilemma. We have no fucking clue what 'mercy' means. And if your only contribution is to yell profanities, well sir, that will be of little help. Now, let's try that again. Do you know what mercy means?" Harry asked the man. The fat man had no response but instead offered a condescending glare.

Harry shook his head, "No, no, no. That will never do, I thought for a second you had something to say, but I can see you don't. Really unfortunate for you. Catch!"

Harry tossed Mark's severed head toward the heavyset man. The head landed in his lap, and the man recoiled in horror. As soon as the man's eyes were off him, Harry pounced. He lunged across the short space between them and grabbed the man beneath the arms. Then he lifted him with ease and held him high so that his head touched the ceiling. A trickle of urine ran down one fat thigh and left a dark spot on his pants. He screamed and wriggled, but Harry's metallic grip did not give. With alarming speed, Harry whipped the man across the room. The man flew over the conference table and smashed into the wall with a thunderous crash. His body fell limp to the floor.

He tried to stand up, but Harry descended on him once more. Harry lifted him again, only this time he held him aloft by the back of the neck. Then he slammed the obese man's head through the wall. Again and again, Harry pummeled the man against the wall. When he was finished, he let the body fall to the floor. Not a sound escaped the fat man whose face was now a bloody pureed mess.

"Now, I asked a simple question that not one of you college educated dipshits seem able to answer. What the fuck is mercy!?" Harry yelled. The group sat silent. A young Asian woman cleared her throat to answer.

"It's w-w-withh-h-olding strength. Not using your full power against someone weaker than you," she stammered. Harry nodded his head while he listened. When she finished, he slowly clapped his hands.

"Ok, now we are getting somewhere, thank you very much Ms. . . ."

"Maggie. Maggie Wu," she answered.

"Ms. Wu. You have been very helpful. Now for another question. Was I merciful to your friend here?"

Her mouth dropped at the question. She closed her eyes, her body quivered as she tried to answer.

"Y-y-yes," she whispered finally.

"Ah. Now, if I was being merciful here, I wonder what I could have done? Can you imagine just what I am capable of? Forgive me, I'm getting ahead of myself. Let's come back to that. Okay? First, your other friend, the one on the *floor next to you, he's missing his body,"* Harry motioned toward Mark Bishop's head. *"Was he a good man?" No one answered.*

"Oh, shucks! You are probably confused by the question, let me explain," Harry paced the room and came to a halt once more in front of the group. *"Now, where do I begin? Your boss Mark there, he was going to help fund a project for me. Great news, right?"*

He gave a long sigh and shook his head.

"Well, not as great as you might think. You see, Mark and I had different opinions on a product I made. We both did things we shouldn't have. He went behind my back, and I tried to kill him. Boys will be boys. What are you gonna do? As you can see, I'm still breathing. And Mark? Not so much."

"But, I don't want to talk all day. Really, I just wanted to get your opinion of Mark. See, I get the impression he wasn't a very nice man. But, sometimes, our own feelings get in the way, don't they? So I need to ask, was Mark Bishop, a really good guy?"

The blond woman in front answered, "No, he wasn't."

"Ok," Harry sighed. *"Well, I am glad we cleared that up. It would have broken my heart to think I killed a good man. So, Mark wasn't good. He was kind of greedy, wasn't he?"*

The group nodded their heads.

"I thought so. It's an evil thing, greed. Wouldn't you agree?"

The group nodded their heads.

"Good. I'm glad we are on the same page. Now, back to my original question about the meaning of mercy. As Ms. Wu just kindly noted, I am merciful. Very merciful. Because of this, I don't want you to suffer the same fate as Mr. Fatty over there or your good friend Mark. Because I am merciful I am offering you a choice, I will admit it's not much of a choice, but it's there for you. You can either work for me or die."

He chuckled to himself.

"I told you, not much of a choice, but it's your decision," Harry said. *They looked around at each other. Everyone nodded their heads in silence.*

It was Maggie, who finally answered, "We will work."

"Good. I was hoping you would say that. Now first things first, we need to fix a few bugs in those armbands Mark was creating. I think we are going to have to make some adjustments. Change them up a little bit."

The memory faded, and Harry was back in the room. Maggie still screamed on the table. Only three of the original group had made it through his rigorous testing. Maggie had been the best of the three. He didn't want her to succumb like the others. He took another long sip of scotch and watched her writhe.

Time was running short. In less than six hours, chaos would reign in New York City. He set the scotch down and got back to work.

Chapter Twenty-Two

John

WHEN JOHN WOKE, the bed in the Mountain Mist Motel where he had collapsed hours earlier was stained red. He rolled from the mattress and tumbled to the floor. The room was spinning, and he felt weak.

"Fuck," he muttered.

He struggled to his feet and lumbered to the bathroom. The man in the mirror looked tattered and worn. John washed his face before peeling the shirt from his body. Using a towel from the rack against the wall, he wet the wound along his shoulder. It burned when he touched it, but he had to clean it as best as he could or risk infection. He doused a washcloth with the alcohol and scrubbed the wound. Then he covered it with a bandage and called it good. It wasn't perfect, but it would have to do.

For now, all he wanted was a clean shirt and a drink. John pulled a white tee from his bag and threw it on. Then he wrapped the bloody one in a garbage bag he pulled from the bathroom trash and stuffed it in a side pocket of his bag. He would throw it out somewhere on the road. It would attract attention here, and he was still worried the police would be looking for him.

He laid the roadmap from the gas station on the bed and scanned the list of rest areas on the back. He knew he was somewhere north of Blisse, but how far? He scanned the map for a few minutes until he found Blisse in Eastern New York. After finding the small town, John found three rest areas within a fifty-mile radius of the town. But of the three, two were southwest of Blisse, leaving the third as the only option. From there, he couldn't be sure what back roads he had taken, but he was almost positive he had been traveling east the whole time. He figured he had traveled eighty to one-hundred miles from the rest stop, which put him somewhere near the border of New York and Massachusetts.

Not bad, he thought as he sat on the floor next to the bed. He could relax a little. The police wouldn't have followed him this far. At least he hoped not.

Whether the police were looking for him or not, John didn't want to stay here any longer. He wanted to move, run, just go somewhere. He could go north again, get out of New York, and head toward Canada. But what was the point now? The only reason he started that way was to get to his brother's, and that wasn't an option anymore. So it didn't matter where he turned from here. He just needed to get away.

Fifteen minutes later, he was in his truck with a cigarette nestled between his lips as he left the Mountain Mist Motel heading south on a two-lane road. He would follow this road and let it lead him where it may.

It was a lonely stretch of road, just idyllic views of the rolling hills gradually fading into obscurity. Beautiful but lonely, John thought. He could see a house here and there dotting the mountains, but otherwise, the landscape was dreary and lonely.

He drove on for a while, lost in thought, and in no hurry to get anywhere. Sometime before the sun fully dipped behind the hills, John saw a faded blue sign that read, Hadisborough. The road rolled smoothly into the main street of the town. Battered houses with broken windows and lawns that were brown and dusty lined the road. In many small towns, the best houses are situated along the main street. If this was the best the town had to offer, John wondered what the other houses looked like.

He continued on. When he first saw the town sign, he had hoped there would be a halfway decent bar where he could get a drink. But, that seemed unlikely now. Then, up ahead on his right, he spied a big grey barn. The paint was peeling, and the roof seemed to droop inward. Near the top, a weathered orange floodlight glowed, the first and only sign of life John had seen in the town. As he approached it, he assumed it must be someone's personal property.

He was almost past the dirt driveway when he saw a blinking red neon sign that read Grey House Pub. John came to a stop in the middle of the road and coasted back a few feet in reverse, eyeing the building.

A porch jutting out from under the neon sign sagged greatly while a shabby wooden door hung haphazardly by its hinges. Small windows high off the ground were obscured through a film of haze and years of wear. The dirt lot was empty, but for an old Pontiac Grand AM that was so covered in dust, the color couldn't be discerned. John pulled into the lot and parked.

He strode across the lot, and sure enough, he heard the distant sound of music coming from the bar. The steps creaked and wobbled dangerously as his boot heels clicked on the wood, but to his surprise, they didn't collapse. He opened the door, and the familiar tangy smell of alcohol and cigarette smoke wafted through the opening and greeted him like an old friend. Don McLean's voice wavered with static from a radio behind the bar. A solitary old man with long hair and a scraggly beard sat conversing with the bartender. Both men turned when John entered.

"How's it goin'?" John asked.

Neither answered with words, but both men nodded in acknowledgment. John took a stool a couple down from the old man.

"I don't know, Daryl, it just seems there ain't room for us round here no more," the bartender continued his conversation with the old man as he walked toward John.

"What can I get ya?" he asked.

"Coors," John answered.

"Original, right? We don't have none of that light shit," the man said.

"I wouldn't have it any other way," John said as a smile spread across his face. He liked this place already.

"Good. Otherwise, I mightin' have to politely tell ya to get the hell outta here," the bartender replied. He was a tall, lean man with thinning blonde hair, a mustache, and glasses perched on a long beak of a nose. He set the beer before John.

"Names Leroy," the man said, extending his hand. John shook hands and introduced himself.

"Small little town ya got here, Leroy. I thought it was a ghost town till I saw your sign out front," John said.

"Might as well be!" the old man a couple of stools down said. He got up slowly and limped toward them, before plopping in a stool one away from their new guest. John noticed as he sat that his right leg was a prosthetic. He wore a weathered leather jacket. Inscribed on the sleeve were the words Vietnam War.

"You served in Vietnam?" John asked.

"Hell yea, I did! Long time ago," the old man stated.

"So did my father," John said as he extended his hand to thank the man for his service. The old man had a strong shake despite the old, knobby-knuckled appearance of his hand.

"I'm Daryl," he said.

"John. It's an honor to meet you, Daryl. You Vietnam vets had it rough. I can't thank you enough for what you went through," John said.

"Well, that was a long time ago," Daryl said.

"What do you drink?" John asked.

"No, no, that's not necessary," Daryl refused politely.

"Get us a couple shots of Evan Williams then," John said to Leroy.

Leroy had three tall shot glasses full to the brim on the counter in no time.

"Here ya are, Daryl!" Leroy said, raising one glass.

John took another and raised it as well. Daryl smiled and shook his head as he took the other one. They downed the shots, and Daryl patted John on the back.

"Thank ya, son," he said, wiping his mouth.

"Thank you, sir," John replied. They sat in silence, sipping their beers while Bob Dylan's "It's Not Dark Yet," hummed through the stereo.

Daryl finally broke the silence, "Ya know people just ain't the same no more. You said this town looked like a ghost town, and damn it, it might as well be. Leroy here got the only place that's still open. I tell ya, there ain't no one left round here. Used to be three different bars all right next to each other. Shit, now ya got this place and a gas station on the other side a town, and that's it."

He leaned deep against the backrest of the stool and took a sip of beer before he continued, "I watched it decline. Yes sir! Kids grow up and have no understandin' of community. I come back from the war and I tell ya, I usta run a garage, right next to Leroy's here as a matter a fact, he'll tell ya. I was busy too! Then, they just stopped coming. Started kinda slow like ya know? A few people here and there stop coming, and before ya know it, I was lucky to get one oil change a week, if that," Daryl stopped and took another long swig from his can of Genesee. He didn't say anything more for a few minutes. John assumed that was the end of his story. Daryl gazed off into space like he might have forgotten what he was talking about. So, it caught John by surprise when he started up again.

"Ya know kids today just don't understand nothin. They're all lost in their phones or those armband things. I was walkin' down the street the other day, and I tell ya, this kid come walkin' toward me and damn near run into me. Not payin no attention, nothing! Just looked at me eyes, all blank like. I says to him, 'Hey! Watch out, kid!' and he just stares at me like he don't hear nothin'. I step to the side, and he just keeps on walkin' like I wasn't there. Damn strange," Daryl finished. Leroy shook his head.

The bar was empty, but for the three of them. As John looked around, he saw dust covering the tables and walls. A pool table along the far back wall looked like it hadn't been touched in years. He wondered if this place ever got busy and what it must have been like years ago, like Daryl was saying when the town was busy. He had an idea that this place was probably a lot like Ted's when it first opened. He could imagine sitting here after work and talking to

Leroy like he did with Ted. Then again, there was something off. Maybe it was just the passage of time that felt more pressing here in a dying town.

He sipped his Coors and yawned. His head felt fuzzy. He could have driven on, but it was probably best that he stopped at this little bar if for no other reason than to clear his head. The beer tasted good, and it helped, but what he could really use right now was another nap. He was sure some of that had to do with the gunshot wound, but besides that, this was when he slept before going to work for the night. That wasn't the case tonight, yet his body was craving that sleep.

His eyelids felt heavy. He yawned again, and a watery layer of tears blurred his vision until he blinked again. He sighed, as much as he craved a good nap right now, he couldn't really take one.

"Another Coors?" Leroy asked, waking John from his stupor.

"Yea sure," he answered. He looked over at Daryl, who was bobbing his head slowly off his chest half sleeping.

"Where you headin'? We don't get too many folks passing through town here. Daryl wasn't lying about that. You must be headin' somewhere," Leroy said.

"I'm just heading to my brother's in Connecticut," he lied.

"So, you got a bit more driving to do, don't cha?" Leroy asked.

"I'm figuring another hour thereabouts," John said. He took a long swig of his beer. Daryl stirred in his sleep, and with a loud snort and cough, he woke from a dream. He nearly fell from his stool; he was so startled.

"Damn it," Daryl muttered.

With a big yawn, he stood up and stretched. A low growl was pushed up and out as he spread his arms wide. John heard Daryl's shoulder joints pop. The old man cracked his neck, then sat back on his stool. With a wet beer burp, he was fully awake again.

"Connecticut, eh?" he said as though he had never left the conversation. "What takes ya up there?"

"Just visiting my brother. Been a couple years and got some time off from work. Think we'll do some fishing," John said.

"Fishing up in Connecticut," Daryl chuckled. "I usta go fishin' at a pond up there. Real nice, just sit down with a case a beer and a coffee can full a dirt n' worms. Nothing better than that, I tell ya," Daryl said.

John nodded. He knew the feeling. He didn't believe he was going to do any fishing anytime soon, but Daryl's reminiscing made John long for that more than anything. He wished this was a vacation.

"Yea," he said finally. "I used to do that all summer. Walk down to the river and spend the entire day just sitting on the edge of the water, waiting for a bite."

Daryl chuckled and shook his head, "Yes, sir. Used to be able to do that. S'pose ya still can, if ya find the right place. I got a feelin' that soon you ain't gonna find places like that no more."

"Yea," John sighed.

The room was quiet as the men sipped their beer. Behind the bar, Leroy dusted some bottles before tiring of the chore and turning on the television that hung in the corner. From what John could see, it was the only one in the place. Leroy clicked through the channels before stopping on the news.

"Oh, not this shit," Daryl groaned.

"Be quiet," Leroy muttered over his shoulder.

It was eight o'clock; the local news program was going through the top of the hour run down.

"Could a resolution to elevated toxicity levels in local water sources be on the horizon? A multi-vehicle accident involving a cattle trailer leaves at least 43 dead. And the Milton high school baseball team is giving credit for their recent playoff victory to a surprising member. But first our top story of the hour, murder at a rest stop. Stanly Chase on the scene," the anchor said.

"Thanks, Lisa. I'm here at the Jackson Lodge just off county Route 54, where locals are saying a pitched gunfight occurred this afternoon around 1:30. Some residents claim this is the culmination of months of drug-related violence. Only, this time the result was death. I spoke with one individual earlier who was at the rest stop at the time of the shooting, and he said it sounded like multiple assault rifles were being fired. Local police have not confirmed what weapons were used, but have asked that the public be on the lookout for the gunman. Details are limited, but police have confirmed the gunman was a white man between the ages of 40 and 60 driving a black truck. Make, and model are unknown at this time. Back to you, Lisa."

"Thank you, Stan. We will have the latest details on the search as it unfolds. Stay tuned for more information when it becomes available. Now, to one of the largest accidents in recent memory. . ." Lisa's voice faded to the background as Daryl began talking.

"Fuckin' drugs. Nobody can just smoke their weed and be happy. Jesus."

John took a sip of beer to calm his nerves. His hand was shaking when he set the glass on the counter. He quickly pulled the pack of cigarettes from his pocket and stuck one in his mouth. The orange burn turned to ash as he inhaled. It seemed like the police didn't have much evidence to go on yet, which was good. Nonetheless, John was nervous. Although he had two hours of driving between himself and the shooting, he still felt too close.

"Drugs, that's just the excuse they use when they don't know," Leroy said.

"How much you wanna bet they didn't even interview anyone? Just ran with whatever they wanted to say?" Daryl asked.

"Oh, I'm sure," Leroy answered.

"'Nother shot?" he asked, turning to John.

"Yea, make it a double," he answered.

"What do you think?" Daryl asked.

"About?"

"The news. Murder at the rest stop."

"I don't know. Nothing surprises me now," John said.

"Ain't that the truth," Daryl replied. "Hey, grab me a shot too Leroy."

That shot led to another not long after. Sometime after the third shot, John began to feel comfortable, the thought of the police on his tail was a distant memory. He was now milking his fourth or fifth beer and approaching the goldilocks zone, that perfect balance between passed out drunk and sober. The room had just a touch of spin, and at least to John, the lights gave off a warm, orange glow.

Everything was perfect, but for the nagging ache in his shoulder. He shifted in the stool to ease the pain. That worked for a moment, but before long, the pain was back. It was probably nothing John thought. Even still, he wanted to take a look at it.

At the end of the bar, he spied the sign for the bathroom. He got up slowly and made his way to the other end of the room and shuffled into the restroom.

It was small and dirty. John peeled off his shirt. In the foggy mirror above the sink, he saw his reflection. His shoulder was purple near the wound and red everywhere else. The skin closest to the injury was tender. There was nothing he could do right now; he would just have to wait and see if it got worse. He slid his shirt back on and went back to the bar.

"Nother drink?" Leroy asked.

John was about to say no, that he needed to get back on the road when he saw her. There sitting in the chair next to his was Elly. She turned and smiled, beautiful as ever.

"You need to stay here, Daddy," she said.

So, John took his seat in the stool and nodded to Leroy.

"Baby girl, what are you doing here?" he whispered after Leroy turned to get his drink.

"Daddy, we miss you," she said.

"I miss you too."

"Daddy?"

"Yea, sweety?"

"Daddy, you are going to die."

He touched the wound at his shoulder; it was warm beneath his hand. The infection would soon spread if it hadn't already.

"I know, baby."

"You need to do something before then."

"What is it?"

"You will know when you see it."

John heard Leroy set a cold glass of beer on the counter. He turned his attention to Leroy for a moment as he thanked the bartender. When he turned toward the stool where Elly had just been, the chair was empty.

You will know when you see it. The words rang in his ears. Please come soon; he thought as he raised the glass to his lips.

Chapter Twenty-Three

Walter

WHERE DID THE DAY GO? In less than three hours, he would be in the church for the midnight service. He was excited to see what Pastor Perry had in store, but he couldn't believe the day was already almost over. *Where had the time gone?*

Walter looked at the empty box of pizza on the coffee table, the Xbox controller stained orange from Cheetos, and the empty two-liter bottle of Pepsi at his feet. That was where the time had gone. Much like the movies last night, this hadn't been his intention.

When he first got home, he had planned on cleaning the house. But before he even lifted so much as a broom, his stomach growled, and Walter decided it would be best to tackle his hunger before doing any chores. Things led to things, and now Walter sat in a stupor, mesmerized by the screen hanging on the wall.

From the kitchen, he heard Mr. Whiskers meow. Had he fed him? Mr. Whiskers cried again, snapping Walter out of his daze.

The cat paced the kitchen anxiously when Walter finally got

around to pouring a bowl of food for him. He sat and watched his pet devour the food.

Although he had gone to the church this morning in hopes of alleviating some of the guilt he felt after last night, his mood was about the same now as this morning. By no means was he a bad person, but he wanted to be more than what he was. He longed to be a man, a real man, like his father.

He wasn't comforted by the elderly ladies in church, telling him how sweet he was. Walter didn't want to be the sweet fat boy. He had been that person his whole life. Walter wanted to know what it was like to be the hero. What must that feel like to be the one to save the day? If he didn't change, he would never know.

Mr. Whiskers jumped on his lap and curled into a purring ball.

"You are right, Mr. Whiskers. I have some work to do, don't I?"

He sighed and scratched his best friend behind the ear.

"That's a good idea, small steps. We will start with cleaning the living room. We can get that done before heading to church, right?"

Chapter Twenty-Four

Melanie

"BRIDGETTE, STOP," Melanie said. "He is a conspiracy theorist. So are his followers. That's all that it is."

"How can you say that?" Bridgette replied through the phone. "The proof is right there. How many posts will it take for you to believe it?"

"That's just it, how do you even know the shit he's posting is real?"

"Mel, come on. You know it's real; you just don't want to admit it."

"Bridgette, I can't believe you are falling for this. It's not real. It's like any good conspiracy theory, you can't prove it wrong, but that doesn't mean it's right. There's like this little bit of unknown, and someone like f_stop39 comes around and says, 'See there's the proof.' But, coincidence doesn't equal fact."

"I can't believe what I'm hearing."

"What? That I am looking at this like an adult?"

"No, that you are too focused about being right that you can't see what's in front of you."

"Oh, come on! Are you serious?"

"Mel, this is the sort of thing we used to spend hours researching in the library. Do you remember how much time we spent reading about the Nephilim? Or the Nazca Lines?"

"That's different," Melanie replied.

"No, it's not. You used to believe that the truth wasn't just what everyone else said it was. You liked investigating. You liked to dig for the answers. Why are you being so stubborn about this?"

Melanie could hear Bridgette starting to cry over the phone.

"Bridgette," she started. "Bridgette, I'm sorry."

There was silence on the other line.

"I don't know why; it just seems too far-fetched. But I'll tell you what. Let's do some digging and see what we come up with. Yea? If there is enough there, I will admit I'm wrong. But you need to promise the same. Okay?"

"I can't wait to hear you admit that you're wrong," Bridgette answered.

"We'll see."

"Yes. Yes, we will."

"I need to get some sleep if I am going to spend the rest of the weekend doing research," Melanie said.

"Yea, me too."

"I'll talk to you tomorrow?"

"Obviously."

"Alright, night."

"Love you, Mel."

"Love you too."

Melanie continued to scroll through Ego, looking at the armband theories after Bridgette hung up. She was fascinated with the information she read. Whether it was true or not, it was definitely interesting.

Chapter Twenty-Five

Harry

"MAGGIE, CAN YOU HEAR ME?" Harry's voice sounded thin in the cool air of the lab. He was nervous. There was no way of knowing for sure if he had fixed the band. At least, not until she was awake and he could really test it.

The sedative would wear off soon. She was already breathing deeper, a good sign. Against the cold silver of the table, Maggie's dark hair glistened. It was splayed beneath her head straight and soft like a baby's.

As Harry watched her sleep, he felt connected to her.

Her eyelashes fluttered as her eyes danced below their lids.

"Maggie," her name hung in the air after Harry said it.

Her lips trembled. She muttered something too soft to hear.

"Maggie, wake up."

"Guhgh," she grunted in her sleep. She was almost awake.

Harry had thought about just taking control and forcing her to wake up, but that wouldn't give him the insight he needed. He had already determined he could control her, but if she could still refuse him, there were still issues. Not that he could necessarily fix them now. It was too late.

If the adjustments didn't work, he would have to destroy her. As much as it would hurt him, there was no other option.

Maggie stirred as the fading remnants of sleep dissolved, and her waking mind rose from the foggy trenches of her dreams. Her eyelids fluttered open. She shifted on the table, rolling her shoulder to work out the ache.

Harry could tell she was groggy and bleary-eyed from the way she blinked and rubbed her eyes. She couldn't have slept well, he thought. The sedatives didn't allow her to get the deep sleep she needed. Harry didn't need her rested though, just obedient.

"Maggie, are you alright?"

She reeled at the sound of his voice and nearly slid from the table. Harry could see the blood pulsing through the veins in her neck. Then their eyes met, and Harry saw just how terrified she was.

"Please, let me go," she whimpered.

"Maggie, it will all be over soon. I promise."

"I just want to go home."

He strode across the room and passed by the table. Maggie turned away trembling, as he passed. But, despite her obvious fear, she remained perched on the table like a cowering child.

When Harry reached the wall at the other end of the room, he lifted a switch that opened a hydraulic door. The light from the lab flooded the grass outside. The crisp night air was refreshing. Harry breathed it in deeply.

Along his left arm, he felt the weight of the band. He ran his right hand over the smooth metal. It was cold beneath his touch. Near his wrist was a button hidden within a small divot in the band. It was barely noticeable. He pressed it.

From behind, Harry heard Maggie slither off the table. She was beside him in no time. Together they gazed through the dark and past the towering evergreens that cast ominous silhouettes in the dim light of the stars. There, beyond miles and miles of dense forest, was their goal, New York City.

"That is where you are going."

Maggie nodded. She understood.

"I will be with you, don't worry."

"Will it hurt?"

Harry turned his gaze to Maggie.

"When you kill me?" she asked.

Part of her was still there. After everything, a part of her remained. He knew that part might never leave, no matter how much he tried to destroy it. So long as he could control her, she would still be useful. She had been with him from the beginning. Despite the recent troubles, he still trusted her.

"No, I will make sure it doesn't."

"How much longer do I have to wait?"

"It will be soon."

"I just want to die. Can't you do it now?"

"No, Maggie. Not now. But soon, I promise."

Her soft eyes met his.

"I will take you to the city, and it will all be over soon."

And with that, Harry wrapped his arms around Maggie, and they ascended in the cool night air. His wings pulled them toward the sky. The chill wind whipped around them and dried the tears that had formed at the corner of Harry's eyes.

Chapter Twenty-Six

Walter

WHILE PASTOR PERRY welcomed the congregation to the taizé service, Walter Makichinski was sweating the seconds away. He was well aware that service started in less than ten minutes, especially as he ran through the dimly-lit street. He pushed his 300-pound frame to make it to his pew in time. His chances were slim.

The night air burned his lungs with every breath. He felt like someone had lit a wood stove in the middle of his chest just to see how much heat he could handle. His Biblical mind thought of Job and the suffering he endured. His skin had yet to erupt in boils, but with the way the last couple days had slipped through his fingers, he wouldn't be surprised.

He thought back on the events that led him to this new low. He still wasn't sure where the time had gone. After feeding Mr. Whiskers, he began cleaning the house, and before he knew it was already 11:30. It took fifteen minutes to get dressed and find the car keys, so by the time he left the house; he was already worried he was going to be late. Then came the squirrel.

At first, he thought it was cute, but as he got closer, the squirrel began the dance of death. It took off to the right, then darted left back into the street, then right and left again before bounding into someone's yard with a nut held firmly in its mouth. The squirrel watched as the Malibu cruised down the street. He was safe, but there was still one fatal dance move left, the cross-traffic sprint. Without hesitation, the squirrel jetted into the road on a kamikaze mission.

There was no time for Walter to change course. He tried to veer, but the squirrel was already under the front passenger tire. Nonetheless, the car swerved from Walter's fruitless attempt to save the poor squirrel. Bounding over the curb on the sidewalk, Walter heard an enormous *POP!* He slammed on the brakes and screeched to a halt. The Malibu sat half on the sidewalk half in the road. He stepped out of the car, fearing the worst. Sure, enough the right front was already starting to flatten against the ground. *Darn it.*

"What is wrong with you!" he yelled at the squirrel.

The body twitched, the big fluffy tail bounced off the ground sporadically. Its head had exploded under the tire.

Walter felt sick. He looked down at his watch to see the time, but it wasn't there. *That's odd. I never forget to wear that; it was my grandfather's.*

He remembered when his grandfather had given it to him for his twelfth birthday. He had told Walter that every man should have a watch. It was part of the daily attire. Since then, Walter had worn it every day. He couldn't think of any reason why he would have forgotten it. But Walter didn't have time to fret about it, so he dismissed it as an oddity.

He knew church would start any minute, and he was going to be late. So, he closed up the Malibu and started trotting down the street. *It's only two and a half blocks. I can do this.*

Two and a half blocks is a long way when you are as out of shape as Walter. He overestimated his abilities. Sweat dripping from his brow burned his eyes. He couldn't remember the last time he perspired this much. Perhaps never. He didn't get this fat by running. In fact, he couldn't even remember the last time he went for a run. Maybe in high school, but even then, he had started to push the scales, and he couldn't remember running much then either. Gym class had been the most embarrassing time of his life. He would change his shirt in the toilet stall so no one could see his rolls of fat. He shook the memory from his head and instead tried to focus on the task before him.

He felt a cramp coming in his calf. If he made it to church, he would be lucky. He pushed himself. Part of him enjoyed the work, and for the first time in his memory, he thought with fleeting optimism that he could lose the weight. He could do it. He would run every morning. The flat tire was a blessing in disguise.

But as quickly as that optimism came, it was just as soon undone by an uneven segment of sidewalk. Walter misjudged a crack in the cement and landed awkwardly, throwing off his balance. He heard his ankle pop before he felt the pain. His foot had rolled to the side, and his ankle had mashed into the cement, tearing a hole in both his pants and sock. Blood was already seeping into his shoe when Walter looked at his foot. He shoved his shirt sleeve into his mouth and bit down to keep from screaming.

The initial wave of pain passed after a minute. Walter took deep, slow breaths to steady his nerves. The pain was sharp, but he didn't think it was broken. Probably just a sprain. He gingerly got to his feet and put a little pressure on the injured foot. It hurt, but he could walk if he didn't put much weight on it. He took his first hesitant step forward, then another and another. Slowly he made his way to the church.

By the time he limped up the front steps could hear the organ playing within. The bells were starting to chime, signaling twelve. He clambered through the doors and found his seat in the back, dripping sweat, just as the congregation settled into pews.

The choir in a uniform line made their way up the stage and sat down behind the pulpit. The bell in the steeple chimed. Pastor Perry waited for the ringing to subside before he began. The reverberating of the bell at each clang sounded dimly in Walter's ears. Each echo was like a distant heartbeat, unknowingly counting each and every second. The bell rang its last, and Pastor Perry raised his head from the Bible in front of him.

"Good evening," he smiled wide, looking the congregation over. "Today is a very special day."

Walter smiled, just hearing Pastor Perry's voice made him feel better. Everything was going to be okay now.

The choir bellowed their praises and sang, "Fill all my vision, Savior, I pray," behind the pulpit while Walter did his best to keep a tune. The organ rang through the church. Each note echoed off the walls and ceiling. Pastor Perry mouthed the words. His eyes were like darts as his glare passed over each person in the congregation. As the hymn ended, the silence in place of the organ was deafening. A pin falling on the carpet would have sounded like a cannon blast.

Pastor Perry waited behind the pulpit. His tall, gangly frame was like a vulture inspecting the surrounding land for a carcass. His long pale neck stretched out from the collar of his shirt, his Adam's apple protruding just below the skin like a lightly veiled golf ball. A thin slimy tongue extended from his mouth and licked his lips before he began to speak.

"Tonight is a different type of service. There will not be a sermon in the usual sense, but we are going to delve into the Bible for just a moment," Pastor Perry began. "In Matthew 4:19, Jesus tells Peter and Andrew to follow him for *'he will make them fishers of men.'* This is almost foreign to us today. How many of you live by the motto of live and let live, or something close to that? Doesn't that sound like us? We say many things like: I won't judge you, or as long as you aren't bothering me, I don't care. This isn't beneficial to anyone."

"But what I really want to ask you is how often do we recruit others to join us in church? Do we ever? The passage I want to read to you is actually from Philippians 2:14-15 *'Do all things without grumbling or disputing that you may be blameless and innocent, children of God without blemish in the midst of a crooked and twisted generation, among whom you shine as lights in the world.'*"

"My brothers and sisters, we sit here in these pews and preach about what's wrong with the world and how we can change it, but are we actually doing anything?" He raised his hands, palms facing up, and shrugged his shoulders.

"We think we are living virtuously by coming to church and

doing our part here, but I tell you now that our Lord is watching us, and he is ashamed." The tone in his voice dropped an octave lower as the last word escaped his lips. The crowd looked intently into the Pastor's dark eyes before them.

Walter was feeling uneasy. This was supposed to be a taizé service, wasn't it? Where was the meditative prayer? There was supposed to be singing and chanting, but that wasn't happening.

"I am ashamed for I have led you astray," Pastor Perry continued. "Standing here before you, I have not spoken the truth. And yet, no one has stopped me. No one has said anything. If I am ashamed of myself, I am ten times as disappointed in you for not being more faithful servants of God."

This was not what Walter had come to see. He had hoped for an uplifting service, a night of prayer and community. He was feeling overwhelmed. He wanted to leave.

"I have been benevolent. I have stood up here and told you everything would be alright. But that is not true!" His voice thundered through the church.

"There is an enemy waiting to catch you unaware. He is patiently waiting to bring you to ruin. The lives you hold so dearly will turn to dust in his clutches. We are meant to be fishers of men. Yet, we sit here, inactive and complacent, and you dare to think you are living God's word. We think we are the light shining in a crooked world, but I ask, is that true? How many of you have actually brought someone closer to Christ?"

The crowd began to fidget in their seats as they looked from one to another. Walter felt the hair on his neck, starting to rise. This wasn't right.

"You have been close-minded! Have you thought once that you are doing what our Lord asked us? We are meant to bring people closer to God. Yet, ask yourself how many times you have actually turned people away with your prejudices," Pastor Perry yelled.

He stood silent behind the pulpit. The aghast faces of many in the crowd stared incredulously back at him. Then, Pastor Perry began ripping into the congregation once more at a fever pitch.

"I know you all very well, having stood up here for the last year. I know which ones of you hold yourselves upon a pedestal. I know who among you goes through the motions. Do you think I am not aware!?"

Walter stood up, shaking his head. This was bullshit. It had been a rough night already without coming here and being yelled at. He didn't have to stay and listen to this. He turned to leave. The pastor's eyes locked on him like a ravenous dog, a smile crept over his teeth.

"Sit down Walter!" Pastor Perry screamed. Walter stopped dead in his tracks. His heart was beating against his ribs like a drum. A fresh layer of sweat formed on his brow again. He turned back toward the front of the sanctuary expecting to see Pastor Perry still behind the pulpit. But, to his horror, the tall, gawky man was right in front of him! His dark eyes nearly bulging from their sockets, his brows slanted into a menacing V above his eyes. There was no way he could get from the pulpit to the back of the sanctuary that fast. No way. Walter had seen him just now behind the pulpit, yet here he stood right in front of him, his teeth clenched behind a crooked smile. This was wrong. Something was off.

"Please, Walter, sit down," Perry's voice was calm and soothing. His eyes still held that remarkable intensity, but his voice was soft, like a lover whispering in Walter's ear. Walter hesitated. Perry held out his arm, welcoming Walter back to his pew. Slowly Walter climbed back into his seat. His cheeks were bright red with embarrassment. He put his head down and choked back tears. He had never been so thoroughly embarrassed in all his life, not even in the high school locker room.

The congregation sat in stunned silence. Perry was back behind the pulpit. He had never preached with anger like this. The crowd was unsure how to handle him.

"I know I have scared some of you and I am sorry for that," he began again. "Our Lord is not as forgiving as I am, though. I am human, prone to the same sins as you. Do you not think I have watched my brothers outside the faith struggle and thought with gladness, *'at least I don't do that?'* We are all guilty of sin in one of its many forms. I cannot stand up here and deny that. But our biggest fault lies in not bringing more of our brothers and sisters to the faith. We cannot do this alone. We cannot plan to live a life of ease while so many are struggling in our midst. As the scripture says, we need to be lights in the cruel and twisted world."

"We are the light. Repeat after me," Pastor Perry said. "We are the light."

"We are the light," the congregation responded.

"Again, we are the light!"

"We are the light!"

Walter felt the excitement coursing through the audience. He was glad he hadn't left.

"Again!"

"We are the light!"

"We are the light!"

"We are the light!"

With each repetition, the energy of the crowd grew.

Walter felt dizzy as they continued to chant. Then, he noticed that the room was starting to dim. At first, it was just his peripheral vision, but it seemed to keep growing. Like a cloud of stormy weather blocking out the sun, a shadow was being thrown over his eyes. In addition to the shadow, he was now getting lightheaded as well. His mouth hung open, his breath coming in slow wheezy gulps. The shadow was growing darker.

Suddenly there was an intense pain in his arm just underneath the armband. Though it burned, Walter was stuck in a daze. The pain shot up his arm and crawled up his neck. It felt like his skin shifted down his shoulders and onto his back as a creeping slithery bug worked its way into his brain. As the pain rattled through Walter's skull, the dark that clouded his eyes intensified until the world was all black.

Chapter Twenty-Seven

Melanie

AS MELANIE SCROLLED through the continually refreshing feed on Ego, she ventured further into the world of the wrist watchers. Though the armbands were technically on the forearm, the name wrist watchers had caught on, and that was the only term anyone on Ego used for the people wearing them. The armbands were pretty much the only thing f_stop39 posted about, so it was the perfect starting point for a cynic.

The first time Melanie read the phrase wrist watcher, she had rolled her eyes. It seemed contrived. But she read on because she had told Bridgette she would. Supposedly, the wrist watchers were being manipulated, and at times their eyes would become completely black. This was all B-movie horror stuff, yet, there was something plausible about it all. The more she read, the more believable it became.

Eventually, her eyes tired, and she faded in and out of sleep.

She awoke to the sound of a metal trash can being kicked over outside. In her sleep, her mind was still racing with the content from f_stop39's page. Were that not the case, she may have ignored the noise. Instead, she climbed out of bed and raced to the window.

There, shuffling along the sidewalk, she watched as a man moved like a zombie. *A tell-tale sign of a wrist watcher.* He walked with great difficulty, his limbs flailing haphazardly with each step. Stumbling over the trash can, the man continued to make his way down the street.

Then, Melanie saw it. In the light of the stars and moon, she saw the reflection of a metallic band on the man's left arm. A chill ran up her spine and goosebumps rose along the flesh of her arms and neck. This wasn't real; she wanted to say. *But what if? What if it was all real?* She needed to know.

She ran to her closet, her nimble feet quiet on the carpet. Her jeans were lying on the floor from the day before. They were good enough; she decided and threw them on. A shirt and jacket were hanging in the closet. She took them off their respective hangers, quickly shed her nightshirt and slipped into the plain grey tee and denim jacket. She pulled the Converse out of the bottom of her closet. They were her favorite shoes. She wore them almost every day. Her mother hated them with a passion, insisting every time they were in Macy's that she get something new. Money was not an issue, and Melanie knew that. If she wanted, she could have a hundred pairs of Converse. There was something about these particular shoes, though, that made her feel invincible. When she was in her Converse, she could run the streets and not miss a beat. She could duck in and out of alleys and through the park. Her Converse were as much a part of her identity as the color of her skin or her name. They could never be replaced.

Shoes tied tight, she crept to her bedroom door and eased it open so that it wouldn't creak. She glanced back into her room and saw her phone on her bed stand. It looked at her like a sad puppy. She couldn't leave it behind. She ran back across the room and pulled it from the charger. It was fully charged. Perfect.

She took off and was just outside her room about to head down the stairs when she saw her parents' door just down the hall from her room. It was open. Someone was up. Her heart jumped into her throat. She could feel each beat move the skin on her neck. If they saw her, she wouldn't know what to say. It was three in the morning, and she was fully dressed, ready to hit the street. She jumped when she heard a noise from downstairs. The toilet flushed. *Shoot. Okay, I'll wait till they're back in the room, then I'll go.* She ran back into her room and slid back under the covers.

Heavy footfalls climbed the stairs. It had to be her dad. She heard the door to her room, creak open. Through squinted eyes, she could see his silhouette checking up on her. He watched for a few seconds. She felt his loving eyes. Not wanting to wake her, just watching her sleep for a minute, his daughter, his only child. She felt a profound love for him at that moment. He turned and walked back to his bedroom. She heard the door close. Instead of jumping out of bed, she remained where she was for a minute. She thought of the danger she could be facing by leaving. Here she had her father, a former linebacker for the Crimson Tide, now a part of the N.Y.P.D. Here she was safe. If she left, there was no telling what danger she would find.

Curled in her bed, she felt her eyes wanting to drift back to sleep, wanting to forget the man. He was probably drunk anyway. A drunk, that's all. Just go back to sleep.

No!

She needed to know the truth. Whether she liked it or not, she had to get up. It was her duty. That was a word her father taught her. Duty to your family, your city, and your country. This was her duty. She sat up, knowing it was the truth.

She pulled back the covers and went to the window. She half-hoped the man would already be gone, relinquishing her of her duty. To her dismay, she could still see him. He was approaching Columbus Avenue, his body still struggling up the road. She sighed and clenched her teeth. If she was going to do this, it had to be now, before the man went around the corner and was lost to the night.

She tip-toed down the steps and then across the hardwood floor as quickly and quietly as she could. The front door towered before her. If she wasn't careful, this could be the end of her nighttime foray before it even began. She unlocked the door, guiding the lock slowly so that it didn't make any noise. Her hands were clammy. Her heart was racing now, faster than before.

Nervous excitement flowed through her veins. She realized she was shaking. Melanie steadied her hand and turned the doorknob, no noise. She pulled the door open and heard a slight squeak as the street opened before her. Standing still for a second, she waited to hear her parents' door open. There was nothing. Hanging from a coat rack next to the door was Melanie's Mets hat, a worn-out, faded piece of cloth. She snatched it off the hanger and threw it over her mess of hair. Closing the front door, she pulled a small set of keys from her jacket pocket and locked it behind her.

Success! She was outside. Hooray for small victories! The man was creeping onto Columbus. Melanie wanted to run, but her inner spy thought better. Taking a leisurely pace, she strode down West 88th toward Columbus, breathing in the brisk air. She pulled out her phone and saw it was 12:08 a.m. Late, but not too late. Even though she had stayed up much later than this, being alone on the street at this time felt a little different. Every little noise was amplified. A rat scurried toward a gutter, and she froze. In her ears, the sound of the pattering feet sounded like someone following her. The rat saw her and disappeared into the city under the pavement. She saw its leathery wet tail wiggle down into the darkness. She was psyching herself out, but she knew the streets at this time were no place for a fourteen-year-old girl.

Columbus Avenue was a block west and parallel to Central Park. As she cut across 88th to get to Columbus, she tried to guess where the zombie-man might be heading. It was an exhilarating and terrifying thought. She had no clue where her chase would take her. For all she knew, it could be like the movies, and he could be limping/running to some abandoned train yard to meet his cronies. The idea that she was hunting what could be some criminal made her feel like she was doing the right thing. Her father would be proud.

Following roughly a hundred feet behind, she tried to remember everything she had read. Some people commented on f_stop39's page, saying the wrist watchers were actually an experimental government project. Of the different theories espoused on f_stop39's Ego account, Melanie felt that theory held more credence than some of the others. It seemed very Orwellian, which scared her and probably solidified her belief. There were other arguments, but none so believable as the government theory in her eyes.

She followed the wrist watcher as he made his way down Columbus Avenue. It was a long walk. The street signs ticked by, 99th, 100th, 101st. Undaunted, she kept her pace, leaving plenty of room between her and the man should anything happen unexpectedly. She pulled her phone out to check the time. It was already almost 1:00 a.m. What if her parents woke up and saw that she was gone? Her Dad was always waking up in the middle of the night, and he was always up super early, well before she left for school. She didn't want to frighten them. She wasn't sneaking out to go to a party. This was something else. She was trying to get to the bottom of a mystery. If only she could tell her Dad.

Why couldn't she? The thought came to her suddenly.

Her dad was a New York City Police Officer. He should be here with her. No, she thought, he wouldn't trust the wrist watcher story. It was too . . . unbelievable? Yes, that was the word, she concluded with remorse. No one would believe such a story. Unless they saw it themselves.

That was it! She needed to record whatever she saw tonight. She would, as soon as something happened.

Marching down Columbus had gotten boring. Nothing was changing. The man limped along, and she followed. Melanie was just watching the streets slowly pass when the wrist watcher stopped. Melanie did the same. Finally, something was happening. But what exactly? The man stood on the corner of 110th as if waiting for something, a sign. Melanie didn't want to just stand here a block away on the 109th street corner, but she didn't want to get closer either. She didn't know how he would react if he spotted her. So, she waited. Suddenly, he turned right and headed east on 110th.

Shit, I can't let him get too far ahead. She raced down the sidewalk to 110th, not knowing what she would find. Her Converse kicked up pebbles as she sprinted along the pavement. She felt alive. The wind blew her hair back. She held her hat down, so it didn't fly away. Her jacket tailed behind her. The bottom edges whipped against her hips. She felt the power in her legs as with each stride, her calves contracted and exploded in bursts of energy. She smiled.

She slowed to a stop just before the corner. A beat-up, old Chrysler slowly pulled up onto the sidewalk behind her. She hadn't seen it following her. It must have come off of 109th and seen her running.

"Where you going, baby? It's a little late, ain't it?" a man with greased back hair and bloodshot eyes called to her. He must have been prowling the streets. The skin along her spine pickled at the sound of his voice. A chill ran through her body and made her eyes water. She wanted to ignore the man, but she was terrified by what the man might be thinking.

She tried to turn her mind back to the task at hand. The wrist watcher couldn't have gotten far, but when Melanie glanced down the street, she couldn't see him.

"Shit," she muttered to herself.

"You lose sumtin? I'll help you look, baby. I'll give you a ride. Just come over here," the man in the Chrysler called.

Melanie felt the hair along her arms stand on end. Another chill ran through her, and she had to blink to clear away the tears blurring her vision. Dealing with this behavior from teenage boys in high school was different than what she faced now. In school, she usually wasn't alone, and it was easy to ignore the catcalls. It was still disturbing, but not like this. This was a whole different level of creepy. Melanie pulled out her phone and pretended to call someone. Out of the corner of her eye, she saw the man scanning her up and down. Her voice shook as she tried to speak loud enough for him to hear.

"Yea. I'm right outside," she said. "You are coming down? Ok, see you in a minute."

The man didn't bite. He continued to watch her.

By the grace of God, a light came on in a room a couple of stories up. Melanie saw his eyes dart to the light above. Then he threw the car into gear and squealed the tires. The Chrysler took off and careened toward Melanie.

"Oh shit!" she screamed and darted around the corner.

The Chrysler bounded over the curb and squealed into oncoming traffic on Cathedral Parkway. Melanie heard the man cackle as he sped by her. The car swerved dangerously through the late-night traffic.

As she watched the vehicle disappear, Melanie felt her heartbeat come back under control. Her knees were trembling, but her breathing had normalized, and as the car grew smaller in the distance, she felt a wave of relief. But now, because of a chance encounter, she had lost sight of the wrist watcher.

"Damn it," she said aloud as she tried to figure out what to do now. She walked along 110th toward the Frederick Douglass Statue. Cars crept by, taxis honked, a bicyclist weaved through traffic narrowly dodging the bumpers.

Melanie felt defeated. This trip had been a waste. She would be in a world of trouble with her parents and nothing to show for it. They would be so worried. There was no explaining this. They wouldn't let her go anywhere now. Maximum security lockdown for this girl. She breathed a sigh. Despite her previous inhibitions about the wrist watchers, she felt that she had really been on to something. All she had wanted was to catch something on video, but her opportunity was gone.

As she walked down 110th Cathedral Parkway, she felt a pang in her stomach. She hadn't realized until just now that she was hungry. The pockets of her jeans were empty. A thin wallet sat in the inside pocket of her denim jacket, but that too was empty. No money, no food, no video of a wrist watcher. *I should have just stayed in bed.* She had fought the urge thinking she was on the cusp of some revelation. It turned out getting out of bed was probably the worst decision of her life. That thought bounced around in her head. Whether it was the immensity of the moment or the truth of the matter, she wasn't sure, but she realized with growing dread if she kept thinking about the failures of this night she was going to cry.

She didn't want to do that, not here, not now. She hated crying. No one had the right words to say. *Sometimes people cry because they just need to get it out of their system,* she said in her mind. Everyone always wanted to tell her it was ok, it wasn't your fault, or you will be alright. None of those answers fit her current situation. It was not ok, it was *most definitely* her fault, and she would not be alright. The tears stung her eyes. She bit her lip and tried to choke them back.

No, don't you dare cry, don't you do it! The tears didn't listen. She blinked, and the world became a blur. She hiccuped, and her defenses caved. The tears fell, and her breath came in ragged stuttering gasps. Using her sleeve as a handkerchief, she wiped the initial tears away, but they were unrelenting, streaming down her cheeks in rivers of regret.

I need to get home. Most likely, it would be too late to assume innocence, but if she ran back, she might be able to avoid worse repercussions. The thought was daunting. She had gone over twenty blocks. The reality of where she was began to set in. She pulled her phone out to check the time, 1:39 a.m. It had been over an hour and a half. But, if she ran the whole way back, she could make it home before 2:00 a.m. She might be able to get home before anyone noticed she was gone. That would take a lot of luck, but it might work. She wiped the tears away again. Staring at the pavement, she took in all the little rocks and pebbles before her feet. This was the calm before the storm, and the sprint home would be a storm alright, of that she was sure. She gritted her teeth. *I got this. I got this!* She turned on the spot, ready to sprint back to Columbus when she heard a loud bang overtop the sound of the late-night traffic.

Turning around and looking back east down Cathedral, she spied an overturned trash can across the street under a tree. She couldn't see who had knocked it over, but she had an idea. Instead of heading back to Columbus and straight home, she took off across the Cathedral Parkway. Her Converse kicked up gravel as she sprinted across the road. Oncoming headlights grew larger as she neared the other side. She leapt onto the sidewalk just as a vehicle sped behind her.

The wrist watcher was just in front of her, not even thirty feet away. Yet, he didn't even notice her arrival. He trudged forward toward Manhattan Avenue. Melanie was back on his trail.

The pace of the man was slower. Melanie could have sworn he was looking for something or someone. He moseyed down the street. It was like he was unsure where he was. *Something was drawing him. He doesn't know where he is, but something is calling him.* The idea frightened her. What would she find when she arrived at the destination with him?

The man turned down Manhattan Avenue. Melanie closed the gap slightly. She didn't want to take a chance of losing him again. When she turned the corner, she was stunned by what she saw. She felt her eyes grow wide with awe, and her heart beat out of her chest.

There were hundreds, no thousands of wrist watchers coming from every direction. She saw multitudes walking down Manhattan Avenue toward her; more came crashing through the brush that surrounded the nearby baseball field. *A hoard of zombies. Real zombies.*

What would they do if they recognized she wasn't one of them? Would they attack? The idea gave her chills. *You need to start filming;* a voice echoed in her head. She turned her back on the gathering crowd and pulled her phone out. She checked the battery: 98%. She opened the camera and switched the mode from camera to video. Her face popped up on the screen, still set to selfie mode. The hair bouncing out from under her hat was messier than she thought, and her face was a little puffy around the eyes where she had been crying. She swallowed, trying to think what to say. Best to just shoot from the hip, she realized, let the words come as they may.

"I'm not sure what is going on, but there is like this huge crowd of people, wrist watchers, I think. I'm gonna try to get a video of them. If I don't return, I'm sorry, Mom and Dad, I love you," she spoke into the camera, cringing at the corniness of the last line. She switched the video to the forward-facing camera and slid the phone in her front breast pocket. The camera sat just above the pocket, giving her a decent vantage point. She casually strode toward the crowd in front of her, anticipating at any moment someone would notice she wasn't one of them. But no one said anything. The crowd shuffled toward 111th, congesting the end of the street.

Melanie felt the crowd closing in on her, like a boa constrictor with a mouse. She felt the air become denser. It was hotter too. So many bodies this close, Melanie swore there was steam rising from the mass. Closer and closer, the bodies gathered. 111th street was one giant cluster of people. Melanie could only see a few feet in front of her. She hoped her camera would catch whatever was going to happen.

With the crowd moving slowly down the street, the congregation behind her continued to grow. A thought came to her. Usually, cars would be going down the street, but she didn't see any. How had they overrun the traffic?

Melanie couldn't see the traffic cones set up at the end of 111th at the intersection of Frederick Douglass Boulevard. Nor could she see the men dressed in the fluorescent orange vests waving off traffic, their vacant eyes oblivious to the curses being thrown at them. Melanie had been too focused on the wrist watcher she was following to see the cones and men at the intersection of Manhattan and Cathedral. Her small stature could never have seen the same cones and men in vests guiding disgruntled drivers away further down at the intersection of 112th. She was still puzzling over the lack of traffic, and so many people undisturbed on one street when the crowd stopped.

Chapter Twenty-Eight

Inside the swarm

WEST 111TH STREET WAS JAMMED. The narrow street was choked with silent statues overlapping the sidewalks. They were waiting for him.

Then, the sound of trumpets rang. The air reverberated, crashing in waves with the sound of each horn. This was it. This was the moment of salvation.

He descended in glory on golden rays from above, clothed in the purest white. Gently he came to rest on a dais that stood in front of the mass. One by one, the crowd fell to their knees in awe. His presence alone was more than they could bear. With arms spread wide, he directed his gaze over each individual. Vibrant like the brilliance of the sun appearing from behind a cloud, he stood in his perfection.

"Rise," he said, his voice echoed through the crowd.

"My sons and daughters, none on this Earth can now touch you. You are beyond their power. Your faith has given you strength, unlike that of which your mortal bodies were capable. Your presence here is because of your belief. You heard the trumpet blast, and you heeded the call. You are saved."

Cheers erupted from the crowd. He smiled at the applause. He raised his hand to cease the praise.

"You are safe now. We are together. We are one." Slowly, like the sound of rain approaching, the crowd began chanting.

"One, one, one," they yelled, growing louder with each cry.

Chapter Twenty-Nine

Melanie

MELANIE'S HEART WAS RACING. She did her best to mimic the crowd, but she did not belong. With every passing second, she felt more out of place. She was in the middle of something of which she had no control. Her only choice was to fit in as best she could and hope they didn't notice her.

Quick glances to those nearest her left Melanie even more confused. Their attention was focused intensely on something she could not see. There was someone leading them, but who?

Their cries grew louder and louder, rising to a fever pitch.

Chapter Thirty

Harry

HARRY WATCHED the crowd from afar. The incident earlier with Maggie had been nothing more than an aberration, he told himself. The crowd proved that the armbands were working exactly as he intended.

Their screams echoed in his ears, beautiful and perfect.

As the chants grew louder, Harry grinned, his mouth a bear-trap of sharp white teeth. He was satisfied. This was exactly what he needed.

Yet, his eyes glowed with hatred. They were burning blue, hot, and intense. He raised his arms above his head, his violent eyes growing larger as he did so. In a roar of caged fury, he erupted, "I am one!"

Though miles away, Harry could see the gathering clearly. He knew precisely what they were seeing when they gazed toward the sky. To them, he was God, right there with them.

From Harry's vantage point, he may as well have been a god. He had created them, at least, who they were now. More importantly, he controlled them. That was the only thing that truly mattered. He wanted to test them once more before he set them loose. He would show them pain, and if they still returned, then he knew beyond a doubt they would never leave.

In one long sweeping motion, Harry raised his arms. Then with his hands stretched wide like the sail on a ship, he sent bolts of lightning down upon the crowd. The shock coursed through them like the sharp sting of fire. Bodies collapsed on the pavement, writhing in pain. All but one.

A young girl remained standing while all the others screamed in agony. Her face was the epitome of fear. She wasn't supposed to be here. She wasn't wearing a band. Harry tried to focus on her, but she faded before his eyes. He didn't have a connection with her. What he had seen was more of a shadow than a physical body. It was enough though.

She would be the perfect test. She would be the first to die, the first of many.

"Kill her," he said softly.

Chapter Thirty-One

Melanie

MELANIE SHOOK WITH FEAR. She wanted to wake from this madness, to roll over in bed and realize none of this was real, but her feet were glued to the pavement. Her eyes were teary, and her nose was cold and runny. She trembled uncontrollably. She had never been so terrified in all her life.

All she had seen since arriving at 111th Street was beyond her understanding. This wasn't on f_stop39's page. No one had mentioned a mass of bodies all convulsing as though they had swallowed poison together. Their mouths foamed as they thrashed against the ground. She wished Bridgette was with her, at least then she wouldn't be alone.

Then, Melanie felt a pair of eyes focused intently on her. She turned and saw one of the wrist watchers clambering to her feet. She turned and saw the others rising likewise. Like lasers, their gaze turned toward her, direct and unflinching.

Whatever had held their attention and caused their pain was now gone. They were now fixated on her. Their teeth snapped in her face as the crowd closed around her. She could almost feel them biting her flesh, ripping chunks of muscle from her bones. She shook her head to get the horrible vision out. *I have to get out of here.*

Without a plan, she started running. The crowd had formed a circle around her while she stood frozen in fear. As she ran, their outstretched hands tried to grab hold of her. She darted left then right, ducking under arms and spinning through a mass of oncoming bodies. No longer did they seem like the clumsy, gangly creatures she had witnessed coming in. They ran with purpose now, clawing at her as she tried to make her escape.

She started east toward Frederick Douglass Boulevard. She couldn't remember ever running with such purpose before. Her life flashed before her eyes. Memories of her childhood played out in slow motion. She saw herself laughing at a birthday party. There was Grandma's house in the country where she learned how to fish. Her first kiss on the lips; it was sloppy, her crush's face now a blur. Then her parent's faces jumped to the front of her mind.

Memories of them were the most powerful. They loved her more than anything. It would kill them if something happened to her. She needed to get away; she needed to get home.

"I don't want to die," she heard herself say.

A tall man with hairy arms reached for her shoulder. She ducked under his hand and elbowed him in the hip. She felt his bony waist give with the force of her blow. That made her smile. Three women and another man ran straight at her. *Damn it.* She couldn't dodge them all. Instead, she frantically looked for the smallest of the four. The woman running nearest to the man was short and looked to have something wrong with her one leg. *That's my target*, Melanie decided as she barreled forward and tried to get as much speed as she could. She lowered her shoulder and plowed into the woman, nailing her right in the sternum. Hearing the air leave the woman suddenly and forcefully, Melanie felt proud. She leapt over the body as it crashed to the blacktop while the other three reached out for her as she passed. The man was able to grab hold of her ankle, slowing her slightly. Melanie kicked her foot free from his clutches and then careened toward the empty street.

She realized with excitement the crowd was thinning.

Tasting freedom, Melanie turned to see the crowd behind her. In so doing, she didn't see the empty milk crate before her and tripped over it. She tumbled hard on the pavement. The adrenaline coursing through her veins left her unaware of the gashes to her knees. She was sure that any second she would feel their grimy fingers around her throat choking the life from her. There wasn't any time to waste. She scrambled back to her feet and felt a hand already upon her shoulder. She spun away and into the waiting arms of another wrist watcher. His arms wrapped around her torso, but just as Melanie felt his grip begin to tighten, she pushed her hands against his chest to give herself the slightest opening. She turned and ducked at the same time and slipped out of her captor's grasp and was once again free.

She turned back toward Frederick Douglass Boulevard and saw the construction workers racing toward her. Their eyes were dark; she was almost sure they were entirely black with no iris or white at all. She steadied her feet beneath herself and took off without waiting to see if she was correct. She juked left, then right, and spun back to her left, mid-spin she saw the nearest construction worker's eyes and noticed they were indeed black like she thought. Her legs pumped, pushing her past the outstretched arms of the construction worker. She leapt over the orange cones and into the street, running under the traffic light before she realized she was in the middle of the intersection. A taxi swerved to avoid hitting her, the driver honked his horn and gave her the finger. Melanie turned south and ran out from under the light to the sidewalk.

She sprinted along the street, afraid to look back, yet curious. She was nearing the roundabout and the Frederick Douglass Statue when she decided to hazard a glance. Turning back, she witnessed the mob scrambling out from 111th Street into the oncoming traffic. An incessant beep now blared through the early morning intersection. Drivers were attempting to weave through the hoard, but more and more people continued to file into the intersection.

The wrist watchers ran toward the stopped traffic. Without warning, drivers and passengers alike were pulled from their cars. Melanie watched in horror as a cab driver was pulled from his taxi, and a crowd of wrist watchers closed in around him. She heard his shrieks as he was beaten to death. Another driver tried to run from the crowd, but they caught him before he got too far. Once in their grasp, Melanie saw the crowd pull him from all directions until his body was quartered in a bloody explosion.

Screams of terror rang out on the early morning street. Men and women tried to run from the hoard, but there were too many. The wrist watchers piled into the intersection of 111th Street and Fredrick Douglass. Melanie watched with growing dread.

A car was overturned. Fire burst from the engine. She heard the taxi driver inside scream. The flames engulfed the car, and before he could unstrap his seatbelt and crawl out, the flames had reached him. She saw his dark shadowy mass squirm within, screaming for help.

"Oh, my God! What the fuck!" she screamed.

Melanie bolted south. She turned her back on the crowd she had spent all night trying to capture. Her slender legs sprinted for home. She wanted to get as far away from this madness as she could. Something inside told her home would not be far enough. Through the middle of Frederick Douglass Circle, she bounded over the brick monuments. Her foot slid on the cobblestone, and she nearly fell. With a quick glance over her shoulder, she saw people behind her. They were chasing her. She couldn't tell if they were wrist watchers or not, but she wasn't going to wait around to find out.

Shots rang out in the distance. She saw the unmistakable flashing lights of a police cruiser whiz past as the officer raced toward the mob on 111th Street. She instantly thought of her father. He, too, would be heading into that deathtrap soon. She had to call him and let him know what was happening.

As she ran along the street, which had turned to Central Park West on the other side of the Frederick Douglas Circle, she pulled her phone out and saw it was still recording. *Good. People need to see this.* She stopped the video and pulled up her contacts. Mom and Dad were one and two. She hit call.

The phone rang in her ear as she ran. *Daddy, please pick up,* she cried in her head. It went to voicemail. Shit! She called her Mom. The same thing.

"Oh no, oh, fuck no!" she screamed.

She tried her Dad again, but still nothing.

Behind her, the footsteps closed in. She looked over her shoulder and saw three men still chasing her, all with those hideous black eyes. She sprinted faster. Her heart beat out of her chest. A cold sweat formed on her forehead. She couldn't shake the terrible ideas of what they would do to her once they caught her.

Their long strides were closing the distance. She had to do something, or they were going to catch her. Closing in on the intersection for 108th Street, she spied a white brick building on the corner, The Park West Café and Deli. That was her goal. She lowered her head and pushed as hard as she could. Every muscle strained to carry her faster. The world around her slowed down. She felt every sense heightened. She heard the sound of her own breathing echoing in her ears; she could smell the sour moisture of the New York City streets. She could taste blood in the back of her throat as her chest was on fire with the pulse of her racing heart. All this she noticed in the blink of an eye. She gauged the traffic along 108th Street and Central Park West. She had to time this perfect, or else it could mean disaster.

A blue pickup turned on to Central Park West. Melanie waved her hands and tried to signal for the man to turn around. Before he could stop, though, she had raced by him through the intersection. Melanie heard the man driving the truck slam on the brakes.

It happened so fast that Melanie couldn't even tell what was going on. She had waved down the truck to try and warn him about the chaos ahead, but the driver must have seen her situation and acted swiftly. She heard the tires screech as the truck spun behind her to cut the men off. It succeeded partially.

She whirled around to get a glimpse and saw that of the three men one had slammed into the passenger door. His head had broken through the window, and a bloody face glared through the cab at the driver. The wrist watcher snapped his jaws and clambered through the window, trying to bite the driver. One man had come to a halt just beside the bed of the truck.

The other had fallen behind some. Instead of stopping at the truck, he picked up speed and jumped onto the hood and catapulted himself onto the other side safely. Melanie was face to face with the wrist watcher now. The café was to her left, but the wrist watcher had blocked off her path to safety.

The man in the truck jumped out and screamed something at him. Melanie couldn't tell what. Her heartbeat was so loud, and fast it blocked everything else out. The wrist watcher dove for her. She ducked and cut his leg out from under him. Instead of falling like she expected, he rolled and was back on his feet facing her again. He dove again. This time Melanie couldn't avoid his arms. She felt the sinewy strength of his grasp wrap around her ribcage. Behind her, she heard the man from the truck as he ran toward them.

Something stopped him, though. There was another sound, the garbled terror of someone choking. Amidst the other sounds at the intersection and her pounding heart, that sound stuck out in Melanie's mind. The wrist watcher that had ahold of her turned around. She saw the man from the truck grope at his neck as blood poured through his fingers. The other wrist watcher looked down at him with blood and flesh clutched in his hand. He had ripped the man's throat open with his bare hands. Melanie felt nauseous and weak.

This wasn't real. This could never happen.

What are these monsters?!

The man behind her squeezed hard so she couldn't take a breath. The world around her was going dark. She had to do something, or she would die right here.

She squeezed her right hand into a fist with her thumb sticking out. She focused all her energy on this one movement. It would succeed, or she would die. She tried to throw herself forward, and when the man hunched closer to squeeze her tighter, she threw her fist over her shoulder as hard as she could. Her thumb connected with the man's eye, just as she had hoped. She felt the gush of warm blood rush over her finger and into her fist. She felt the jellylike plasticity of his eye around her thumb. But the man did not recoil as anyone else would have. He squeezed harder.

The world around her faded and disappeared. It felt like she was falling. A buzz sounded through her ears. She gasped as she desperately tried to breathe, but there was no way the wrist watcher had her squeezed too tightly. She felt numb all over.

There was a loud bang behind her. The body around her loosened and fell at her feet. Melanie collapsed to her hands and knees next to the body and gulped lungfuls of air. The other wrist watcher with the man's throat in his hand turned toward the sound. In an instant, he too was dropped with another loud bang, a bullet hole through his head.

She scrambled and tried to get to her feet, unsure what had just happened. The next thing she knew, she was being hoisted up under the arms and was being squeezed again. Her first thought was to try to escape. Then she realized the man holding her was her father.

"Daddy! I'm so sorry!" she cried.

Tears cascaded down her face for the second time this night. She clung to her father's neck, unable to fully believe he was here.

"It's okay, honey. But we have to go now. Come on," he stood her on the pavement next to him. "My cruiser is just down the street, let's go."

Chapter Thirty-Two

Gino's Pizzeria

THE SWEET STALE smell of the dumpster in the alley didn't affect Jeff anymore. The tangy scent of rotting meat in the trash from the Asian restaurant next door used to roil his stomach. It was just a part of life now.

Jeff sat on a short stack of milk crates and enjoyed a smoke with his co-workers before they started cleanup for the night. Bella sat across from him in a fold-up chair, and next to her stood Dale. Besides Gino, the owner of the pizza place, Dale was the oldest crew member. He pulled a couple of cans of beer from his jacket. He had nabbed them from the cooler before coming outside. He tossed one to Jeff and Bella each before cracking open his own.

"Feels good out here," he said. Jeff nodded in agreement as he sipped on his beer.

"Shit, I'm glad the night's almost over. I thought those people were never gonna leave," Bella said.

"They leave a decent tip?" Dale asked.

"Course not," she replied.

"Figures," Jeff said. "How much did we make overall?"

"In tips, 430 dollars. Which is what, like 130 something each?" Bella asked.

"143," Dale said, slipping his phone back into his pocket.

"Not bad," Jeff said.

"We made 250 the other night," Bella sighed.

"You were working with Heather, though, weren't you?" Dale asked.

"Yea, why?" Bella asked.

"Nothing. She's just the biggest tease I've ever met. But, shit, she makes money, so I don't blame her," Dale said.

"She's nasty," Bella asked. "You think she's hot, don't you?"

"Hot? No, not really. I mean, she's got a pretty nice body. But, she's got that pug face. All I can think of is my girlfriend's dog when I see her," Dale said.

"Well, that's a little harsh," Bella said with a laugh. "What about you? You think she's hot?"

Jeff looked up from his cigarette.

"What's up?" he asked.

"Never mind," she said. "What are you thinking about?"

"I don't know," he answered.

"You don't know?"

"Nothing in particular. I mean, just a book I was reading," he asked.

"Is it good?" Dale asked.

"Yea. It's different, but it's good."

"Different is good," Bella said before she took a slow drag on her cigarette.

"What do we have left?" Jeff asked, changing the subject before either of them asked about the book. He didn't want to explain it.

"Not much," Dale said. "Trashes, mopping and wiping down the counters. That's it, I think."

"Did you make the sauce already?" Bella asked.

"Yea. When we had that lull earlier," Jeff replied.

"Nice. I'm pretty much done with my cleanup stuff, so I'll help you mop," she said.

"Alright, you ready then?" Jeff asked.

Dale snuffed out the last of his cigarette on the brick wall of the pizza shop. He shook the beer can in his hand before draining the last of it in one gulp.

"Yea. Let's get this over with. I wanna stop by Marco's. They were supposed to have a new beer coming out today," Dale said.

"You still go there?" Bella asked.

"Damn right. You have to try it," he answered.

"I'm good."

"You don't know what you are missing," he replied.

From further down the alley, they heard someone scream. The sharp cry was followed almost immediately by a gunshot. Jeff quickly looked to his co-workers then down the alley. More shots rang out. A shower of sparks lit the ground near Jeff's foot. Then, something hit his knee.

"Jeff!" Bella screamed.

The pain didn't register immediately. It was only when he looked down and saw his kneecap covered in blood that the hurt came. It started hot and stinging before changing into a deep dull ache. The gunshots grew louder.

Suddenly, Dale and Bella were carrying Jeff through the door and into the kitchen. Behind them, Jeff heard more screaming and shooting.

"What the hell is happening?" Bella yelled.

"Here. Set him down," Dale said as he and Bella laid Jeff in a booth. "I'll be right back."

Dale ran back through the kitchen and closed the inside door. Then he threw the latch and locked the entry. By the time he returned to the dining area, Jeff was rocking back and forth, holding his leg. Blood covered the seat and floor. He was losing too much blood.

"Here," Dale took off his belt and wrapped it around Jeff's thigh and cinched it tight.

From the front of the pizzeria came the sound of shattering glass. There was a thud as the body hit the floor and rolled across the shards of glass. Outside the pizzeria stood a woman covered with blood. She leapt through the broken window and lunged at Bella.

Dale jumped up quickly and blocked the woman's path. Instead of stopping, she charged straight at him. At the last second, she ducked and drove her shoulder into his diaphragm. He stumbled back and fell over a chair.

She was on him before he hit the ground. Dale tried to push her away, but the woman was relentless. Dale was bigger than his attacker and should have been able to get rid of her. But she was fast and tireless. Her fingers found his throat and dug into his skin

Bella grabbed a chair nearby and hurled it at the woman. The metal leg of the chair smashed against the woman's head and left a deep gash through which the white of her skull was visible. However, the woman didn't stop. It was like she didn't feel anything.

Dale's face was already turning purple. Bella needed to do something. She sprinted across the dining area and threw herself on the woman. She was able to get her arm under the woman's chin. She locked her other hand around her wrist and squeezed tight.

Beneath her, Dale's eyes rolled back in his head. His face was ashy grey.

"No!" Bella screamed.

She was too late. Dale's head rolled to the side. His open eyes dimmed, and then he was gone.

There was noise coming from the street.

"Bella, look out!" Jeff screamed.

Bella turned as a man with a huge knife clambered through the broken window. The man with the blade was already upon her. She let go of the woman and spun away from their new attacker. His knife flashed in front of her face as he swung for her head. Blood dripped into her eyes from a gaping wound along her forehead.

"No, please!" Jeff screamed.

The woman that had killed Dale scurried across the floor and pulled Jeff from the booth seat.

For a moment, Bella was distracted by her co-worker's screams. That was all it took for the man with the knife to launch a second attack. His knife came down across her neck. Blood poured down the front of her shirt.

Jeff saw Bella try to close the wound, but he knew there was no hope. She slid to the floor and collapsed with her arm outstretched toward him. Jeff struggled to free himself from the woman, but her hands were like a vice grip that tightened more every second. As the room began to dim, Jeff turned his gaze back to Bella. She struggled to get closer. Their eyes met. The last thing Jeff saw was a fleeting smile that passed over Bella's lips as she died.

Chapter Thirty-Three

John

THE VIDEO on the television screen was incomprehensible. The camera jerked every which way. The sound faded in and out, so John couldn't understand what he was hearing. It sounded like sirens. For a moment, they watched the crowd of people run down a busy street. Then the picture faded to snow. Leroy smacked the side of the box, and the picture came back. The camera was somewhere in a crowd of people now. The sound gradually became clearer. To his horror, John now realized exactly what it was. It wasn't sirens, but the sound of people screaming. Sweat formed along his forehead.

The events of the other night replayed rapidly in his mind. He watched in awe as a cluster of people huddled together only to be mowed down by a woman with a submachine gun. He was stunned to see this on live TV.

"My God," he muttered as he gazed up at the television screen.

The three men were glued to the butchery. No matter where the camera focused, someone was being killed in any number of ways.

John could see no rhyme or reason for the attacks; there didn't appear to be protestors or anything like that. It was like all of a sudden, this huge group of people just snapped and started killing everyone they saw. Through the chaos, John was on the lookout for opposition to the attackers. Where were the police?

As the images on the screen rapidly shifted. John searched for any clues as to what might be happening. The camera changed so quickly that it was difficult to differentiate those that were killing from those that were fleeing. He remembered the man that had attacked Ted's.

"I'm gonna turn it off, I've seen enough," Leroy said.

"Wait!" John yelled.

Just as Leroy reached up to turn the television off, John caught a glimpse of something different. Directly in front of the camera, stood a man holding a huge machete. His body was covered with specks of blood. His right leg twisted grotesquely backward, obviously broken, yet the man was still standing. His face was cut open with a deep gash from his ear through his nose to his other ear, blood streamed from the wound, and covered the bottom half of his face in dark red ooze. Despite the jarring appearance, John was focused on the man's eyes. Like two dark pits, those eyes stared into the camera. He felt the heat from that gaze through the screen, as though those two black eyes could see him through the miles between.

"Jesus," he whispered.

John's heart sank as he now understood the man that attacked Ted's was one of many. Thousands maybe. Somehow, they were connected. This was some sort of sprawling attack beyond his understanding.

Leroy clicked off the television and said, "What the hell was that?"

"You will know when you see it," John muttered.

"What's that?" Leroy asked.

His daughter's words hung in the air. This was it. He knew it, without a doubt.

"Nothing," he said to Leroy.

"No. This gotta be some sorta prank or something," Daryl said.

Leroy clicked the television back on and changed the channel, but it was the same thing.

"My God. What is this?" Daryl groaned with disgust. The same question was running through his head. For a moment, John had hoped that the screen would show something different. That it was all just some weird prank. But it wasn't, and he knew this was what Elly had meant. John wanted to tell them about the other night. They would understand. But it was something he didn't really want to confront himself. Since yesterday night at Ted's, he had purposely been running away. If he were to tell them the story of what happened and where he was going, he would have to admit that he was afraid. Afraid of the consequences, afraid of the future and afraid of the past. It was easier to hide the fear. Sweep it under the rug and forget about it. But with what was happening on the television, he realized running would never provide any sort of escape.

There was also the problem of the man from the rest stop. He must have followed John from the diner in Blisse. If that were the case, there might be others.

The only option was to go to New York City. For reasons he couldn't explain, he knew that he was where he needed to be.

"I'm gonna need another shot," he said to Leroy.

"Me too," Leroy said. He poured three shots full to the brim.

"I'm gonna go to New York," John said.

"Fuck that," Daryl growled.

"You might better take the bottle 'cause you ain't coming back if you head that way," Leroy said.

"Yea. You might be right," John sighed

"You're serious, ain't ya?" Daryl asked.

"I think so yea," John said. "I feel like I need to do something."

"Ya know something? I went to war for this country. I got shit when I came back, but ya know what? I'd do it again. I've always loved this country. I'd do anything for it. You might be right. Whatever this is, I can't sit here and watch," Daryl said.

John looked him in the eye and held his gaze for what seemed like a long time. He nodded and downed his shot.

"I have no idea what we're getting into," John said.

"No. We can't really know what we're gonna find, can we?" Daryl said.

He reached out his hand, and John shook it.

"There ain't much left here for me anyways. Leroy and I been talkin' about that for some time. Feels like we've lived past our time, watchin' the world change around us."

"Are you really going to throw your life away?" Leroy asked, pointing to the screen behind him. "You see what's going on there, right? My God, you're just asking to die."

"Then, I should sit here and wait instead?" Daryl asked.

"If you go there, you know what will happen. Look at that? It's madness," Leroy argued.

"Leroy, what if it don't stop? If this is just the beginning? They destroy New York. Then they are gonna move on to Boston, or Philly. Hell, they probably already started! Eventually, maybe not tomorrow or the next day, but eventually, we will be in the crosshairs. I don't want to live in fear, waitin' for them to come and slit my throat in the middle of the night. I won't; God damn it!"

"If you're so damn sure this is the only way, then go! I don't believe the city will fall because of this group of rabble-rousers. The police will show up and round those bastards up. I know it. You bein' there will just get in their way," Leroy said.

"When has that ever been the answer? Let's not help because someone else is gonna do it? Come on, Leroy! Use your head. You saw the TV yourself. Did it look like they had it under control?" Daryl said.

"You go ahead if you want, I'm staying here. I might be old, but I'm not ready to die yet. No. No, I'll stay right here," Leroy said.

Daryl reached out to shake hands with Leroy. John saw the emotion in their faces. He knew the pain of their parting dearly. He had felt that same pain when he left Ted. Although neither man was dead yet, John knew that Daryl was accepting his fate and acknowledged he wouldn't be coming back. Daryl planned to die in New York, defending his country.

Chapter Thirty-Four

At Daryl's

IT WAS 2:00 a.m. when they arrived at Daryl's house. It was dilapidated and looked for all the world to be vacant, but Daryl assured John it was his home. Upon entering, his assertion was reinforced by pictures that hung on the wall that showed a much younger Daryl standing next to a beautiful woman and three children. John didn't ask about the picture. It was obvious from the way the house was kept that Daryl lived alone.

In the lone hallway that extended from the living room stood a large wooden gun case, where Daryl kept "the necessities" as he called his cache of firearms. John waited in the living room while the old man rummaged through the cabinet. Daryl threw a blanket on the floor and situated an array of firearms on it. Among his weapons, he laid a large rifle with two boxes of bullets, a double-barrel shotgun, not dissimilar from the one John had stashed in the truck, another rifle slightly smaller than the first but with a larger clip attached to the stock, a 9mm handgun, and a larger Smith and Wesson revolver with a polished steel barrel and wooden grip.

Lastly, he laid an old shoebox on the blanket. John wasn't going to ask what was inside, but Daryl had the eager look of a child who was desperately waiting to show off some ill-gotten goods. John reluctantly obliged and asked him what was in the box, much to the older man's delight.

"Wasn't supposed to bring these back from the war," he started. "I've held on to 'em for the last fifty years just waitin' for a moment like this."

He opened the lid to the shoebox, and John saw a dozen shining grenades. They were stacked neatly, one on top of the other. The black casing of each grenade shined in the light. They looked too perfect, almost like toys.

"Will they still work?" he asked.

"I think so. Been kept safe in this box all this time, no water damage or nothin'," he answered with a huge grin.

"Alright," John replied. "But I'm leaving that to you."

They were able to just barely squeeze everything behind John's bench seat except for the box of grenades, which Daryl was happy to hold on to. From where they were in northeastern New York, it was about a three-and-a-half-hour drive to the city if they went straight south. They would arrive just before dawn, so long as they weren't held up. Little did they know that the television scene that they had witnessed was only a portion of Harry Davis's army. A vast horde worked continuously to sabotage all entry and exit from the city, a fact that the two men couldn't have foreseen, and one that would ultimately cost them dearly.

Chapter Thirty-Five

Isaac

THE POLICE CRUISER sped down Central Park West. Isaac hadn't said anything to her since they got into the car. She was sure she had a thousand questions to ask. He had to get her to safety first and foremost.

"Dad?" she asked.

He didn't look at her. His lips were a thin tight line, his eyes intensely scanning the road ahead.

"Dad, where are we going?"

The trees of Central Park to their left were a blur of shadows. The police siren was a dull buzz in the background. The cruiser darted in and out of traffic, the red and blue lights reflecting off other vehicles.

The radio crackled, a woman's voice echoed through the car, "10-34S repeat 10-34S. 10-51, 10-66, 10-50G at 111th and Frederick Douglass. Multiple homicides being reported. Officers be advised."

Isaac Parker looked at his daughter. Her knees were bloody, she was covered in dirt, and her hair was a mess beneath her Mets hat. But she was alive. He wanted to scream at her, to tell her how stupid it was to have gone out this night. *Twenty blocks from home?! What had she been thinking?* He knew that would get him nowhere, though. She was a smart girl. She never got in trouble. There was a reason for her going out this morning. She wouldn't be let off the hook, no, no, no, not after this; but he had to know what drew her outside this early.

"Tell me your story before we get home, don't leave anything out. I need to know everything. If I hadn't shown up, you'd be dead right now. I want to know what would draw Melanie Parker twenty blocks from home in the middle of the night," he asked, his voice remained smooth and calm.

"Daddy, am I in trouble? I'm so sorry. I shouldn't have gone out," Melanie pleaded.

"Melanie, answer me," Isaac said.

He could see that she was scared and tired.

"Daddy, do you know what Ego is?" she asked.

He turned to her, his eyebrows furrowed at her question.

"It's an app," she said.

"Go on."

Melanie explained the previous three and a half hours to her father. He listened closely to every word like he would an interrogation with an eyewitness. He needed to know where these people came from. When she had finished, he sat silent. They were a little less than two blocks from home. He pulled the cruiser over and turned the lights and siren off.

He turned to look at his daughter, his own flesh and blood sitting next to him. Her eyes were glazed with tears that had not yet fallen. He reached over and pulled her to him. Isaac kissed the top of his daughter's head and felt her sobbing into his shoulder.

"It's alright. You are with me now, Melanie. I got you," he whispered. He held her tight to him. She cried, releasing her fear bit by bit with every tear.

"Listen, Melanie," she looked up into his eyes. "Life isn't a baseball game. There's no such thing as three strikes. You were lucky today. I was lucky. I could just have easily been a minute too late. Something is going on right now. Something big, alright? I think your instincts were right on. We are gonna figure this out. Whatever is happening, we are gonna put a stop to it. But right now, I need you to be home with your momma. Let me handle this," Isaac explained.

She nodded.

"I'm gonna take you home. You are going to have to explain to your mother what happened and believe me; she is going to take this a lot worse than me," he said.

He put the cruiser in drive and looked in his mirror before he pulled onto the street. There was a sudden explosion behind them just as they entered the roadway. The cruiser jolted forward, and the back half lurched off the ground. It sounded like thunder as the rear end was crumpled with the force of the impact. Isaac and Melanie flew forward and smashed into the airbags blasting out from the dashboard. The cruiser was thrown to the right into a parked car. The hood accordioned as the quarter panels gave way under the pressure. The windshield spider-webbed. Melanie's body was thrown back into her seat. The car swayed like a boat on water, as she settled from the jarring impact.

The van that had rammed into them was fuming black smoke from underneath its hood. The damage to it was much less pronounced than the cruiser, but nonetheless, the impact had fractured a fuel line in the engine. The black smoke bleeding into the night sky would soon erupt in flames.

Isaac opened his eyes. The world was red. He wiped his face with his hands to clear his vision. Blood filled his mouth. He spit a wad of red gunk as well as a cracked tooth into his palm. His head was throbbing, and there was a dull pain in his neck. He looked over at Melanie. She appeared lifeless in the big seat. He scrambled to unbuckle his seat belt.

"Melanie! Hey!" he yelled. He whipped the belt off and pulled himself over the computer and radio console in between the seats. He unhooked Melanie's belt and tapped her lightly on the cheek to see if she was responsive. Her mouth hung open, and her head drooped down onto her chest. Suddenly, she gasped, and her eyes opened wide.

"Ummff," Melanie moaned. Blood spilled from her nose. It was broken.

"Don't move," he told her.

He pinched her nose in his fingers and snapped it back into position.

"Oye!" she yelled. "Ouch! Damn it!"

"Pinch it, so it doesn't bleed more," he told her.

The driver's door was closed tight from the impact. Isaac had to ram his shoulder against it before it finally creaked open. He stepped out of the cruiser into a pool of gasoline leaking from the van behind them.

"Oh fuck," he muttered.

He crawled over the front of the car as quickly as he could and yanked Melanie's door open.

He heard the whoosh of igniting gas before he saw the fire. The van jumped from the pressure of the explosion.

There was no time. He grabbed Melanie. She latched onto his shoulders, and he clasped his hands around her back and pulled. The heat was on them before she was out. The car ignited in a blaze of bright red. Isaac spun as a wave of fire blasted his back. He managed to run only a few steps before the blast threw them forward. He squeezed Melanie tight to his body to shield her from the flames. They collapsed on the cold pavement while the fire burned the air above them.

On the sidewalk, they braced against the blaze. Isaac saw the terror in his daughter's eyes and pulled her closer. Above, the fire burned for what seemed like an eternity. Once the inferno died, the only thing left burning was the cruiser.

Isaac rose from the ground clutching Melanie to his chest and approached the tall white brick building on the corner of 88th street. Less than two blocks from home. They could walk and be there in five minutes. He set Melanie down next to the building.

"Just wait here, I need to see what the hell is going on," he told her. Her eyes were wide. She nodded slowly, and Isaac understood. She was shocked; for the second time today, she had narrowly escaped death.

Isaac approached the burning wreckage. He was confused as to where the van had come from. He had looked in his mirror and seen nothing. *They must have been flying to have hit us that hard.* Even though he had a pretty good idea no one would have survived the blast, he had to check.

He slid by the remnants of the cruiser to get a look inside.

His ears were ringing from the explosion. But even through the white noise, he heard a fire siren off in the distance. Closer, he heard something more ominous. As he approached the charred remains of the van, the noise got louder. Then he saw it. Behind the van was a crowd of people running toward him, screaming.

"What the hell?" he muttered.

His hand was on the butt of his pistol as soon as he saw the mob heading toward him. Melanie's story, coupled with the call over the radio just a few minutes ago, had him on edge. He pulled the gun out. A woman at the front of the crowd spotted him and ran toward him.

"Officer! Help!" she screamed.

He waved her over, but before she reached him, a man grabbed her neck from behind. There were too many bodies, too many people to make sense of what was going on. Before Isaac realized what was happening, the man had a knife to the woman's throat. In the second it took for Isaac to yell stop. The knife was gone, and a thick line of blood was pouring down her chest. She collapsed and died on the road.

The man behind her came full into Isaac's view. His arms were covered to the elbows in blood. Streaks of red were smeared across his face. Isaac's stomach turned at the sight of him.

Without hesitation, Isaac raised his pistol and shot twice. Both shots hit the center of the man's chest, the second one taking him down. He knew there were more. He understood now why the van had collided with him. They had been fleeing this immense horde.

The crowd was on him now, hundreds of people pushing, trying to run through the street to escape whatever terror was chasing them. A man screamed from Isaac's left. He turned his head in time to see the man fall to the ground with another man on top of him, ripping at his face with his mouth. He raised his gun and fired two more shots. The attacker fell on his victim. Isaac ran to see if either was still alive.

As he approached the men, Isaac's heart sank. From somewhere in the midst of the crowd, he heard the unmistakable *RAT-TAT-TAT* of semi-auto gunfire. He quickly glanced at the bodies on the ground, there was too much blood, and neither was alive. The crowd raced past.

RAT-TAT-TAT! RAT-TAT-TAT! RAT-TAT-TAT!

He couldn't see where the gunman was, but bodies started to fall left and right.

"My God," Isaac whispered.

He ran toward the crowd, his eyes scanning the scene for the shooter. Someone hit him hard from the right side and knocked him back. Before he could take another step, a tall, lanky man lowered his shoulder, charged hard into his chest. There was no time for Isaac to think; he could only react. He grabbed the man's shoulders and threw him to the ground.

The eyes that stared back at him were black. Dull and lifeless, like a deer, once it's been shot. Suddenly, the man was tearing at Isaac's face. His fingers, like thin daggers, dug into his flesh. Isaac thrust his pistol under the man's chin and squeezed the trigger. Blood exploded everywhere. His face and body were covered with the sticky red mess.

He had to get out of here. He needed backup. He clambered to his feet and ran with the crowd. He pulled the scanner from his shoulder to radio for help, and that's when he noticed the wire had melted and frayed in the fire. He couldn't call anyone. He was alone. Then, his thoughts turned back to Melanie. He needed to get her out of here.

Bodies ran alongside him. He couldn't tell if they were attacking or fleeing. At this point, it didn't matter much. He had to get away. Getting Melanie to safety was all that mattered. He didn't know where they would go. *Was anywhere safe?* He needed to get to her first, then he would figure the rest out.

The entire street was crowded with bodies. Just minutes ago, he had pulled out into traffic, now there wasn't room to squeeze a bike, let alone a car, through this mass of people. If he could only get out of the crowd, he could run so much faster. As it was, whenever there was a crowd, the movement was reduced to the slowest possible speed.

Isaac turned to a man near him. The man's face was bloodied, but beneath the blood, Isaac saw fear. That was good; at least he had wits enough to be afraid.

"Where did they come from?" Isaac asked the man.

The man spun toward him, fist upheld. Isaac raised his hands and pointed to his uniform.

"Oh, shit, man! Shit! Help me outta here, man, help me!" the man screamed.

"I will. I will. Listen, I need to know where this all started," Isaac explained as they trotted. Earlier, the scanner woke him with the chaos on Fredrick Douglass and 111th. He wanted to find out if this was the same mob.

"I was coming from the Starbucks on Columbus and 100th," the man said while they continued to run. "I get out the door, and this woman runs into me, screaming her head off. Her boyfriend was just shot, she says. So, like I grab her right, but I'm looking around like 'where did this dude get shot' ya know? I ain't about to get shot. Then all of a sudden, she slumps over into me. I move my hand and see blood all down her back. So, I fucking ran."

"So, you ran down 100th. Where did all these people come from?" Isaac asked.

"As soon as I got to Central Park, a bunch of people were already running this way, so I followed them. I'm fucking scared, man. I saw a dude get his eye gouged, man! Fucking gouged out his head, man! One of those freaks with the weird eyes dug his claws into his face," the man said.

Isaac thought of the man he had just seen. He knew the look.

Black smoke was rising ahead. Isaac couldn't tell, but he thought it might be from the van. He had to get out of the road and back on the sidewalk where Melanie was.

"Hey! 88th Street is right over here, I'm gonna get the fuck out of here!" he yelled to the bloodied-up man. The man looked at him and nodded; he would follow.

Isaac saw the wreckage of the van ahead. The crowd was giving it a wide berth. *Better for me.* He ducked behind the back of the van and was able to squeeze between it and a parked car that had taken some fire damage from the explosion. The mangled mess of his cruiser lay ahead of the van. As he looked at it now, he realized how lucky he was to be alive.

"Is that your car, man?" the guy following him asked.

"It was," he replied.

Isaac ran toward the white brick building where he had left Melanie. She was right where he had left her. Her face was vacant. She was in a daze.

"Melanie!" he yelled to her. Her head shot up at her name.

"Dad!" she jumped up and ran to him; she was crying again. "I thought you were gone, I heard someone shooting, and I got scared."

He held her close and felt her little body shake. He kissed her head. *Now what?*

He saw the bloodied man that had followed him run down the entrance to the subway. He hoped the subway was safe, but he wasn't sure of anything now. He grabbed Melanie's arm and looked her in the eye.

"Can you run?" he asked. She nodded. "C'mon then."

They rushed around the corner of the white brick building onto 88th street. The crowd that was running down Central Park West split in two at the intersection; some remained on Central Park West while others turned the corner and embarked down 88th. The vehicles that had stopped at the light were abandoned. The drivers must have taken off when they saw the chaos, Isaac realized. What must they have thought, he wondered? Then he thought of Melanie and what she must have felt at the intersection of Fredrick Douglass.

Isaac and Melanie jumped into the throng that had worked its way down the street. They shuffled their feet and tried to break loose from the growing crowd. Home was only a little ways away. They could make it. *Hell, I can practically see our house.*

"Does Mom know what's going on?" Melanie asked.

Isaac laughed. He couldn't help it. While the crowd around them dissipated, Isaac and Melanie slowed to a stop while Isaac tried to compose himself. But, it was no use. He held his gut as his cheeks turned red, and his eyes watered. It wasn't funny, but it was.

"Melanie, I don't even know what's going on!" he laughed.

Melanie glared at him.

Behind them, a woman's scream rose above the muffled sounds of the rest of the crowd. Shortly after her scream came the *RAT-TAT-TAT* of gunfire. Isaac was afraid to see who wielded that gun. He saw Melanie's eyes widen at the sound. She was terrified, and so was he. They stood frozen in place, his laughter gone. He closed his eyes. The shots rang out again *RAT-TAT-TAT*, only this time closer. He grabbed Melanie's arm.

"C'mon!"

They ducked behind a Ford, off the street, and onto the sidewalk. They were on the same side of the street that they lived on. They knelt behind the vehicle. *RAT-TAT-TAT RAT-TAT-TAT!* Bullets peppered the cars nearby. Some shots sailed high and chipped the brick houses behind Isaac and Melanie.

"We should run," she said.

He shook his head and held up his hand. With his right hand, he brought out his pistol. He pulled a fresh clip from his belt and replaced the near empty one. He raised his finger to his lips. Melanie nodded. Isaac turned to the rear of the car and remained low as he approached the opening behind the Ford's trunk.

Isaac waited by the rear of the car. He wanted to get a clear shot at the gunman whenever he came into view. He would catch him by surprise. Hopefully, that would buy him enough time to get a kill shot. He didn't want to think about what would happen if he didn't get a clear shot and gave away his position. He knew he was outgunned.

More gunfire echoed from the end of the street. Isaac's heart sank. He knew behind those shots there were bodies falling to the ground right now. Then, he saw his target. It was a fleeting glimpse, not enough for him to shoot, but at least a visual. The man strode behind a parked car on the opposite side of the street. Isaac would have to wait for him to come out from behind the car before he would have a clear shot.

The waiting is the hardest part. The gun in his hands felt hot, and his palms began to sweat. He made a conscious effort to breathe slowly to keep his composure. One shot was all he needed. One shot.

Melanie was crouched by the front tire of the Ford. Isaac turned to her and knelt down, so they were looking at one another on the same level.

"If anything goes wrong, you need to run back to the house. To your Mother. Do not stop for anyone," he whispered.

She nodded.

Isaac looked her over once more before he stood up. She was short but strong, inside and out. After this morning, he would expect most girls her age to be in shock. Granted, she had been shocked earlier, but now when he looked at her, he saw that same determination that colored everything she did. She didn't argue with him now. He knew she must be thinking of what could happen. Yet, she stayed quiet. Isaac leaned over and kissed the top of her head. Melanie turned and kissed him on the cheek.

Isaac rose and peered through the back window of the Ford. Still nothing across the street. It was too dark to tell for certain, but Isaac thought he could see a shadow behind an SUV where the man stood on the other side of the street. There was no movement. He sighed.

Up the street, he heard more screams. There was a loud *BANG* followed by the whoosh of fire, which forced him to turn his gaze from the car across the street. A car had exploded on Central Park West. He couldn't tell how, but he could see the fire caused by it now. Black smoke billowed into the night sky. *This city is going to fall if we don't get control of this soon.*

He turned his attention back to the car on the opposite side of the road. The man was no longer hiding. He was out in the open as he watched Isaac. His face contorted into a crooked smile. The AK-47 held loosely in front of him, dangled toward the ground. In one fluid motion, the man wheeled the gun up to his shoulder and fired.

"Shit!" Isaac dropped behind the Ford. "Fuck."

He held the pistol tight in his hands and rested his forehead along the smooth cold barrel. The bullets pierced the Ford and rang loud as the metal turned in on itself. The man bellowed into the night as he sprayed bullets left and right. His voice echoed off the buildings nearby, but he didn't sound human. His screams were wild, like that of an animal.

As suddenly as it had started, the shooting stopped. Isaac took the opportunity to once again stand behind the car and look for a clear shot. But he was too eager. He realized once he stood, that he should have waited. The man lifted the gun again and started shooting. Bullets whizzed by Isaac.

He relaxed his shoulders and raised the pistol. Isaac aimed and fired three quick shots. The first hit the man square in the chest but didn't stop him. The second sailed to the right and missed entirely. The third went straight into his forehead, and the gunman fell dead.

Isaac collapsed behind the Ford. He felt weak.

"Dad!" Melanie scurried over to him.

"It's alright baby I got him, we can go home," Isaac said.

Melanie looked down at him. Her eyes were filled with tears.

"Melanie, it's okay," he said again.

She shook her head, and more tears fell.

He couldn't understand why she cried. It was over.

But as the seconds ticked by and the adrenaline subsided, Isaac struggled to catch his breath. Something was wrong. He looked down, and that's when he realized why Melanie was crying. His chest was a pool of blood. He saw two holes in his uniform, one by his sternum. That bullet hadn't caused any damage as it had connected with his vest. It would leave a bruise, but that was all. The second bullet grazed the collar of his shirt and missed his vest. That one had lodged itself at the base of his neck just above his collarbone.

"Oh," he sighed as he tried to keep his breathing under control. "Melanie, it's ok. We just have to get back home."

Chapter Thirty-Six

Melanie

EVERYTHING HAPPENED SO FAST. Melanie was dizzy. She wanted to scream. There was a knot in her throat that made it difficult to speak.

"Dad," she cried.

"Mel, listen," he said. "Help me stand up."

It was hard to focus. Melanie heard her father speak, yet his words seemed distant. She didn't move right away. Instead, she sat, watching him breathe, slow, and ragged. She could tell he was in a lot of pain. It wasn't until Isaac reached out and took her hand that Melanie broke from her stupor.

"Yeah, Daddy?"

"Help me up," he sighed.

She pulled him up to a sitting position. His blood ran down the front of his shirt. Although his uniform was dark, Melanie thought she saw where the blood had soaked the fabric. Maybe it was just in her head, but it didn't matter.

"Alright," he said. "Pull hard, baby."

Isaac winced as she helped him up. Melanie steadied him and helped him balance against the car. He was really weak. She knew right away; she would have to help him walk.

"C'mon," he grunted. Melanie tried to support his weight as they made their way across the street. She was too short to really be of much help, but she did the best she could. They crossed the street to the dead man.

"Dad, look at his arm," Melanie pointed to the black band on his forearm.

"That's what it looks like?" he asked.

She nodded.

"Grab the gun," he told her.

She pulled it off the limp body. Crouched next to the dead man, she looked at his arm. The band didn't look special. *Why would you want to wear one if it did this to you?* She didn't understand.

She stood up and strapped the gun around her shoulder. Isaac looked down on her with a smile on his face and chuckled.

"You look ridiculous."

"So do you," she spat back.

They both laughed. Isaac coughed into his palm. Melanie saw the gob of blood but didn't say anything. They both knew their time was limited.

"Let's get home," she said.

"Just help me walk, I'll be okay," he said.

Melanie wrapped her arm around his lower back, and they began the short journey home. Isaac staggered with each step. His eyelids started to slide closed. Melanie couldn't support his weight alone. If he fell, they would both go down.

"Hey!"

"What's that, baby?"

"Keep your eyes open. You can't fall asleep."

"I won't," he muttered.

"Keep them open!"

Melanie watched him struggle to open his eyes. It took a second before they focused on her. Brown, with streaks of silver, his gaze was gentle and loving. Melanie smiled.

"Let's go," she said.

They trudged on. Melanie knew her Dad was getting weaker. She could feel it in his steps. He was leaning on her more and more, and he was slowing down. She was afraid to look behind them in case they were being followed.

This couldn't be real; she tried to tell herself. She would wake up and hear her Mom calling her from the hallway, saying it was time to get up. That voice wasn't coming, though. As much as she didn't want to believe this was real, there was nothing to convince her otherwise.

She could see their front porch, only three houses down now.

"Dad, we are almost home," she said.

"Unhmm," he mumbled.

"Mom! Mom! Help!" Melanie screamed. Her Dad was too heavy. Her mom would hear her and come help. She would know what to do.

"Mel don't yell," her father said with difficulty.

It was too late. The front door of their house opened. Melanie waved her hand in the air and signaled for help. She saw the look of shock envelop her mother's face just before she screamed.

"Oh, my God!"

Delana jumped down the front steps and ran toward them.

Suddenly, Melanie saw a blur jet past her left side. It was too quick to make out. By the time Melanie whipped her head to the left to see, it was already past. She turned back to her mother and realized too late what had rushed past.

The man speared her mother square in the gut. Melanie heard the air rush from her mother's lungs as her body slammed into the blacktop.

"Mom!"

Isaac slid from Melanie's shoulder and tumbled to the ground. Desperately, he scrambled forward using his hands to push himself up once more. He didn't get more than three steps before he was tackled to the ground as well. His face smashed into the blacktop and pebbles ground into his skin.

All the while, Melanie was frozen. She couldn't think fast enough. She needed to help her mother, but her father needed her at the same time. Then as she felt the weight of the world crashing upon her, an idea came to her.

Melanie groped at the rifle hanging around her shoulders and wedged the butt against her shoulder. It was enormous against her little body. She had never fired a gun before and only vaguely knew what to do. She squeezed the trigger. The recoil against her shoulder knocked her back a step. She would have fallen over were it not for the wrist watcher that slammed into her backside.

She felt her knees give out with the force of the collision. Then, she smashed into the ground; her head bounced off the blacktop, opening a great gash along her forehead. She still held the gun and was unable to put her hands out to break her fall. Her right wrist was pinched beneath the barrel. She felt the bones in her hand, cracking under the pressure.

Melanie twisted under the weight of the wrist watcher. The skin on her wrist peeled back and exposed the shining white bone. Nothing had ever hurt so badly. She screamed. Then a fist struck her hard in the middle of the face. Her nose cracked for the second time, and fresh blood cascaded over her mouth.

She looked into the eyes of a monster. Black orbs stared back at her. The face showed no emotion. Melanie watched the man rear back for another punch. Instinctively her head jerked forward, and the fist sailed high and smashed into the ground behind her head. She looked back up to see the wrist watcher's reaction, but as before, he was unfazed. She realized then that they didn't feel pain whatsoever. They were zombies.

She turned again as best she could to loosen the gun that was still under her. The barrel poked out from under her shoulder. The body above her lunged for it. The rifle was the only hope Melanie had. If she lost it, she was dead. She spun the rest of the way to her left, rolling in the strap of the gun, and rotated her body so that the stock was against her hip. The wrist watcher had a hold of the barrel. When he tried to rip the gun away, Melanie reached for the trigger and squeezed.

His head disappeared in an explosion of blood. The body collapsed on the ground next to her. Melanie scrambled to her feet and wheeled the gun in front of her. She aimed for the wrist watcher over her father, this time prepared for the recoil. The shot rang out and echoed off the buildings. The body over her father went limp and collapsed in a heap. Over her mother, the wrist watcher turned just in time for Melanie to see his dark eyes before his head caved in like a wilted pumpkin with the impact of her shot.

Melanie ran to her father, sure it was too late, but hoping beyond reason, he was still alive. She got to him and saw the blood around his neck and knew she was too late. His eyes were closed.

"Dad," she shook his shoulder.

His head rolled to the side, and Melanie knew he was gone. Her only hope now remained in her mother.

She turned and ran toward Delana Parker, but before she even reached her, Melanie could tell she had suffered a similar fate. Her neck was ripped open just below her jaw. Blood still trickled down her throat onto a yellow blouse.

Melanie collapsed on the pavement. Her chest heaved up and down as she struggled to breathe. She couldn't get enough air. Her ears buzzed, and the street was a dim blur. She fell on her back. The next thing she knew, she was floating. The night sky above was streaked with wispy cirrus clouds that stretched across the moon and felt so close like she could reach out and touch them. This was all just a dream. This didn't happen. Not in New York. Minutes slowly passed. She focused on the sky, how peaceful it seemed. Eventually, her breathing came under control as she watched the clouds move across the sky. She waited to wake up.

Except, the dream never stopped. Eventually, she sat up. The streetlights spun as she tried to focus. She was numb, body, and mind. Faintly, she heard police sirens and screams whisper on the wind from somewhere far away. Further down the street past her father's body, she saw her Mets hat rumpled and lonely. When she finally stood up, pain shot through her knees. Blood caked her jeans. Her right wrist was a bloody mess. She was sure her face looked wretched as well. She walked over to her hat and put it on.

Melanie looked at the splayed bodies of her parents, now lifeless. She couldn't leave the bodies out here. It wasn't right. If the roles were reversed, they would take her inside. She decided that was exactly what exactly would do.

She first went to her mother. As she looked down at the body, she realized how large her mother was. Not fat, but tall and strong. She was easily 5'10" with lean muscular arms and legs. There was no way Melanie could lift her, let alone her father. There had to be another way. After a few moments, a thought came to her. She raced to the front door and bounded through the empty living room to the sofa. There she found a few blankets stacked neatly on the backrest. She took two and ran back outside.

Carefully she laid the blanket out next to her mother and slid her onto it. She grabbed the blanket and pulled. It stretched and looked like it might rip, but just when Melanie thought there was no more give, the blanket obliged, and she was able to pull Delana Parker back to her home. Melanie navigated the steps cautiously, lightly lifting the blanket higher on each step so as not to let her mother catch on the cement.

Melanie ran back outside and followed the same procedure with her father.

At last, when his body was in the living room next to her mother's, she closed and latched the front door. She covered them with another blanket from the couch. It wasn't proper, but it would have to do. It was all she had.

She had never been to a funeral and was unsure what people said at such times. She knelt down next to their bodies and peeled the blanket down enough to see their faces. There was a vase full of roses sitting on the end table next to the sofa. Melanie reached and took two flowers and placed them on her parent's chests. Finally, she kissed each of them on the forehead.

Tears rained down her cheeks. She didn't say anything. Instead, she sobbed quietly over their bodies until her eyes were red and puffy, and no more tears would come.

Chapter Thirty-Seven

Harry

PERCHED on the topmost branch of a pine tree, Harry Davis admired the glow of the city in the distance while the caravan weaved its way along the highway. His eyes glistened in the light of the moon, which hung above the horizon. Its white glow reflected off the traffic. Still, a solid hour away from their destination, this line of traffic was one of many approaching New York City. The city was reeling from the devastation of the first attack. It worked as he had planned. He knew military personnel were already on their way. That was fine. In this line of traffic alone, Harry had four-hundred and eleven new soldiers. All told he had over three thousand migrating to the city from New York and Pennsylvania.

Once New York fell, the attacks would become more difficult. He anticipated that. By attacking the city first, he hoped to dictate where the impending attacks would take place. He knew that soon after the city fell, there would be reclamation squadrons sent to win it back. He would get as many of his troops as he could inside the city before then. In this process, it was important to not only kill, but also to turn as many people as possible to his side. The bands were nearly perfect in that regard. Maggie had been the only flaw, and she was doing much better.

Harry leapt from the tree. His wings caught the air, and he rocketed high into the sky. Clouds above him turned to mist as he flew through them. High above the traffic, he found peace within the clouds. Here, even better than the forest back home near Dunker Pond, he was able to feel the cosmic energy gently run through him. He understood his place in the grand scheme of time. He embraced it, for he understood what evil humanity was capable of. Julianna's death need never have happened. But it did.

It was here above the clouds that he could escape his rage and fully embrace the wonder that existed outside human comprehension. The day would soon come where he could experience that celestial freedom without the constraints of his human body. There was work yet to be done. These momentary escapes into that high haven were just that, escapes.

He descended back below the clouds. The line of traffic still weaved its way along the highway. He would leave them for now. They knew where they were going. He had other matters to attend to. With a few strong beats of his wings, he raced through the sky well past the front line of traffic and disappeared over a hill a few miles ahead.

Chapter Thirty-Eight

Walter

THE ROAD WAS dark as they wormed their way through the miles of highway to New York City. Walter had never been to the city. It was one of those trips he always intended to take but hadn't yet. This wasn't a trip he would remember. In fact, as the caravan ticked past the mile-markers, Walter was unaware of anything.

The congregation was packed systematically in vehicle after vehicle. Silent and organized, they sped into the night. Their destination was clear on the mental map they all shared.

There were no stops on this train. It was killing time, and the night was just beginning.

Chapter Thirty-Nine

John

THE STARS SPARKLED on the water as John and Daryl crossed the Hudson on Interstate 287. Their light reflected off the water and highlighted each ripple in shades of silver. On the horizon was a dazzling display of oranges and reds where the light from the city glowed. The wind through the windows was fresh and cool. It gently whipped against their faces. Traffic was at a standstill as they waited to get to the thruway ahead.

"I hate traffic," John said.

"That so?" Daryl laughed to himself.

He had slept for a good portion of the ride. Upon waking, he had been in a jolly mood. John was aggravated. For the last hour, they had barely moved. A semi in front of them blocked his view so he couldn't see what the holdup was.

"We haven't moved from this spot for at least 15 minutes," he said.

"I'll get out and see what's goin' on," Daryl offered.

"Leave the grenades in here. Last thing we need is to be seen with a box full of explosives."

Why had he agreed to let Daryl bring them? Their entire plan was a half-baked concoction destined to get them killed. What if they got there and it wasn't anything like what they saw on Leroy's TV? Persistent doubts had made the drive drag on. He was grateful Daryl had slept most of the way because his chatter reminded John how ill-prepared they were and just how ridiculous this entire scheme was.

"I'mma take one just in case," Daryl said.

Before John could reply, he was out the door. The box of grenades sat in the seat; its lid was propped open slightly. John sighed. Part of him wanted to turn around and head home. He no longer cared if he got back to his little house in Ebron and found a S.W.A.T. vehicle there. He was tired and felt old. He ran his hands over his face and through his hair and groaned.

What they needed here was a hot dog vendor. Like at a baseball game. Vendors would make a killing just walking through the lines of traffic. He could see it now.

"Hot dawgg! Hot dogs over here!"

"I'll take two, and while you're at it, what do you have to drink?"

"Ice cold beer! Five dollars!"

"Five dollars! You train-robbing bastard. I'll give you two bucks."

"Five or nothing," the vendor said.

Oh, what the fuck, I'm getting ripped off in my own daydream.

Through the windshield, John saw Daryl lurking near the back of the semi.

"What the hell Daryl? You may as well have stayed in here for all the good you are doing," John muttered.

He leaned back and stretched his arms behind his head. Just then, something shook the entire truck. He reached for the pistol under his arm without thinking. The .44 was already out of the holster and in his hand, as he looked in the mirrors. There was nothing behind the truck that he could see. His eyes raced over to where Daryl stood.

The old man's eyes met John's. He shook his head. John didn't understand. What was going on? He opened his door and stepped out into the cool night air. Daryl mouthed something, but it was too dark to read lips. What did he say? When next their eyes met, Daryl left no doubt as to what he said.

"Run!"

John watched him pull the pin on the grenade and hurl it toward the thruway. He ran around the side of the semi to see what happened. He suddenly understood why traffic hadn't moved. There was a pile of cars in the thruway blocking all movement. There had been a major accident. Where were the ambulance and police? An explosion of dust, debris, and fire lit up the road. The grenades still worked.

"What the fuck!" John yelled as he stumbled backward.

He turned and ran toward the truck. Daryl beat him there.

"What the hell are you doing?"

"John, let's go!" the old man yelled.

"No shit!" John jumped in the driver's seat. "What were you thinking?"

"It's them. I saw 'em like on the TV," Daryl said between breaths. "Drive fast!"

"Where?" John asked.

"There was a little space on this side."

"Enough to get through?"

"Maybe," Daryl replied.

John looked in his mirrors. There was no way to go back over the bridge; it was jammed. Forward was the only option. But there wasn't room to turn past the semi. He would have to back up some to make room. The car behind them was too close, though. The man at the wheel was on the phone, not paying any attention at all. He probably hadn't seen Daryl throw the grenade. *Fuck it*. He threw the truck in reverse and slammed on the gas. The Dodge revved loud. He let off the clutch, and the truck careened backward into the car. He had turned just enough so that the truck avoided any major damage. The passenger side bumper was ruined, but that didn't hurt much of anything. The man in the car seemed unaffected by the collision.

John thrust the shifter into first and hit the gas. The truck rolled forward. There was barely enough room to get by the semi now.

John saw the space Daryl had mentioned ahead. It was just outside the actual thruway; they would be lucky if they fit.

Then he saw the scene at the highway more fully. It was not just an accident. The cars were purposely blocking all the lanes.

"What the hell?" John said.

"I know," Daryl replied.

"Why are people just sitting here?" John asked.

"The truck driver's eyes were black," Daryl said. Then John understood.

The truck weaved between the parked cars. The little space that Daryl had seen wasn't completely cleared. They wouldn't fit if they tried to squeeze through. But it was the only option they had because turning around now was impossible.

The cement guardrails that separated each lane would pose the greatest hurdle. If John approached straight on, they should be fine, but that meant he had to cut across lanes of traffic and create an impossible angle to maneuver the truck through the cement guardrail and maintain enough speed to crash through the blockade on the other side. As they got closer to the lane, John saw that it was more jammed than they originally thought. It was obvious they wouldn't make it.

He cranked the wheel hard and just scraped the cement on the driver's side. He was in the lane! He slammed on the brakes.

"What are you doing?" Daryl asked.

"We need more speed," John answered. "We'll never make it through from here."

He put the truck in reverse and backed up as far as he could. For half a second, John wondered if he was falling for a trap, like a Venus fly plant luring an insect to its death with the sick-sweet smell of decay. But the thought was fleeting, and this seemed like the only option they had. John stopped the truck. He hoped he had enough room to get some speed.

He stomped on the gas. Smoke and dust kicked out from under the tires. The RPM gauge shot into the red before he shifted. Their speed climbed, 25, 30, 35, and then SMASH! The truck barreled into the car that was half blocking the exit. They were wedged between the car on the left and the cement barrier on the right.

John cranked the wheel while he stood on the gas pedal, hoping to loosen the truck. It was hopeless. It was wedged too perfectly. He tried to reverse. If they hit it again, maybe they could breakthrough. Only, they couldn't back up. The truck tires squealed and refused to move.

"Fuck!" John screamed.

"John, we have to move," Daryl said.

"Yea, no shit!" John replied.

"No. Look!" Daryl pointed past the car that had them pinned against the cement. A crowd of people stared at the truck.

"Oh, shit," John sighed.

Even from a distance, John could see their vacant eyes in his headlights. There were thirty of them, maybe more.

"Can you open your door?" he asked.

"No. You?"

He pushed the driver's door, but it wouldn't budge, "No."

John looked out the back window. It was small, but maybe they could squeeze through. Then he looked over at Daryl and his leg. *No, that would never do.* He twisted in his seat so he could reach behind and pulled the shotgun off the rack.

"Hold this," he told Daryl.

He grabbed the bag that held all his supplies and placed it in the empty seat between them. From the bag, he pulled out a box of shells. He handed them to Daryl.

"Load it for me," he said.

Daryl snapped open the barrel and set the shells in. John pulled the Ruger from his bag and hooked it between his belt and pants on his right side. He wished he had a holster, but this would have to do. Daryl's guns were still in the back. John reached back over the seats and pulled them forward.

"Here, trade," he said to Daryl, who took the rifles and handed John the shotgun.

"Watch your eyes," he said.

John laid the gun on the dash. He turned his head. He didn't really need to aim. He squeezed the front trigger. *THRACK!* The blast was deafening, and the air smelled like gunpowder now. He looked at the windshield. It had spiderwebbed, and a couple of chunks broke loose, but it had not broken completely. He squeezed the second trigger. *THRACK!* This time the glass did shatter. There was a gaping hole in the windshield, large enough to crawl through. It was their only way out.

Through the busted windshield, John saw a man standing in front of the truck. His dead eyes gazed into the vehicle. His face and chest were bloody.

John opened the barrel and ejected the two empty casings. Without taking his eyes off the man, he reached for the box of shells and placed two more in the barrel before clicking it closed. The man at the front of the truck jumped on the hood and clambered toward the broken windshield. John leveled the shotgun. He had the man lined up and was just about to pull the trigger when the air to his right exploded. He felt something wet splatter across his face. The man was sprawled on the dash; his head looked like the inside of a watermelon. To his right, John saw the smoke still rising from the tip of Daryl's pistol. He pushed the dead man's body to the side with the barrel of the shotgun. The body slid down the front of the truck and back to the pavement leaving a bloody streak behind.

"Think you can climb out?" John asked.

"Don't have much choice, do we?" Daryl replied.

John would climb out first. If need be, he could pull Daryl out. He set the shotgun on the hood ahead of him. It was a struggle to squeeze over the dash and through the windshield. Daryl was going to have a hell of a time with his leg.

"Throw me my bag," he yelled to Daryl once he was completely out of the truck and on the hood. Daryl shuffled around in the cabin behind him. John looked toward the group of vacant eyed men and women standing some fifty yards away. A good-sized group of them was heading toward the truck. He quickly counted, fifteen, maybe sixteen, but he wasn't sure he saw all of them. Daryl pushed the bag through the windshield. John grabbed it and slung it over his shoulder.

"We have to hurry," he told Daryl. He reached through the windshield and offered his hand to the old man. Daryl was too busy setting his guns through the window to notice. He placed the grenades on top and began climbing out. John was surprised with the ease at which the old man was able to crawl through the tight space.

"I'm old," Daryl said. "But not that old."

"Alright, I'll climb down first. You keep watch. They're coming this way. We need to hurry," John said.

"I see 'em," Daryl replied. He pulled a rifle from the hood and set it in the groove of his shoulder. "Go on; I got 'em."

John climbed down the hood. It was only a second before he felt the solid pavement beneath his feet. From above, Daryl's rifle rang out. *CRACK! CRACK!* Once fully on the ground, John pulled the shotgun from the hood of the truck and, in one swift motion, raised it to his shoulder and spun toward their attackers. Already the fifteen he had counted were within twenty yards. Damn it, he thought, we don't have enough time. He rested his cheek against the wooden stock and felt the therapeutic kick of the gun once then twice. *THRACK THRACK!* He snapped open the barrel and loaded two more shells.

"Daryl come on!" he shouted. More shots from above *CRACK! CRACK! CRACK!* He heard the old man shuffle on the hood.

"Here," Daryl called.

John turned and behind him, on the hood of the truck, was Daryl's .30-30. John set the shotgun to his right and took the rifle. It rested easily against his shoulder. John looked through the scope and fired three shots in quick succession. One was a headshot, the other two body shots, all immediate kills. The crowd had lessened significantly. John was feeling better about their odds, but they needed to get moving.

Then to his left, he heard the screech of Daryl's boots on the still wet blood that covered the hood of the truck. The old man slipped. John first heard the thud as he fell on the hood of the truck. Then, more disheartening was the crack like the snapping of a branch that echoed in his ears as Daryl crashed in a heap on the pavement next to him.

The old man wailed in agony.

John cringed. He knew it was bad. He didn't want to look, but he had to. Daryl writhed on the ground cradling his good leg.

"Oh God, my leg! My leg! It's broken! Fuck! It's broken!"

John saw Daryl's leg bent forward just below the knee. The old man held it in his hands and screamed. His gut-wrenching cry made John's hair stand on end. But he knew there was nothing he could offer. *What solace was there? This was a death sentence.* John sighed and knelt next to Daryl.

"Go, John, you're not dead yet," Daryl said.

"Daryl," was all John could say.

"Go. I'm dead, John," he said through gritted teeth. "You have work to do."

John knew there was nothing he could do. He stood up. To his right, he saw the crowd advancing. He pulled the rifle up and shot twice, two more bodies fell. The clip was now empty. Only three more people remained from the group of fifteen. He reached for his shotgun; the blasts rang out in the dark. Two more bodies fell. The last one charged onward. John pulled his .357 from his belt and waited for the last one to get closer. He was ten yards away then eight then seven. John squeezed three times for good measure. The body fell. A second wave of attackers was already on their way.

"John," Daryl called.

"Yea," he answered.

"Leave the rest to me," Daryl said. "You get while ya still can."

On the hood of the truck were Daryl's guns and the box of grenades. John pulled all of them from the hood and set them next to Daryl.

"You take the box. They're wasted on me," Daryl said, pushing the box of grenades away. John pulled one out and handed it to the old man. Their eyes met, a somber smile spread across Daryl's face as he took the grenade.

"Go!" he said.

John nodded and slid the box into his bag. He ran to the right as far as the road allowed. A cement barrier bordered the edge of the highway. John used that as a guide in the darkening night. For the second time in two days, he was told to run, and so he did.

He ran toward a city balanced precariously on the edge of a razor blade, with only the slightest glimmer of hope in a world of absolute darkness.

Behind him, shots reverberated. To his left, John heard footsteps.

The crowd had split in half. Some were drawing close to the truck and where Daryl lay, but seven or eight that had broken off were following him and gaining.

He could try to shoot them, but he would have to stop, and if he missed, they would be even closer. So, instead of stopping, he ran faster. The road ahead was desolate; even in the growing darkness, John could see there was little in the way of cover.

The footsteps behind him grew closer. The soft pattering of sneakers against pavement grew louder each second. *The grenades.* He could drop one without stopping and perhaps buy himself some time. He reached for his bag. The zipper was still open, and he felt the box sitting on top. He slid his hand in and felt the cool metal casing against his palm and pulled it out.

Far behind him, he heard a *POP!* Just over his shoulder, he saw the slight flash of fire. Daryl was dead. He felt sick inside. *This was not how it was supposed to happen;* he screamed in his mind. Although Daryl had said he was ready to die back at the bar, John had privately held out hope that nothing so dire would come to the old man.

He pulled the pin on the grenade and dropped the heavy ball. It clanked on the ground behind him. John ran faster, not knowing how much time he had or how big the blast would be. He still heard the footsteps behind him until *BANG!* The explosion shook the earth. John stumbled. His knees bashed against the pavement tearing holes in his jeans as layers of skin peeled away, leaving an area of deep dark red. His hands instinctively reached out to save him from the fall and were rewarded with deep gashes from the gravel and dirt.

Although his hands and knees burned, John tried to ignore the pain and quickly turned his body to see the road behind him and the effects of the grenade. A small fire burned on the ground, not even thirty feet behind him. There were the mangled bodies of at least four, maybe five of his attackers. Despite the pain throughout his body, John hoisted himself back to his feet.

Through the flames, he saw the silhouette of a man approaching him. John reached for the .357. He still had bullets in the cylinder. The man continued toward him. Then, to his right, John heard someone scream, and the wind was knocked from him as he was thrown to the ground.

His attacker lay on top of him. She was tiny but strong. His right arm, which held the revolver, was pinned across his midsection. He tried to push the woman away, but she clung to him. Then something sharp stabbed his thigh. A wave of pain tore through his leg. He twisted his hand and rotated the gun before he squeezed the trigger. Her body jerked forward from the force of the shot, and John was able to free his arm. He saw the hole in the middle of her back where the bullet had exited. She should have been incapacitated. Instead, the woman's small fists rained down a frenzy of punches aimed at his head. The first one caught him off guard, a hard-right hand above his eye. He turned in time to avoid the next one. Before she could get another punch in he quickly pulled the revolver up from his side and shoved the barrel in the woman's face and squeezed. Her head exploded, and she fell in a heap on his chest. He wanted to vomit. He pushed her lifeless body off and looked down at his leg. A jagged piece of metal stuck straight out of his thigh.

"Shit," he grunted.

John had barely moved the woman off of him before the man he had initially seen was on top of him. Huge meaty hands grabbed him around the neck and lifted him easily off the ground. The pistol fell from his hands with the suddenness of the attack. His feet dangled inches above the road. John felt weak and helpless, like a child in the hands of a grown man. He gasped for breath while the hands around his neck squeezed tighter. Then the man threw him. John crashed hard against the pavement. Fresh pain jolted through his body as his spine struck the road. He coughed and gasped for air.

He saw a glimmer of steel, his pistol, only a few feet away. He scrambled toward it. The man kicked John hard in the ribs. His side went numb. John fought against the pain and reached out and grabbed the gun. Another solid kick to his ribs. He collapsed. The pain was gone; everything was numb and weak. It took all his strength to focus the .357 on his attacker. His hand trembled. There was no time to get a perfect shot, so he squeezed the trigger.

His attacker recoiled against the blow but remained largely unphased.

Then, the man jumped on top of him; his fist was cocked back, ready to throw a devastating right hand to John's already bruised head. He squeezed the trigger again. A hole appeared where the man's eye had been. A large gaping wound that ripped through his skull. The body slid to the right and fell on the road. John heaved a sigh of relief.

His eyelids wavered then closed. He wanted to sleep. He needed sleep.

"Daddy, stay awake," John heard softly in his ear. His eyes blinked open ever so slightly.

"Your leg, daddy. It's bleeding," Elly said. She sat next to him on the highway, the moon reflecting off the bright yellow summer dress he remembered so well.

"I know, baby," John said. "I just need to rest a little. I'll be okay."

"No. Daddy, you need to fix your leg, or you will die," she said. John gazed into her soft blue eyes.

"Help me, Elly," he said. He felt her hand on his.

"It's okay, Daddy, you can do this," she said. He groaned and sat up. Elly was still there next to him. Her big eyes watched him intensely. She looked at his leg.

"I know," he said. He grabbed the metal with both hands, drew a deep breath, and pulled. John bit his lip to keep from screaming. Blood poured from the wound. He would bleed out if he didn't do something. He unbuckled his belt and slid it out from beneath the loops on his pants. Then, he wrapped it around his leg and pulled it tight, to fashion a makeshift tourniquet. Blood still seeped from the hole, but it seemed a little better. His leg was numb. That wasn't a good sign, but he didn't know what else to do.

"You need to keep going, daddy," Elly said.

"I know, baby," he said. John felt his daughter's little arms wrap around his neck.

"I miss you," he whispered.

"You'll be with us soon," she said, and then she was gone. John's stomach sank.

He gingerly rose to his feet. It felt like he had been hit by a truck, his body ached everywhere. He put pressure on his leg. Prickly pain shot through his nerves. It hurt, but it would hold.

He pulled a Marlboro from the pocket on his jacket. The cigarette was bent and battered. John straightened it slightly and stuck it in his mouth. He pulled the lighter from his pocket, lit the cigarette, and drew a long deep puff.

The bag with all his supplies laid at his feet. He knelt next to it. He needed the .357 and shotgun shells buried within. It would be best to reload now before he ran into more danger. It took a second, but John found the bullets and reloaded both guns quickly. Then, he slid the pistol in the small of his back and tucked it between his shirt and pants. He slung the shotgun over his shoulder. Then he patted the holster that held the .44 under his arm. He was ready, at least, ready as anyone could be.

He had never stopped to think what it would be like carrying all the guns he owned at one time. By no means did he have some enormous arsenal. But with the three guns and the bag hoisted over his other shoulder, John felt like he was going to war. In a way, he was. No one had asked him, and he hadn't signed up. He was just a civilian doing what was necessary. Would he have willingly gone on this journey even just a week ago? Probably not, he thought. He probably still wouldn't have chosen to go were it not for what happened at Ted's. He could see himself sitting at the bar right now, watching the Pirates game with Ted. Was this how it happened for those people that went on to do great things in their lives? Did it start with one event, like the last domino in a line, as everything else fell in order? If so, why him? He was no one. He had spent the years since that night at Harry's trying to fade away, trying to hide from who he had been and who he could have been.

Something glistened in the light of the fire and caught his eye. The body of the big man lay only a couple feet from John. The fire was slowly dying some distance away, yet the reflection John had just seen was closer. He walked over to the man and looked the body up and down. The reflection was coming from the man's arm. John knelt next to him to get a better look at it. His leg screamed out in agony, but he tried his best to ignore it. A black metallic band was strapped across the forearm. John took one final puff of his cigarette before he snuffed it out on the dead man's back. He lifted the forearm and felt the smooth metal. On the inside of the forearm, John saw a clasp that locked the device. He pried at the connection. It took some effort, but he was able to pop it open. Copper pins stuck into the man's skin. John pulled the band away from the man's arm, and the long pins slowly withdrew from beneath the flesh.

The hair on his neck stood on end. He had seen this before. This was almost exactly like what he and Harry had made all those years ago. Larger and positioned slightly different on the arm but almost identical. The copper pins were the same as he and Harry had used to help combat dementia. The nearly imperceptible electrical pulses that fired through the nerves kept the grey matter in the brain active and limited the effects of the debilitating disease.

If the electrical pulses were manipulated, someone could, in theory, control others wearing the armband. John now knew, somewhere, on the other end of these armbands, someone was directing the attacks. But Harry was dead. The only other person who could have had access was Mark Bishop. Could he have altered the early design to create this? If so, why?

He had to find out.

John looked around; he saw the outline of a big green sign hanging above the road a little way ahead. He went towards it to see where he was. EXIT 9 TARRYTOWN SLEEPY HOLLOW it read. That wasn't much help. He wasn't familiar with this area at all. Daryl had been his navigator. Somehow the old man had known exactly where he was going. John assumed he must have traveled here often. They were heading this way in the truck, so it only made sense to keep walking this way, John decided at last.

So, he continued down the highway. His leg became more reluctant with each step. After ten quiet minutes, John came to another sign. By now, he was breathing heavily and ready for a break. He leaned against the cement barricade to his right and rested his hands on his knees to catch his breath. Once he had caught his breath and felt the cool night air blow gently against his cheek, he felt better. Still leaning on the barricade, he looked up at the sign. 87

SOUTH SAW MILL PKWY NEW YORK CITY ¾ MILE. How far had he just walked, he wondered? A tenth of a mile? Maybe. Three-quarters of a mile would take him an hour at this rate if he even made it. John looked further down the road past the sign above. He saw what looked like a couple of vehicles a ways off.

It took another ten minutes to get there, and when he did, he was breathless and held his leg with both hands to quell the throbbing pain. Three vehicles were parked haphazardly along the highway. One, a big Ford Eco-van, still had the driver door open, and the lights inside dimly reflected off the cement. Another van, much older than the first, had rust marks along the wheel wells and side skirting as well as a flat front tire. It was useless.

In front of the vans, and close to the center barricade was a big Chrysler. John could tell it was new from the shape of the body and how the angular contours of the hood and roof worked gracefully toward the rear of the car. He walked over and looked through the passenger window.

The seats were leather. They looked comfortable. He opened the door and threw his bag in the driver's seat, and collapsed in the passenger seat. It cradled him like a cloud. This was more comfortable than his bed at home. There was no way he could drive this and stay awake. John's hand slipped off the door, and it automatically shut. With a soft click, it was closed, and the dashboard lit up. John stared wide-eyed at the display behind the wheel. An array of symbols and numbers were lit up in bright blue. It was dizzying to look at. Suddenly the wheel shifted, and the entire dashboard seemed to move. The wheel slid across the dash until it rested in front of John.

"Where are we going today, sir?" a woman's voice asked. John jumped. He could have sworn someone was in the vehicle with him. He looked in the back seats and over to the driver's seat, or was it now the passenger's seat? But there was no one.

"Sir?" the voice asked again. John realized it was the car talking to him. He fell back in his seat and laughed. He laughed until his belly hurt, and tears were rolling from the corners of his eyes.

"Should I call an ambulance, sir?" the voice asked.

"No. No, I'm good," John coughed.

"Then where can I take you?" the car asked.

"New York City?" John asked.

"Anywhere in particular?" the car asked.

"Let's just get there first, then we will talk about specifics," John said.

"Okay, we will be there in forty-five minutes," the car said. "Would you like to listen to some music while I take you there?"

"Let's just keep it quiet," he said.

"Okay, let me know if you change your mind."

The car sped forward into the night. John had never imagined riding in a vehicle that could drive itself. It felt unnatural. His nails dug into the armrests. The highway whizzed by. It was a good ten minutes before John actually felt comfortable as the vehicle propelled them toward the city. Even then, he couldn't let himself fall asleep. As soon as his eyes started to close, he would snap awake sure the car had taken them off the road and into a ravine somewhere. But that didn't happen. The ride was smooth and went by quickly.

Chapter Forty

Melanie

SHE SAT at the kitchen table for hours, unsure what came next. There were signs of life all around her, from the coffee pot to the television that hung over the counter.

When she finally broke from her daze, Melanie decided she couldn't sit in the kitchen any longer. So, she climbed the stairs and peered into her parent's room. The hair dryer was still on her mom's dresser, where she had left it the night before. Papers for the upcoming court case were spread along the dresser. A white blouse, freshly ironed, hung in the corner. Delana would have worn that today. From across the room, Melanie could smell her mother's shampoo, coconutty. She had always loved that smell.

In their bathroom, Melanie gazed at her reflection in the mirror. She looked wild, her hair every which way. Her face was caked with blood. Her nose was still bent to the side from when she was punched. She grasped it like her dad did earlier and pushed. It snapped back into place, bouts of blood spewed from her nostrils. She rinsed her face in the sink, but still felt grimy. It was like the blood and dirt had seeped through her clothes and burrowed under her skin.

Melanie turned on the shower and let the water run so that the room got steamy. She went to her room and got new clothes and a backpack. She laid the backpack on the bed and started packing whatever she could find, clothes, a charger, a snow globe her mother got her from a trip to the zoo. There was more she wanted to pack, but she couldn't think straight.

She went back to her parents' bathroom with her clothes in hand. A thought ran through her head, and she trudged downstairs and grabbed the rifle she had used earlier. She brought it upstairs to the bathroom with her and leaned it against the wall within arm's reach if she needed it.

Finally, she undressed and got in the shower. The water cascaded over her shoulders. Like a video on fast forward, she relived the events of the past six hours. She shook uncontrollably with a mixture of anger and sadness. The shower could wash away the blood and tears, but the memory of what happened would never fade.

When she finally pulled the curtain open to dry off, the room was a haze of steam. The hot water helped. She could think a little more clearly and was no longer covered in blood and dirt. She got dressed in much the same attire as before. The only difference was her jacket, as the other was covered with blood. She grabbed another denim jacket, a little older, but still good. She slid into her lucky Converse and threw her hat on over her wet hair.

She went back to her room and looked through all she had packed. It was a good start. She went downstairs to the kitchen and took some bottled water from the fridge to take with her. In the cupboard, she pulled out a box of Strawberry Pop-Tarts and stowed them in her bag. She had always liked the fruit flavors more than the dessert ones. She looked over the counter at the coffee pot. She had never tried it before, but until this morning, she had never fired a gun either.

She filled the pot half full of water and poured it into the back of the coffee maker. Mornings before school, she would sit at the table and watch her mother make the morning brew. She knew where to put the water and the filter and the grounds. But, she had no idea how many scoops to use. She could have looked on the coffee container; instead, she just guessed and put four heaping scoops into the filter. Then she pressed the on button and waited.

The smell of the percolating coffee was like a remnant of the past. Welcome and refreshing, the aroma was a reminder of how alone Melanie was.

It took about ten minutes before the half pot was done brewing. She waited patiently. She had always wondered why adults liked it so much, so now that she was making her own, she was eager to try it.

When the pot gurgled to a finish, Melanie grabbed a mug and poured a cup. She had always watched her mom stir milk into her own drink, so she did likewise. She took a sip and immediately cringed at the bitterness.

"Yummy," she muttered and poured the rest of the cup down the drain.

She ran back upstairs to her parent's room. In the top drawer of her Mom's dresser was a box. Melanie pulled it out and opened it. Inside was all the Christmas money her parents set aside each week. She counted out over six hundred dollars. The cash was held together with a money clip. Melanie stuffed the wad in the inside pocket of her jacket.

Then, she went to her father's dresser and opened the top drawer. Under piles of socks, Melanie saw the box she was looking for. She pulled it from the drawer and laid it on the bed. On the side was the digital lock. She typed the number 7-4-8-9 and waited. There was a moment of silence followed by a ding that acknowledged the correct code. That had been her father's code for everything; she never knew why, and now she would never be able to ask.

She opened the box and found her Dad's Smith and Wesson revolver. The silver barrel glistened in her hand. Two boxes of shells were stowed in the box as well. Her father had shown her this gun a couple of times, in case she ever had to use it in an emergency. She breathed deeply to steady her nerves before she opened the cylinder and carefully slid a bullet into each chamber. Her fingers trembled as she loaded the bullets. She left the remaining bullets in their boxes and put them in the front pocket of her bag.

In the closet, she found the holster her Dad kept as a keepsake from his father. It wasn't Velcro like the one he wore with his police uniform. This one was supple leather emblazoned with a rose on the holster that was woven in intricate lines along the belt. Melanie slid the holster around her hips, but her waist was too small, so she ended up wrapping it around twice before it was tight enough that it wouldn't slide off. She slid the pistol into the holster. It looked massive, saddled next to her thin legs. It was nearly the length of her thigh.

She felt awkward walking with the extra weight. She adjusted the holster and pulled it a little tighter. The revolver sat higher on her leg and wasn't as awkward. She paced back and forth, trying to get a feel for how it moved with her body. It would take time before she was completely comfortable with it.

I'll just have to get used to it.

She walked across the room to the mirror, hanging on the back of her parent's door. In the mirror, she saw her reflection and marveled at the girl looking back at her. The gun on her hip looked like it belonged there like it should have always been there. She was awestruck by just how much she looked like an old-time gunslinger. She just needed some boots and an actual cowboy hat.

As she gazed at the gun in her reflection, she decided that revolver was the only gun she would take with her. The AK-47 was big and awkward to shoot. The Smith and Wesson she now had strapped to her side was her father's, and that alone was reason enough to choose the pistol over the rifle.

She looked over her room one last time. She saw her phone lying on the bed and picked it up. She wanted to post the video on Ego. By now, the app was probably abuzz with videos of the riots. She pressed the button on the side of her phone to turn it on, but nothing happened. She tried again with the same result. The battery was dead. She plugged it into the wall and waited to see the charging symbol, but again nothing happened. She flipped it over in her hands and inspected it. A deep crack ran down the middle of the screen.

"Oh," she sighed. There was a knot in her stomach. She felt hollow.

This entire night had been for nothing. She had no video for all her efforts. Fresh tears formed in the corner of her eyes, but before they could escape, her sorrow turned to anger. Melanie glared at the phone in her hands. Then threw it across the room. It shattered against the wall, but she didn't feel any better.

She screamed and slammed her fist into the wall. There was no pain, only a desire to kill. Left then right, she punched and punched. The drywall gave way under the force of her knuckles. It felt good. Over and over, she pummeled the wall until her knuckles were bloody and crusted with the white debris.

She collapsed on the bed. The adrenaline running through her veins left her muscles tense and shaking. She felt a little better. Melanie rubbed her hands over her face and sighed. She felt the urge to do something. The word duty swam through her head again.

On her desk was a notebook. It was mostly blank because school was online for the most part. Melanie started jotting down what she knew.

Black armbands.

Black eyes.

Violent.

No pain.

Not in control of themselves.

The last words stuck in her head. She needed to know who was controlling them and who started this.

Once she found them, she would kill them.

Chapter Forty-One

John

"SIR," the woman's voice sounded through the speakers.

The world outside the window was a blur. John looked back to the dashboard, he was dizzy.

"What's up?" he asked.

"I set our destination for Central Park," the car answered.

"Okay," John said and waited for the rest of the information.

"There is an unexpected delay, sir. I cannot find any construction or events that would cause such a delay. But it appears that every entry into the city is blocked," the voice said.

"I know," John said.

"Are you sure you still want to go to the city?" the car asked.

John sighed. He pulled the pack of Marlboro's from his pocket, stuck one in his mouth, and lit it. Looking back out the passenger window, he could only see to the edge of the highway before the dark consumed the scenery. How easy it would be to disappear into that darkness.

"Keep going. Let me know when they are right in front of us," he replied.

"When who is in front of us?"

"Anyone."

The car continued through the night. John waited for the moment when it would stop. His mind thought of the group he had just escaped. *Would the others be like that? Worse? What if there were more?* His eyes drifted back across the dash to the bag next to him.

How many grenades did he have? *Not enough. It would never be enough.*

For ten minutes, the car drove steadily into the night with no disturbance. John had finished his cigarette, and his chin was bobbing off his chest as he fought to stay awake.

"Sir?" the car asked. John didn't move.

"Sir?" it asked again. John stirred slightly.

"Sir!?" His eyes opened halfway. Then he blinked. A cough rolled up his throat, raspy, and dry. The wake-up kiss from years of smoking. He was up now.

"Yea?"

"There is a disturbance in the road ahead. One mile from here," the woman's voice said.

"What do you think we should do?"

"I cannot make that decision," she answered.

"Then what are we looking at?" he asked.

"There is a large group of people standing in the road. Blocking both north and south bound lanes," she said.

"How do you know that?" John asked.

"Satellite images show the road ahead," she said.

"So, if I asked, you could tell me what is happening right now in Central Park?" John asked.

"There is a few seconds delay, but for the most part, yes," the woman's voice replied.

"Are there vehicles blocking the road?" John asked.

"Yes, partially. The road is mostly blocked off, but there does seem to be a few places where a vehicle could fit through."

"Okay. Find the spot that we can fit through the best and go through there. Do not stop for anyone," John said.

"If a human is in my path, I must stop. I cannot hit a person."

"They aren't people," John said.

"They are," she replied.

"I have seen them up close. They aren't human anymore," John argued.

"But they were once."

"Once, but they aren't now."

"Then what is human?"

John didn't know what to say.

The tires screeched. His stomach continued forward with the momentum. A wave of nausea passed over him quickly and then was gone.

He grabbed his bag, threw open the door and slung the shotgun over his shoulder as he stepped out of the car. In his left hand, he pulled a grenade from the box and held it at the ready.

The lights from the Chrysler shined over a large crowd. Some turned toward John. Others shied away from the light. His heart was racing. There were so many people. If he was quick, he could throw this grenade and get another one into the crowd before they turned on him. How many could one grenade kill?

At the back of the crowd, nearest to John, someone turned in the car's lights and raised their hand. John froze. He was just about to pull the pin on the grenade when the person's hand went up in the air. Was he waving?

"Help!" a man's voice carried through the still night air. John didn't move. He still held the grenade in his hand. He was ready to throw it. But what if?

"Help! We need help!" the voice cried again. John saw the man walking in his direction. He was still a ways off, but John could see his silhouette growing larger in the blue glow of the headlights.

They cried for help. Images from Ted's flashed through his mind. The bodies strewn across the bar. Blood covered the wooden floor, the walls, the counters. It seeped through the cracks between the wooden beams and dripped to the ground below. One man had done that. What could the group before him do?

The grenade was heavy in his hand. How easy it would be. Just a flick of his finger. But what if?

The man was less than a hundred feet away now. John thrust the grenade back in his bag and instead pulled the revolver loose from the small of his back.

"Don't move," he called to the man. The silhouette froze. Its hands went up on either side of its head.

"I'm not armed," a voice replied.

John waited to see if anyone else from the group moved forward. After a few seconds, when it appeared no one else would come near, John slowly walked toward the silhouette. He kept his eyes on the man; past him, John could make out the shadows of the others. It was too dark even with the light from the car to see which direction they faced. They could be watching him. There could be a hundred guns pointed at him right now, and he wouldn't even know it. He continued toward the man.

"Honest, I don't have any guns," the man said as John got closer.

"Don't talk," John said.

He was close enough now he could make out most of the man's features. He was a short man, with a bit of a belly, thin arms and legs, and balding. It was too dark to see much else. John was only a few steps away from the man now. He raised the revolver. The end of the barrel focused between the man's eyes. The man flinched as John raised the gun. Carefully, John pulled the hammer back. The metallic click was loud in the silent night.

"Do they have weapons?" John asked.

"Some do," he said.

"How many?"

"Maybe half."

"Do you?"

"Do I what?"

"Have a weapon?" John asked.

"I told you I didn't," the man replied.

"I'm asking you, do you have a weapon?"

"There's a snub-nose, in my boot," the man said with a sigh.

"Is that it?"

"Yea, that's it."

"No lies?"

"No lies."

"Give it to me. Slow now," John said.

He watched the man closely as he leaned over and reached inside his boot to pull out the revolver. He waited for the slightest provocation, but the man was slow and smooth. He extended his hand with the revolver. John took it and slid it in his back pants pocket. He slowly released the hammer on his pistol, so it was no longer engaged. He kept it in his hand all the same.

"Why are you here?" he asked.

"We got stuck," the man answered.

"You were all together?" he asked.

"No, we are from all over, but there's a barricade further on up ahead. You can't get through."

"Why'd they send you out?" John asked.

"No one sent me. I saw your lights. I thought you could help."

"How many of you are there?"

"We are one," he laughed.

John saw his teeth, reflecting the light of his car. A smile curled at the corner of the man's lips. A shadow passed in front of the lights behind him and covered the man's face for a split second. John aimed the pistol, but it was too late. The man lunged. A bony shoulder rammed John hard beneath the ribs, and they fell. He heard footsteps behind him.

He rolled to his right and scrambled to his feet. Hands grabbed at his back and legs. He tried to run, but there were too many hands slowing him down. *How had they gotten this close?*

The grenades. He reached in the bag. He felt the cool metal against his palm. Just then, something hard came down across the back of his neck. His legs gave out, and he landed face first on the pavement. John saw feet all around him as the world went to black.

Chapter Forty-Two

Melanie

FOR AN HOUR, Melanie had contemplated the realization that the wrist watchers were being controlled from afar. Maybe f_stop39 had been right from the beginning. That meant Bridgette was right too. Melanie had tried to call her on the landline phone, but the call hadn't gone through. She hoped her friend had found a way out of this madness. The madness where she was about to return.

She wanted to inspect one of the armbands. If she was lucky, maybe she could figure out how it worked.

Luckily, only a few feet away from her doorstep, there were three bodies sprawled on the pavement. She held the pistol firmly in her hand as she approached the nearest body. It was the one that had attacked her mother. She knew the man to be dead. She had watched his head collapse in on itself when she shot it. Nonetheless, as she drew closer to the body, her heart began to race. At any moment she expected the body to jump up and come hurtling toward her. She was now within arm's reach of the body. She hesitated and looked up and down the street for any sign of life. She didn't see anything.

She knelt down, next to the wrist watcher, and poked its shoulder with the revolver. It didn't move. The body felt stiff against the gun. He was dead.

The armband looked like a solid black bar on the wrapped around the forearm. Melanie moved the arm to get a better look. On the inside of the man's arm, the device clasped together with a metal latch like you would find on a watch. She felt the band; it was smooth and cold. The shiny black surface looked so unremarkable, so common. Nothing about it screamed danger. As far as she could tell, it was just a black band. Maybe it wasn't the bands that controlled them. Maybe it was something else. Maybe the bands were just like a symbol to help recognize each other, like a club.

What a club! She pictured the signs for weekly meetings: *Are you feeling lonely? Do you want to kill? Give us a call!!*

She rolled the arm over in her hands, inspecting every inch of the apparatus, but she found nothing. Then an idea struck her.

She looked at the inner clasp that held the band together. If she lifted that latch, the band should fall off, and she could look at it more thoroughly. The latch was closed fast, but if she used her fingernail, she might be able to pop it open. Sure enough, with her fingernail bending, almost to the point of breaking she was able to snap open the latch. When she did, the armband didn't fall off like she expected. Instead, it stayed clung to the man's arm. The inside of the band was completely open; she could see the man's discolored flesh where the band had been clasped for so long that the skin had turned a pale, sickly white from lack of sun. The part that rested on the outside of the forearm still clung fast. *That's odd. It should have just fallen off.* She pulled on the device, and it slowly separated from the man's skin. As she pulled up, Melanie watched two copper prongs lodged deep in the arm reluctantly give way and slide out from under the skin.

With the device fully removed, Melanie inspected the copper pins, which looked like a snake's fangs protruding from the inside of the band. *This was what controlled them.* She wasn't sure how but she knew, as there was nothing else about the band that signaled control like these two small prongs dripping blood. Melanie looked at the two red pinpricks in the man's arm and wondered what would happen if she had been able to pull the armband off while he was alive. Would he wake up from a trance and not know where he was, like in a movie? Would he continue to attack? She desperately wanted to find out.

She crossed her legs and sat down, thinking how best to do this. It's not like she could just wave to a wrist watcher and have them come over and wait patiently while she pulled the armband off. She tried to picture that. She imagined the wrist watcher like a zombie trying to scramble free as she tried to help it. Then she looked down at the armband in her hands. If she just slid it on, she would look like one of them. Disguised as one of the gang, she could probably get close enough to a live one to remove their band. It would be dangerous. By putting the band on, she would not only look like a wrist watcher but to anyone like her, who recognized the armband as a sign, she would *be* a wrist watcher and, thus, a target. She contemplated her choices for some time. If she wanted to know what would happen, she would have to at least pretend to be a wrist watcher. She took the metal prongs and bent them backward until they snapped, then slid the armband on and closed the latch so that it was tight to her arm and wouldn't slide. *There, now I am a wrist watcher.*

Where should I go? I could head back toward Central Park West, then maybe South, and try to catch up to the crowd. That is if there is still a crowd. From what she saw of her father's reactions to the insanity, the police had been caught completely off guard. She couldn't be sure that even now, hours after it started, the police would have a handle on the situation. It had been such a rapid and well-organized assault that Melanie feared just how effective it may have been.

She would need to find out for herself how bad things were. She stood up, her body one constant ache from head to toe. She stretched her arms above her and arched her back, which caused a series of pops to run down her spine, releasing a good deal of pressure. She sighed at the relief, although there was much that still hurt. Pain just meant she was still alive.

Melanie headed toward Columbus Ave.

What would make someone want to kill all these people?

When she read about the wrist watchers on Ego, there was always a level of separation. She had been able to step away. But in the dim blue light before the sunrise, Melanie walked with the disturbed confirmation that only physical proof created. She was no longer the curious fourteen-year-old girl watching all of this from home, for now, she had seen the danger firsthand and knew its power. Melanie had touched the flame and felt its keen burn.

Evidence of the morning tumult lay strewn across the street. Debris and bodies littered the pavement, yet the only sound Melanie heard as she strode along the sidewalk was the rubber *slick slick* her Converse made with every step.

She wondered if there were families hidden in the houses she passed. It was easy for her to imagine, a mother huddled together under the kitchen table with her wide-eyed dirty faced children not yet in school, like a still shot from a Time magazine cover meant to tug at your heartstrings. There were no words that Melanie would have to console them, but she wished she could just let them know it would be alright. Then Melanie remembered the dangerous game she played. To all the world, she was a target. To that family huddled under the table, she was just another one of the killers.

The street continued on, and Melanie walked her soft squeaky march toward whatever doom awaited her. As she crossed Columbus Avenue, she stopped and looked left then right. The street was much the same as 88th. Ominous in silence. She continued on; Central Park West had been the primary route through which the entire crowd seemed to have squeezed. Chances were, she would find a straggler or two there if she were lucky. Melanie was still struggling to think exactly how she was going to approach a wrist watcher when her silent world came crashing down in the reverberations of a rifle blast.

The echoing bang tore through the still air. Melanie's ears burst as the pressure of the shot split the air like a bullwhip. The hair on her arms stood on end as gooseflesh prickled along her skin. She immediately recognized the danger she was in and quickly raised her pistol to chest height and held it with both hands ready to fire. Her eyes scanned her surroundings. There was no movement.

Another shot from a rifle cracked the silent street again. This time Melanie felt the whoosh of the bullet brush her pant leg. Behind her, she heard the bullet ricochet off a brick building with a whizzing screech. She flinched, and her eyes hunted for the slightest movement. *Where were they hiding?* Parked cars on the side of 88th blocked some of her view. She realized the shooter had to be behind a vehicle. There wasn't time to weigh her options. She ran toward the sidewalk. Then she heard another bang.

Melanie Parker dove behind the first vehicle she came to. She tried to compose herself by closing her eyes and counting to ten. The Smith and Wesson was clutched firmly between her sweaty palms; her head leaned against the cool steel barrel. The cold metal touching her skin gave her the comfort she needed. No human love could have been as reassuring as the protection the revolver offered in that moment. Whatever came next, she would be ready. With one final deep inhale Melanie, spun around the front of the vehicle. There, roughly a hundred feet ahead, Melanie saw a man lying on his stomach with a rifle wedged against the crook in his shoulder.

She knew he was too far away for her to get a clear shot. She would have to cover most of the distance between them to have any sort of a chance with the revolver. As soon as she jumped out from behind the vehicle, the man had spotted her, and in the split second, she took to decide whether to shoot or not he had turned to face her full on. She made a dash straight at him. Caught by surprise, the man twitched just enough to make his first shot sail wide over Melanie's right shoulder. She charged toward him, looking all the while for an opportunity to dive back between the parked cars. The man lined the sight on her once more and pulled the trigger. Just as Melanie dove in front of a parked truck, she heard the rifle echoed once more.

She waited there and caught her breath as she leaned back against the front bumper of a Ford. An idea crossed her mind, and she acted on it.

"Hey!" she called out.

There was no reply. She tried again this time a little louder.

"Hey!"

Silence still greeted her. She waited. Finally, ever so quietly, she heard a voice, a man's voice, reply.

"Hey!" was all he said.

But to Melanie, it was a relief just to hear another human voice. Her heart fluttered. A broad smile spread along her face. She reached her hand out from behind the truck and waved in the direction of the man down the street.

"Lay your guns down and step out from behind the truck slowly so I can see you!" the man yelled to her.

How big a fool does he think I am?

"No. I am going onto the sidewalk. If your gun is not set to your side, I will shoot to kill," she yelled back.

She was met with silence.

"Okay," she heard the man reply softly after a few seconds. Her heart wavered. She was relieved to be talking to someone, but she couldn't let her defenses down. She knew the consequences of trusting a complete stranger, yet as she stepped out from behind the truck, that was exactly what she had to do. Even with her revolver raised at chest height, there was much that could go wrong. She needed to trust that for the half-second it took her to step out and onto the sidewalk that the man would keep his word.

She moved quickly, ready at the slightest provocation to jump back behind the truck or to squeeze the trigger on the Smith and Wesson. Her heart beat furiously against her ribcage. The world materialized before her as soon as she was out from behind the truck. Melanie saw the street, clear and bright. Before her, some six or seven car-lengths away, she saw the man lying flat on the ground. The rifle was moved just to his side; obviously, he had listened and pushed it away. His face lay flat against the ground, and his hands were raised in submission. Melanie approached him cautiously. With each step, she waited for him to move, but he never did.

"Let me see your face," she said.

The man lifted his head from the ground, keeping his hands raised. He had soft brown eyes that looked pleadingly up at Melanie. Yet, there was something off about him. He was pale; his skin looked grey. Then, Melanie noticed the pool of blood beneath him.

"How bad does it hurt?" she asked.

"I don't know. I can't feel anything now," he replied.

There was a pause where neither spoke, just looked at one another.

"I thought you were one of them," he said, pointing to her armband.

"No. It's just for protection," she said as she took a step closer and knelt next to him.

Melanie put her hand on his shoulder. He was cold. He would die soon. The man smiled at her touch, just that little bit of humanity seemed to ease him.

"I'm Wallace," he said quietly while he extended his hand.

"Melanie Parker," she replied while she gently shook his hand.

There was silence between the two of them again. Wallace stared at her arm until Melanie started to feel awkward and casually slid it out of his sight.

"That's all it takes, huh? Just a little band," Wallace mused.

"I guess."

"He sees everything, Melanie. You know that, right?"

"Who sees everything?"

"You mean, you don't know?"

"No. What can you tell me?" she asked.

Wallace coughed, spittle with droplets of blood sprayed into his hand, covering his mouth.

"Oh, shit," he moaned. "That one hurt."

He coughed again, this time harder. His body shook savagely with each cough. Melanie's hand still rested on his shoulder. She wished she could offer him more comfort than just her hand, but she didn't know how. After a moment his coughing episode stopped, his breathing came in short rapid breaths until his heartbeat slowed back to normal.

"Melanie, he will find you if you wear that," he said, pointing to the armband. "Take it off while you can. Or he will find you and make you one of them."

Melanie looked down at Wallace. The pool of blood beneath him was enormous. She realized he was dying fast. There was still so much she wanted to ask him. What did he know that she didn't?

"Who is he?" she asked simply. Wallace closed his eyes and moaned as the thought rolled around in his head.

"He...is...death. Take...it...off," Wallace whispered through gritted teeth.

He forced each syllable just as he began another round of painful coughs.

"Ogh, damn it."

From the back of his throat, Melanie heard him spit up a bloody wad of phlegm. Then with his dying last breath, his eyes rolled back, and his head lolled forward onto the pavement. Melanie shook his shoulder, but he didn't move. She scooted back away from his body. He had to be somewhere in his thirties, she thought as she looked at his face. She wondered if there was a family waiting for him to return. Or maybe he was alone. *Alone.*

That was a word she was becoming very familiar with.

Alone. It was a dark word with strong connotations. There was a time when she had loved being alone, but now, she couldn't think of anything worse.

She didn't want to travel down that rabbit hole. Melanie stood up and removed her hat. She ran her hand through her hair, so it all fell back on her shoulders, then she slid the hat back on. She made a cross symbol across her chest like she had seen some people do in church when she went with her mother. With that as her prayer, she slipped back onto 88th Street.

Melanie looked back the way she came; the street was still empty. Ahead of her, less than a block away, was Central Park West. Once there, she would travel south until she met the hoard or found some sign of them. She still wasn't sure how exactly she would get one wrist watcher away from the group, but that was a bridge she would have to cross later.

Chapter Forty-Three

Maggie

HOW DO you oppose an action when you have no control? Maggie grappled with this dilemma. Her mind still searched for some way of escape. But in her heart, Maggie had given up her resistance a long time ago. She was conscious of what she did, but no matter how she tried, there was nothing she could do to stop herself. Her only hope was that she would die soon. That was all she wanted now.

From miles away, Harry Davis looked through her eyes.

Maggie clambered over the fence at the edge of the park and tumbled onto Central Park West. The crowd was gone. Remnants of their destruction remained, but Maggie was alone.

Then a little way off, she heard footsteps.

She dove behind a tree and waited. A young girl emerged through the dark and walked slowly past where Maggie hid. Maggie stepped out from behind the tree after the girl was past. She kept a distance between herself and the girl.

Chapter Forty-Four

Melanie

THE AIR WAS silent and heavy, as though even the buildings along Melanie's right were unaccustomed to the quiet. *How far could they have gone?*

There was a crunch of pavement as sneakers tread over loose gravel some distance behind her. Melanie's heart raced. The sound was faint, barely audible, but she was sure she heard something. She looked down at her arm, and the band strapped tightly there. What danger might it signal to others in the city? What if the person following her was like Wallace and thought she was actually a wrist watcher? Or what if the person behind her was the wrist watcher she was searching for? She would have to turn around.

Just a glance. That wouldn't hurt. Just a glance. She turned her head slightly to the left, but she couldn't see far enough behind. She turned a little further and still nothing. She gave up and turned back ahead. It was too dark to see anyway. Unless they were right on top of her, she wouldn't see them.

As soon as Melanie turned back around, Maggie lunged

forward. Her arms and legs sprang to life. She was six or seven strides into her sprint before the girl finally turned completely around. Her eyes grew wide, and she spun forward and took off. The effort was too little too late, though, as Maggie was already on top of her.

Melanie scrambled to break into a sprint. Her legs betrayed her, and she nearly fell. Still, she tried to push forward. Her feet skidded on the gravel, and she struggled to gain traction. Then there was a sudden jolt from behind her.

Iron arms gripped her torso and pulled her to the pavement in one fluid motion. Although thin, the arms wrapped around her squeezed tightly. Melanie swung wildly as she attempted to break free. Yet, the snakes around her midsection only grew tighter.

"Let go!" she screamed as she twisted her body hard to the left. The arms gave way just slightly. Melanie plunged through the small gap she had created. She felt the arms let loose. She was free! Then a sharp pain ripped through her scalp. Her hat was on the ground below her, and her hair was caught in the hands of her attacker.

What happened next felt like slow motion. Melanie saw her attacker's leg bend back and the hands pulling her hair tight loosened. For a moment, she was free again. Then she felt fingers dig into the back of her skull. Out of the dark, her attacker's leg emerged, bent at the perfect angle to deliver a deadly blow. Maggie's knee swung forward and smashed hard into Melanie's forehead. Instantly tears blurred her vision. At first, there wasn't even pain. Just pressure.

The fingers dug into her skull once more.

NO! Maggie wanted to scream. *Let her go!*

Her hands grabbed the young girl's head once more. She threw her knee into her face again, and she felt the girl go weak. If Maggie let go, she knew the girl would collapse. Was she even conscious?

"*What do you say? One more should do it, right?*" Harry's voice rang through her mind.

You bastard! No! No more!

Ah, you're right, Maggie, more it is!
Stop! No!

Her leg swung forward again. In her hands, the girl felt limp, weak, like she was already dead. It was only when Maggie threw her knee forward again that the girl moved. She spun to the right just in time to avoid another blow to the head. As she spun, she pulled away hard. Hair ripped from her scalp, and she was free. The tufts of hair were still held firmly in Maggie's hands. Melanie crumbled to the pavement.

Maggie lurched. Her hands found the girl's neck.

There was a loud *BANG*, and a searing pain shot through her stomach. Then, she felt a similar pain in her arm. She squeezed harder. Again, a blast echoed through the night, and with it, Maggie collapsed into the waiting arms of Melanie Parker.

"I'm sorry. Oh my God, I'm sorry," Melanie cried.

She tucked the revolver back into the holster at her side.

Maggie tried to breathe but couldn't, at least, not fully. She clung tightly to Melanie, who brushed her hair with her hand and tried to calm her.

"Let's lay down and see if it helps," she said.

Maggie nodded and let the young girl gently slide her down on the pavement. Her breaths were still short, but she felt better laying down.

"I'm gonna die," Maggie whispered.

"I'm sorry! I didn't mean to. I was aiming for your arm, but I didn't get the gun turned enough, and the first shot went into your belly," Melanie said.

"It's okay," she said.

"It's not," Melanie cried. Tears rolled down her cheeks. "I was trying to save you!"

"You did," Maggie said. Her voice was weak. "I feel . . . better . . . now."

For the first time she could remember, she didn't feel the constant pressure that came with the armband. The pressure had been like a paralysis that wouldn't let go.

Now, she actually felt herself moving. She lifted her arm. There was a hole in the metal casing. The first shot had passed through the side of her stomach and lodged in her forearm. It was the most beautiful thing she had ever seen. She squeezed her hand, weakly. Then the laughter came. Joy, beyond any she ever remembered, overwhelmed her. She was free! It hurt so much to laugh. She could barely breathe. Yet, it felt natural and was the only thing that came close to expressing how ecstatic she was.

"Calm down. Just breathe," Melanie tried to tell her, but it was no use.

Maggie continued to laugh. It was only after a coughing spell that she was able to calm down enough to speak. Melanie handed her a bottle of water from her bag. Maggie swished the water in her mouth before she guzzled the whole bottle. When she finished, her throat was still dry, but she felt somewhat better, enough to talk anyway.

"What's your name?" she asked.

"Melanie Parker. You?"

"Maggie Wu," she said. A few seconds passed in awkward silence.

"How long have you. . ." Melanie asked, pointing toward the armband.

"I don't know," Maggie said just before she erupted in another coughing fit.

"You feel different now, though?" Melanie asked when Maggie had regained composure.

"Yea. A lot," Maggie said. "The bands are a connection."

"To what?" Melanie asked.

Maggie thought about how to describe him. He was a monster, like something you would find in a horror story. He knew everything you thought or did. It was like he lived inside you. He would have seen what happened. He could be on his way right now. She had to get the girl to leave her.

"Melanie, he's coming for me. For us," she started.

"Who?" Melanie asked.

"He's a monster. He's the one who controls all of us," she pointed to the armband, which was now cracked and broken.

"Then we have to stop him," Melanie said.

Maggie looked down at her body. She was thinner than she

remembered. There was nothing to her. Even if she wanted to help Melanie, was there anything they could do?

"I don't know how," Maggie conceded.

She tried to think. He could be here any second. She had to get Melanie out of here.

"Go to the bushes and wait for my signal."

"Then what?" Melanie asked.

Maggie pointed at the pistol. Melanie nodded.

"Okay. What's the signal?" she asked.

Maggie made a pistol shape with her index finger and thumb. Then she squeezed her finger like she was pulling the trigger.

"Okay, got it!" Melanie said. She ran to the overgrown fence across the street. She leaned into the greenery and disappeared from view. It was still dark out but a streetlight nearby cast enough light that Melanie could see Maggie clearly. A dozen thoughts ran through her head. What if she missed her shot? What would he look like? Would she recognize him? It was a challenge to calm her thoughts. She closed her eyes and took a couple deep breaths. She felt the revolver against her hip. She was ready. Then she heard the sound of wings.

The wind around her swirled. Trash and leaves danced on the sudden breeze. The heavy beating of metallic wings set Maggie's heart racing. She remembered the last time they had met. He promised it wouldn't hurt when she died. She wondered if he would stick to his word. It didn't matter though. Whether it hurt or not, it would all be over soon. She only hoped that Melanie remained in the bushes. As long as she wasn't seen, she might be safe.

Light glistened on the metallic armor as he descended upon Maggie. He landed just a step away from her head. The heavy silver suit was almost silent as it touched the ground. His gracefulness was a contradiction to the power Maggie knew he wielded. Mingled, with her fear, was awe for the man standing next to her. He was like a god. His face was strong, his thick black beard shined in the streetlight, and his eyes gleamed the darkest shade of blue. His lips curled into a wicked smile.

"Hello, darling," his voice was smooth and deep, his eyes focused on Maggie's.

She didn't dare say anything. Instead, she would wait; he would speak again; she was sure. His eyes left hers, and he sighed while he looked around the abandoned street.

"What have you done with our new friend?" he asked.

"She left," Maggie said simply, her voice calm and even despite her fear and pain.

"Now, you don't think I really believe that, do you?" he said.

She didn't reply, but kept her eyes on his face and waited for any sign that he saw Melanie.

"Did you know you were my favorite?" he asked as he gazed out at the darkness around them.

"No," she said quietly.

"It's true."

He knelt down next to her. A cold steel hand gently brushed the hair away from her brow. He sighed. His dark blue eyes watched her intensely. They shone bright, almost watery.

"You must be what, twenty-five?"

"Twenty-six," she said.

"Ah, close," he laughed. "Sometimes I wonder what it would have been like to have a daughter. I imagine she would have looked something like you, Maggie."

Maggie was silent as she grappled with the thought. He was lying. He had to be. But Maggie also noticed as he looked down at her, his face was a mixture of emotions. His forehead was wrinkled, and his mouth was turned down at the corners in the slightest frown. There was sadness there and pain also. Something was buried deep behind that expression.

Then it was gone. As if woken from a dream, his countenance shifted. His eyes focused on her once more, and his lips curled up in a smile again.

"Tell her to come out," he said softly.

"She won't listen to me," Maggie replied.

His hand was fast and strong, his fingers wrapped around her throat and dug into the sides of her neck. The metal against her skin was cold and hard. *Kill me now. End it all.*

"We can make this happen fast or slow," he said.

He then let go of her neck. The sudden release of pressure was accompanied by searing pain in her abdomen. His hand was pressed firmly where the bullet had passed. A sharp white heat washed over her. Everything got bright, and she was sure she would faint. Then the pressure was gone.

"You decide Maggie. Where is she?" he asked again.

She tried to focus on his face, but there was an urge to check on Melanie to make sure she was still hidden. For a split second, her eyes drifted toward the fence that bordered Central Park. She blinked and brought them right back to the monster before her. His face was a broad sneer. He knew.

"Melanguhhffmp," was all she was able to yell before his hand quickly covered her mouth and smothered her voice.

"Thank you, darling. That was fine," he said. Maggie felt his fingers tense over her mouth. With his other hand, he held her nose fast. She fought to suck in air, and his grip tightened. She couldn't breathe. She hoped Melanie would run. She wouldn't stand a chance if she tried to fight him. Even with her pistol, he was too fast and too strong.

The world around her began to fade and was replaced with a soft glowing light. It pulsed gently in time with her heart. There was a thrum in her ears that beckoned her to sleep. It felt like she had closed her eyes, but the light remained. In fact, it seemed a little brighter. Instead of waking her, it seemed to put her to sleep. The light surrounded her. Nothing remained but the light.

Her eyes drifted back in her head. Harry watched her body struggle and then go limp. She was gone.

He rose and turned toward the overgrown bushes that grew through the fence surrounding Central Park.

Melanie waited in the bushes and watched. As the metallic figure stood, she felt a chill run up her spine. *Run!* Her mind screamed. Her body was tense. Every muscle was on edge. She wanted to run, but she remained frozen. Then he turned. She could see his eyes in the street light; they searched for her. He knew she was here.

Soft rays of light glistened along the smooth metal suit as he raised his arms. Melanie squinted her eyes to see more clearly what he did, but it was too dark. He stared into the bushes. Melanie could feel his eyes on her.

Bright orange fire sparked in his palms. The little flames breathed the night air and grew until, in each hand, Harry Davis held a glowing orb. He strode across the street. His large long strides covered the ground quickly. Melanie remained hidden, now mere feet away from him. She watched the red-orange flames lick and sputter, then gently roll over upon themselves. Consuming and conceiving. New life and old mingled as one.

Harry closed his eyes. With a squeeze of his fingers, the fires grew. He snapped his wrists, so his palms faced the bushes. The flames sparked and danced eagerly. He took one final deep breath, followed by a slow exhale before he released the inferno. The fire burst forth in a frenzy of chaos. It was intense and furious and devoured the bushes before him in seconds.

Melanie remained frozen in place far too long. As the bushes before her disintegrated, she finally broke her stupor and rolled to her left. The flames followed her. She felt their heat along her back. She raced through the thickets looking for an escape. The deeper she dug, the thicker and more difficult the bushes became to navigate.

A sharp pain in her palm stopped her dead. She glanced at her hand, which was now awash with dark blood. A large gash ran from her thumb to her little finger; blood was spewing from the open wound. The heat intensified behind her. Melanie looked down and saw a jagged piece of metal fencing hanging loose. The cause for the cut on her hand. One moment a curse, the next a blessing. The fence had been cut, leaving sharp loose ends, but also a hole just big enough for Melanie to climb through. She carefully stepped through into Central Park.

She took just a second to glance back and see the bushes engrossed in fire before she took off across the wet grass. Melanie kept her head down and barreled forward, unsure just how much time she had to get away; she zigzagged between trees and across the smooth cement of West Drive before ducking behind a tall oak near Bridle Path.

She used to walk the park with her mother when Delana was

home early from the law office she owned. Melanie could almost create an accurate map of the entire park in her mind. She knew just behind her was the reservoir. If she followed the edge of the water south, she would come to the 86th Street Transverse, which she could use to travel east or west back to where she came from or to the other side of the park.

Behind her, the blaze spread quickly from the shrubbery to the overhanging trees that bordered the park. While Melanie leaned against a tall oak tree and caught her breath, she watched the bright orange blaze cast its sinister glare over more of the park. Then, a shadow rose high above the trees. The metallic suit shimmered bright scarlet-orange in the darkness as light reflected from the fire below. His giant silver wings spread wide. Melanie watched in amazement.

Her hand fell to her side and brushed against the holster hanging against her thigh. Her fingers found the grip and pulled the revolver free. Melanie snapped open the cylinder and saw four bullets still inside. She knelt down and unzipped the front pocket of her bag where she had stashed the boxes of ammunition. She placed two more bullets into the empty slots and clicked the cylinder closed.

She had been frozen in fear when she saw him converge on Maggie. At first, she couldn't believe he was real. That had been the perfect opportunity, and she let it slip through her hands. It wouldn't happen again.

Melanie watched and waited. The beast flew higher until he was no more than a speck in the night sky then disappeared. Her heart sank; she failed again. Then from behind her, a deep voice whispered in her ear.

"Hello, child."

Chapter Forty-Five

John

JOHN WOKE SOMETIME LATER. His head was pounding. A dull ringing sounded in his ears. His leg was throbbing. He looked down to see blood caked to his jeans with a spot in the middle of the dark red stain that was still damp. If he could just fall back asleep and wake up in his bed at home, he would be alright, he thought.

"Hey. Hey, you alive, man?" a voice near him asked.

"Am I?" John asked.

"I'm Jackson. Guess we're sharing a cell," the voice said.

"That so?"

"Where'd they pick you at?"

"I don't know," John said.

"Hey, since you're up, you can help me try to get outta here," Jackson said.

"I don't know where here is," John said.

"Open your eyes," Jackson said.

Above him, a bright fluorescent light blinked on and off. It hurt his eyes and made his headache even worse.

Three of the four walls were brick, with the other being the steel barred door of a jail cell. As he sat up, John realized he was on the bottom mattress of a bunk bed.

"Where are we?" he asked as he rubbed his eyes.

Jackson leaned against the wall on the other side of the cell, only a few feet away.

"That's the question, ain't it?" his cellmate answered. "I was trying to get out of the city when they got me."

"Who?" John asked.

"Them fuckers with the armbands," Jackson said, tapping his left arm. "Where were you?"

"I was coming into the city," John said.

"Why would you do that?" Jackson asked.

"I don't know now. I thought I would help."

"Well, lotta good that did ya."

"Yea," John sighed. "How long you been here?"

"Couple hours before you, best I can figure," Jackson answered. "Listen, I been watchin' 'em bring people in. It looks like everyone they bring in here is like you and me. No armbands. Ya, dig?"

"So?" John said.

"I think they are catching anyone they don't kill. Anyone without an armband. I don't know why though. They killed enough of us already."

"You've seen them up close?" John said.

Jackson rubbed his forehead with his large hand.

"Yea," he started. "Yea, I saw 'em up close. Fucking scariest moment of my life."

He shook his head and buried his face in his hands.

"She had her hands round my neck, ya know. Felt her thumbs digging into my Adam's apple. Thought she was gonna break my neck right there. I just kept feeling this pressure gettin' worse and worse. Then, I saw her eyes, man. They were black. Like they were fucking dead. Then, I blacked out and woke up here. Thought I was dead, man. I don't know how I got here. Hell, I don't even know where the hell we are. No one talks. I tried yellin', ya know? See if anyone would answer, but no one does. It's quiet. Like I was the only one here except I seen 'em bringing more people in. Then you showed up. They carried you in. One of them held a gun on me while the others carried you in and dropped you on the floor. I put you in the bed after they left," he smiled a little and shrugged his shoulders.

"Thanks," John said. He looked around the room for his bag, knowing that it was useless. It was gone. His guns. The grenades. All gone.

"Shit," he mumbled.

"Yea, fucking blows. I been trying to think of a way out of here, but they got us locked down hard."

"I want my shit back," John said. For a second, Jackson stared at John, his head cocked sideways slightly. Then he started laughing. Deep belly laughs.

"Don't we all, man," Jackson said with a sigh. "Shit, yesterday you know what I was doing?" John shook his head with a smile and waited for Jackson to continue.

"Man, I had this girl, right? Like she's the girl I want to make the move on, ya know? It's just been hard, we been seeing each other, but the timing's been off and shit. Anyway, she's over to my place, and I'm ready to make my move, ya know? Like it's been months. We been hanging out when we can, we go to movies, we go on walks ya know all the mushy stuff ya do to get a girl. Shit man, you know this stuff. How old are you?"

John smiled, "Old enough to know where your story's going," he said.

Jackson laughed.

"Yea, well, I doubt that old man. See, I have her over to my place. I pull out all the stops, bottle of wine, I make us a seafood pasta, cause she likes that. I hate it. But she likes it. So, I make this pasta with clams and shrimp and a creamy sauce. It's going perfect. Finally, I ask her. After dinner. After the wine. We are there in my apartment, and I say to her, 'Nikki, I want to be your man. I want to make this official.' And she just smiles. Man, she just smiles at me. Raises her eyebrows a bit, then she says, 'Prove you can be my man.' Next thing I know, no joke, we are on the floor naked. When I wake up, we are still on the floor; she's there next to me. I don't remember getting a blanket, but there we are with a blanket over us. And I hear sirens going off on the street below. Happens all the time you get used to it. But man, I start hearing gunshots. So, I jump up and throw on my jeans and a shirt, and I'm like 'Yo Nikki, you gotta get up something's going on,' and she fucking looks at me and she has those dead eyes that I was telling you about. She just looks at me like she don't even know me. Man, I thought she was gonna kill me right then. Her eyes were just stuck on me. That's when she reached out and grabbed my throat," Jackson stopped and took a deep breath. "I didn't even notice till right then she had one of those armbands on. Next thing I know I wake up here. Man, I don't understand what's going on."

Jackson's head fell against his knees, and he cried. He was young. His whole world just turned upside down in the blink of an eye. There was nothing John could say that would make the situation better. Then the memory of Abby slowly dying in his arms passed through his mind. He knew Jackson's pain. Part of him wanted to pat the kid on the shoulder and tell him it would be alright. But could he offer those empty words while knowing in his heart that nothing would ever be alright again? Something had changed. The fabric of society, the threads that held the world together, were frayed and thin, stretched to the point of no return. There was nothing they could do.

He should have pulled the pin. He should have thrown the grenade and not thought twice. At that moment, however, something inside told him to wait. Maybe it was human nature.

What is human? The computer in the car asked.

He didn't know then, but if she asked him now, he would say, it was that moment of hesitation. It wasn't hate or curiosity that caused him to hesitate, no, it was love. It was love beyond any he had recognized before. With his wife and daughter, John had known love in that deep familial sense. That love was unending. Even now, when he thought of their faces, it was that love that welled up in him and broke his heart. But when the man raised his hand and cried for help, John had put the grenade away. There was still caution; that's why he held the .357. But now he realized it was human nature that told him to tuck the grenade away. It was the reason he had traveled to New York City in the first place. Human nature had called him to help someone in need. He couldn't just ignore it. John understood human nature, that need to do the right thing for someone else, would be the death of him.

Jackson dried his eyes on his shirt sleeve. He pulled himself together. *Good. I'm going to need him if we have any hope of getting out of here.*

"What about you? You seen them up close?" the young man asked.

"Yea. Couple times," John said.

"That's it?"

"That's it."

"Come on, man, I told you my story," Jackson said.

"What do you want, kid? I'm sorry about what happened to you. I am. But don't ask me to tell my story. I lived through it once, I don't want to talk about it," John snapped.

"I'm sorry," Jackson said. "It's just; I've felt so alone since all this started happening. You're the first real person I've talked to about any of this. I just want to know I'm not the only one that's seeing all this."

"You're not alone," John said. "We've all got a story. Now just isn't the time for mine."

A trumpet sounded off in the distance. The sound ricocheted off the walls and echoed along the corridor. It was loud and shrill and out of key. John looked over at Jackson, who shrugged his shoulders. They waited for more. From far off, they heard a voice through a megaphone.

"Rise and shine, fuckers!"

"Here we go," John muttered.

"In just a moment, the doors to your cells will open. Do not stampede through them like the filthy animals you are. I repeat, do not run from your rooms. You will be shot immediately."

Just like the voice said, there was a metallic click, and the cell door slid partway open. John stayed seated on the bed. Jackson rose to his feet but remained close to the wall. From only a little ways away, the sound of a machine gun cut through the air. *RAT-TAT-TAT.* Instantly Jackson turned to John his eyes wide with fear.

"They are going to kill us," he muttered. "We gotta run."

"Don't you fucking move," John said through gritted teeth.

"Come on!" Jackson pleaded.

He started toward the cell door. John jumped to his feet and ran toward him. He grabbed his arm just as Jackson stood on the precipice of the hallway beyond the cell door.

"Don't move," he repeated.

"You are gonna get us killed, old man," Jackson said. He pulled his arm from John's grasp and strode into the hall. He looked left, then right, then bolted. There was no one to the right. Jackson was only a handful of steps from the cell when John heard more gunfire. *RAT-TAT-TAT.* The young man fell in a heap face first on the cement floor. John watched the blood pool along his back. Three clear bullet holes stood out clearly amid the blood. John closed his eyes and stepped away from the cell door. Jackson was dead, and he would be too if he wasn't careful. *Just do exactly what they ask, maybe you can get out of this alive.*

For what seemed like an eternity, John listened as gunfire echoed through the halls. He knew the urge Jackson and others like him felt. It had surged in him when the door opened. For a split second, he had thought about running. But he had fought the urge. It was difficult, but he had pushed it out of his mind and waited. The sound of gunshots and screaming told him how difficult it was for others to push that feeling aside.

Seconds ticked by. The gunshots became fewer. The muffled sound of dying men moaning in agony replaced the echo of the machine guns. There was no help for them now. They had lost the fight against temptation.

"Apparently, a lot of you have trouble listening," the voice sounded once more. "I thought I was very clear. Well, those of you still in your cells come forward. You will not be shot."

John rose from the bunk and stepped toward the door. His heart beat against the wall of his chest. He kept his breathing smooth and calm, but really, he was terrified. He stepped slowly out of the cell. To his right and left, he saw other men doing the same. In the cell to his left, an old man looked at John nervously. John nodded his head once. The old man stepped into the hall like everyone else.

"Now, I want you to slowly make your way to the dining area.

Those of you on the floors above take the stairs down to ground level. I will be waiting here. When you get to the dining area form two lines. Lastly, I shouldn't have to say this, but don't try to escape. You saw what happened to your friends," the voice said.

John turned to the left and followed the men in front of him as they walked slowly toward the stairs. To his right, John passed innumerable bodies. The floor was covered with their blood. He thought of trying to talk to one of the men in line near him. Maybe a couple of them together could overwhelm whoever held the guns. He looked over the shoulders of those before him and tried to catch a glimpse of a guard. He didn't see anyone. *Where the hell are they?* If he could get his hands on a gun, he might be able to get out of here.

It was hopeless though. *Just keep walking*, the voice in his head told him. *You saw Jackson. If you listen, maybe you will live. Otherwise, you know they will kill you.* So, he followed the other men down the stairs.

The line snaked slowly into a wide dining hall. Tables had been pushed to the side, so the men worked their way around them to stand in two lines at the center of the hall. John was somewhere in the middle of the line. There were maybe twenty people ahead of him, as far as he could tell. They waited. The squeak of sneakers against pavement finally faded into nothing; they were all there now.

"Good, hopefully, I don't have to use this anymore," the voice called from the front of the room. John couldn't see his face; there were too many bodies in the way. He saw a megaphone raised in the air, then heard it crack against the floor as it was thrown against the pavement. "You will walk two at a time through the double doors behind me. Afterward, you will be free. Simple as that. Don't raise a fuss, and we'll be cool. Okay? Any questions?"

It wouldn't be that simple, John knew. Something was behind those doors.

"Okay, good," the voice began again. "Let's go, first two."

The line inched forward. John heard the double doors open. A second later, they clicked shut. He held his breath and focused all his attention on listening for any sound behind the doors. He couldn't hear anything. After a few seconds, the voice called for the next two. The line moved forward a little more. John leaned forward, just slightly and whispered in the ear of the man in front of him.

"Hey."

The man looked over his shoulder.

"Hey," he replied.

"Can you see any guards?" John asked.

"No," the man said.

"Damnit."

"Wait, is that one?"

John followed the man's hand as he pointed to a pillar at the end of the dining hall. John squinted, just behind the pillar he saw the outline of a body, it looked like there was a gun in his hands. It wasn't clear. He assumed it was a guard. Now what? That was only one. How many more might there be?

"Next two," the voice called.

John's heart raced. He stepped forward with the line. If he could get his hands on that gun . . . what? What would one gun do against countless guards? He thought of Jackson, how it only took a second for them to find and shoot him. If nothing else, it would give him a fighting chance. It was also suicide, but if he did nothing, he would die anyway.

Just then, he heard something. Behind the door, he heard the muffled cries of someone screaming. The guard stepped away from the pillar and toward the double doors. Now was his chance.

"Follow me," he whispered to the man ahead of him.

"Fuck you, man," he said. "You're gonna get killed."

"So be it."

He ducked to the outside of the line and ran straight for the guard. The man was facing the double doors and couldn't see John as he ran toward him. There were maybe thirty yards between them. This was the only chance he had. If anything went wrong, he was dead. He sprinted past the men in line. His long strides carried him quickly toward the guard. He felt a sharp pain shoot through his leg, where he had been stabbed. Fresh blood poured from the wound. He tried to block it out, but with each step, it grew worse.

The guard stopped and turned toward John and raised the machine gun to his shoulder. *RAT-TAT-TAT.* The shots rang out loud, but they were off target and lodged into a wall somewhere behind him. John lowered his shoulder and crashed into the man.

They fell as one. Suddenly he heard more shots echo from around the hall. The guard still held the gun tightly, but he couldn't angle the barrel enough to get a clear shot. Bullets flew from every direction; they pinged off the cement floor and walls near them. There was no time to think. John threw a hard-left hook. His knuckles smashed into the man's temple. Despite the devastating punch, the guard seemed largely unfazed. Instead, his black eyes narrowed on John. Against his stomach, John felt the barrel of the gun twist. *RAT-TAT-TAT.* The barrel was hot against him, but the angle was still off, and the shots went harmlessly to the right. He grabbed the guard's head with both hands and smashed it against the ground as hard as he could. He screamed, primal and angry, as he bashed the head against the cement again and again. The man's head cracked. Blood oozed through John's hands, and chunks of white bone emerged between his fingers. John let go and fell away from the bloody mess. He reached over the dead body and pulled the gun to him as he crawled behind the pillar.

In the seconds it took John to kill the guard, the dining hall had erupted into a frenzy. Shots rang out from every direction. John leaned against the pillar and drew a deep breath. He had to get out of here. He looked toward the double doors. Finally, he could see the man who had called them all here. He was tall and thin, the armband on his pale forearm stood out. John aimed the gun at him and fired. *RAT-TAT.* Two shots, one through the chest, the other to the head. He fell instantly.

Now, how to get out of here? It was a long way to the double doors. He looked down at his bad leg. He pulled open the hole in his jeans and laid the still hot barely against his skin. The smell of burning flesh filled the air. The hot metal stung against the open wound. John fought the burn, and until he couldn't take another second. He glanced down and saw the barrel had worked almost as well as he hoped. It had cauterized some of the skin, but it wasn't perfect.

"Just get to the doors," he said. "We'll figure it out from there."

He used the pillar to shuffle to his feet. Behind him, the two lines descended into a rush for the door. Bodies fell left and right as guards from the other end of the hall and the floors above sprayed bullets in every direction.

"Here we go," John muttered.

He sprinted toward the doors and weaved into the middle of the pack as the other men charged the nearest exit. The double doors flew open. Immediately the men at the front of the pack fell as guards behind the doors opened fire. John raised the machine gun to his shoulder and dove against the wall beside the doors, out of the line of fire.

He could just barely see through the opening, but it was enough. He pulled the trigger. One guard fell, then another and another. He slid into the opening. He scanned the room to his left and shot. Instinct guided his hands. There had been nine guards in the small room beyond the double doors. None remained. John fell forward into the small room. Men piled in after him. Shots continued in the dining hall behind.

John wanted to run to the door at the end of the small room, but something pulled him back. He looked over the bodies of the guards and men from the dining hall, all dead in the little room. So close to freedom. Then John noticed a large box in the corner of the room. He looked in it. Around him, men cried out in pain, the sound of gunfire echoed endlessly, and still more men rushed past him toward the next exit, but amid all the chaos, the world seemed silent and frozen to John. In the box were armbands, hundreds of them. All black and metallic. His heart sank. He realized now how close he had been to death. Being shot would have been a welcome end compared to these armbands.

He ran to the door. It was propped open now; the men rushing through had broken the hinge at the top, which left it lodged open.

Behind the door was a long hallway with rooms on the left and right. He couldn't think straight; his mind was racing. Men ran past him, but he was in too much a daze to focus. A door on his right was open. He fell into the room and closed the door behind him. There was an old leather couch against the wall. He collapsed into it. The room was spinning. He glanced down at his leg. It was drenched in blood. The cauterized skin had torn open as he ran. Blood was spewing from the wound. He had lost too much blood. He wouldn't make it much longer. John leaned back into the couch and watched the ceiling spin above.

Chapter Forty-Six

Walter

THE BLOCKADE WAS SUCCESSFUL. Their piece of the puzzle was complete. Now they waited.

Bodies were strewn every which way. The congregation had killed more than one hundred people. By and large, it had been a perfect slaughter. Only a handful of church members had fallen in the process, and they were generally the weaker individuals.

Walter stood near the front of the group. Dried blood covered his face. His sweater was torn, revealing his hairless chest. But for a few cuts here and there he was mostly unhurt.

The same couldn't be said for Pastor Perry. His jaw had been broken in the melee. His mouth now hung open to the side. A deep cut near his throat continued to bleed. Eventually, he would die from blood loss. For now, he waited for the next orders.

They all waited.

Chapter Forty-Seven

Melanie

MELANIE SPUN TOWARD THE VOICE. As she did, she felt heavy metallic fingers dig into her shoulders. With one heavy downward thrust, she was thrown to the ground. She landed on her pistol and scrambled forward to free her hand. Melanie whirled around, ready to shoot only to realize he was no longer behind her. From her left came a heavy blow to her ribs. She heard the bones crack and immediately collapsed in agony. The pain was sharp and intense. She struggled to her knees; the pistol still grasped firmly in her hand. Another blow, this time from her right, paralyzed her. She felt her entire side go numb, and she fell face-first again. With her left hand, she tried to push herself off the ground, but the right side of her body refused to cooperate and dragged against the ground. Suddenly, he had Melanie's hair and lifted her by it. A new pain shot through her head. Her eyes were squeezed shut as a cold heavy hand gently petted her face.

"Look at me," he said.

She opened her eyes. The face staring back at her was wrought with pain. His eyebrows were furrowed, age lines ran along his forehead and under his eyes, his beard sprouted a few coarse grey hairs, and his dark blue eyes looked almost sad.

"You will never understand how much this hurts me," he said, setting her gently on the ground and kneeling beside her. He brushed a bundle of hairs back from her face. Melanie was dumbfounded.

"Tell me, how did you know about the armbands?" he asked.

Don't answer him, a voice in her head screamed. *Shoot him now!* The pistol was still in her hand; all it would take was a flick of the wrist. But something in his voice, maybe how smooth and gently he talked to her, made him sound almost human. His eyes gazed deep into hers. He waited patiently for her to speak.

"I saw someone outside my window," she said in one breath. She closed her eyes to gather her thoughts and tried to let the pain fade away before she said more. "He was a wrist watcher."

He nodded his head. "But the armbands, how did you find out about them?"

She met his eyes. The voice of the dying Wallace rang through her head. *He will find you if you wear that. . . He is death.*

"You made them," she said at last. "You are the one they worshipped in the alleyway."

"Yes."

"Why?"

"It was time," he said.

He slowly shook his head, and his gaze turned away from Melanie. She thought for a moment; he was crying. Then, his eyes turned once more to her only this time they no longer looked soft and calm but full of rage. His hand sprang forward and grasped her throat. Melanie heard a *WHOOSH* as flames erupted in his other hand. She tried to squirm free only to find herself totally trapped. He raised his hand with the fire, so it burned Melanie's eyes. A garbled scream weakly escaped her throat.

He had lulled her into complacency. She should have shot him as soon as she saw him. The pistol was heavy in her right hand, but she twisted the barrel toward him and squeezed the trigger.

BOOM!

The blast echoed through the night. His fingers around her neck loosened slightly, and the fire in his other hand went out. Melanie wiggled loose and fell to her feet. Then, without hesitation, she squeezed the trigger again. *BOOM!* He stumbled backward and raised an arm to shield his body. Melanie fired again. *BOOM!* A look of panic swept over his face.

The suit had absorbed most of the blow from the first two shots. Harry looked down quickly. There were two deep indentations on his torso. The third shot though, had missed his body and lodged itself in his arm. There was a hole where the bullet had pierced his armband; it oozed black. Fear and fury consumed him.

Melanie had the pistol raised and focused on his face. Harry tried to ignite the flames along his palm again. They sputtered and went out. He tried again, and this time the flames struggled slowly to life, fragile, but there nonetheless.

Melanie squeezed the trigger again. *BOOM.* The shot-blasted Harry in the shoulder. Except for another indentation, there was no major damage. She adjusted her aim a little higher. Before she could shoot again, Harry raised his palm, and a rush of fire exploded from his hand.

Melanie spun away from the blaze. She felt the heat to her left side and covered her face with her arm. Quickly, she raised the pistol again and fired once. *BOOM.* Immediately the fire stopped.

Harry stumbled to his knees. The shot broke his armor, just below his ribcage. The armor had failed to block this one. There was a hole where the bullet had entered his body. He drew a shallow breath. The girl had ruined everything.

Melanie staggered a step closer. Her entire body trembled. She was afraid.

"I hate you!" she screamed. Harry glared into her watery eyes. Her face was shining, where the tears streamed down her cheeks.

"You took everything from me!" She clicked the hammer back and took another step forward.

"No, darling," he said calmly. His words left his lips smooth and perfect despite the pain.

"You killed my family. My parents are dead because of what you did to those people," she pointed out toward the city.

"You took everything from me," she repeated.

"No, my dear. You are still breathing," with that, he rose in one fluid motion to tower above the young girl. Melanie squeezed the trigger, but she was a second too late. He took her wrist, and with one quick backward snap, the bones cracked. Melanie cried out in pain as the gun fell from her hand. He let go of her wrist, and it fell limp at her side. She couldn't move her hand. Suddenly, his metal fingers were around her throat again. She struggled to break free, but this time there was no loosening his grip. A thin gasp escaped as she tried to breathe. Her face felt hot, and water blurred her vision. Everything started to go dim. She struggled frantically to break free. She clawed at his arm, but he only squeezed harder. Melanie felt herself slipping away. The further she faded, the less she felt. Like a fog that obscured her vision, everything before her faded to a hazy grey before going white.

Chapter Forty-Eight

Harry

HARRY DAVIS WAS CROUCHED atop a great stone church on the corner of the 90th and 5th. The white stone where his palm rested was cool and damp. A pool of blood had formed below him. He was oblivious to everything except the pain coursing through his chest and arm. Between that and the deep-seated rage at this unforeseen failure, he couldn't think straight.

He should never have come to the city. He should have watched the events unfold from a distance. At least then, he could have ensured a constant connection with his army.

He glanced down at his arm. Blood and oil still dripped from the bullet hole. She hadn't killed him, but she may as well have. He assumed the damage that bullet had caused. He had yet to find out for certain, though. Running his hand over the wound, Harry winced, he felt the sting of the copper prongs deep in his arm. His connection with the others would most likely be lost. He needed to know for sure.

He stood and instantly felt nauseous. Vomit rose in the back of his mouth. He coughed to clear his throat. Then, he stepped off the edge of the building and fell for a moment before his wings caught him and lifted him. The wind cleared his head. He didn't feel dizzy anymore, just weak and tired.

There wasn't time to focus on himself, not now. He needed to find at least one person wearing an armband. Their reaction might not be indicative of the group as a whole, but it was nonetheless important to know how just one of his followers had been affected. If they were still under his control, not all had been lost, but if they weren't . . .

So, Harry went North. There were groups clustered throughout the city. Each one numbering anywhere from one hundred to over a thousand, not to mention those outside the city who had worked to block the roads coming in. It took a herculean effort to bring this city to its knees. That had been the plan from the beginning.

Back when Harry laid on the operating table in Mark Bishop's laboratory, the vision of this day materialized. For months prior to regaining the use of his body, he was forced to stay alive. Forced to breathe and eat, day in and day out. He longed for death and could not attain it. While in that state, all thought of helping society disappeared. Any positive thoughts of humanity died on that table. All he had worked for was taken from him. All he wanted was gone. Eradication was the only answer.

But something went wrong. Or maybe, it was wrong from the start. It didn't matter.

There, where 5th Avenue crossed the Duke Ellington Circle, a crowd was clustered. Harry swooped down and landed gently behind them. They were all turned toward a central figure who stood on some sort of pedestal. No one had heard him land. They were too focused on the man in the middle.

"We must stand together now more than ever!" he shouted. Harry saw the black band along the man's forearm.

Harry smiled. If he could just have incited violence without the armbands, how much easier that would have been. But it wouldn't have worked. They would have killed themselves in a blaze of glory, and the revolution would have died and left only a memory. At least with the armbands, they were mindless killers not swayed by danger or alternative ideas.

"We are free! We must help the people still alive. We must! It is our duty!"

A murmur spread through the crowd. Harry saw people nodding their heads.

No, this will never do.

He took to the air and converged on the pedestal. Now that he saw it, he was underwhelmed. It was just some bricks cobbled together a couple feet high. Harry saw the man's fear before he heard him scream. The man turned a ghostly white, and his eyes bulged huge and bright. Harry landed on the pedestal and grabbed the man by the throat. Quickly he wrapped his fingers around the man's skull and yanked upward. He felt the bones in his neck pop as the head was severed from his body; blood ran down his metallic hand. He pushed the body off the pedestal and turned to the crowd.

"I missed the first part of his speech. What was he saying?"

The crowd was silent. Mouths hung open in awe. Harry tossed the head into the crowd. It splattered blood down a woman's blouse and fell at her feet.

At that, the crowd erupted in chaos.

People ran in every direction, clambering over each other to get away. Any idea of helping others was instantly forgotten. It was every man, woman, and child for themselves. Weapons lay strewn across the ground. If just one person had thought clearly, they could have saved them all. But that was not to be.

Harry jumped high into the air. A rush of heat ran down his arm. The flames came to life in his palms. Anger boiled within. He unleashed the fire, and with a furious *WHOOSH,* the blaze spit forth and consumed all in its path.

Harry flew just above their heads. They were once his slaves. They had been necessary. Now he wanted nothing more than to kill every last one of them. In his wake were strewn bodies, blackened and disfigured. They ran helter-skelter, only to be picked off one by one.

This was just the beginning. He would have to kill every single person still alive in this city if he were to be successful. The task was unimaginable. It would be impossible. But then, everything Harry had done was nearly impossible. The fact that he was alive at all was a miracle. That and the suit and the armbands. He was a living embodiment of that which should not be.

To his left, he heard a fresh cry of fear. He turned quickly and saw the people streaming from the prison exit. He raised his palms, and a wall of fire cascaded upon the men and women before they had time to run back inside. They fell in a heap outside the door, their charred bodies a shadow of life.

Chapter Forty-Nine

John

JOHN LOST track of time as he watched the fan spinning above. It was only the eerie quiet outside the office that broke his stupor. John listened close and waited for someone to say something or for more gunshots to blast, but there was nothing. He lifted himself gently off the couch; everything hurt. His leg was so weak it could barely hold him. Using the rifle as a crutch, he was able to limp to the door and open it. Outside the hall was empty. He staggered to his right, the way the other men had gone.

At the end of the hall, he could see dim rays of morning sunlight shining across the tile from a doorway on the left. He felt a cool spring breeze coming through the door, and with it came an acrid odor. John covered his nose in the crook of his arm to block the smell.

He limped to the doorway and peered through. Just outside, John saw a mass of bodies. As he looked, the scene became clear. The men had been ambushed. But they hadn't been shot. Their bodies were black, charred.

Just then, he heard heavy clinking footsteps cross the pavement outside.

A shadow stepped into the doorway. John fell against the wall and raised the rifle.

"Put the gun down, John," a deep familiar voice said.

"Who are you?" he asked.

The shadow was dark against the sunlight. His face was hidden.

"You already know."

Chapter Fifty

Walter

AS THEY WAITED, something inside, Walter shifted. All of a sudden, he felt confused and heavy. His head felt like it would explode as a great pressure built up in his temples.

Walter reached his hand out to steady himself against the van. Next to him, a woman fell. He looked over and realized it was Betsy, an old friend from school.

Walter staggered toward her. The world was spinning, and he nearly fell himself.

"Are you okay?" he asked.

She looked up; there was sadness in her light blue eyes.

"Walter. Where are we?" she asked.

Walter looked over his shoulder and saw the church van and the smoke from the bridge, but this didn't look like home.

"I'm not sure," was all he could answer.

"Walter! Are you bleeding?" she said, pointing toward his blood-covered sweater.

"Huh?"

Betsy crawled over to him and inspected his shirt. When Walter looked down and saw the blood covering him, he wanted to vomit.

"Hey, take it easy."

A hand lightly touched his shoulder. Walter turned and saw Pastor Perry looking down at them. His jaw was crooked, making him slur as he spoke.

Then, something inside clicked. Walter remembered the worship service last night and Pastor Perry's odd demeanor. But he couldn't remember coming here. But somehow, Pastor Perry was the reason they were here now. He brought them here. Rage welled up inside Walter. He dove at his pastor's feet and brought the tall gaunt man to the ground.

"Walter! I'm your friend!" Pastor Perry pleaded.

Walter crawled on top of him and placed his knee on the man's chest so he wouldn't move.

"What did you do?" Walter yelled.

"What are you talking about?" Perry answered.

"You brought us here! Why? Why are we here?"

As he screamed, Walter noticed a light reflected on the black band on his arm. *Deus lux mea est.*

"You gave us these bands. What were they really?" Walter asked. Betsy had crawled up beside him.

"Walter, what are you doing?" she asked.

"Do you remember where we got these?" he asked, pointing to his arm.

Betsy's eyes went to the pavement; when she looked up, her eyes were wide.

"This thing!" she yelled, grabbing her arm. "We got these at church. We all did."

"What are these things?" he pointed to his arm and looked at Perry, who struggled to breathe below him.

"I don't know," Pastor coughed. Walter moved from his chest, so he could speak, but remained close to him.

"I don't know what they do, Walter. I don't remember getting mine," Pastor Perry said. He gazed past Walter and Betsy, his eyes focused on the sky.

"Did I hurt anyone?" he asked.

Walter glanced over to Betsy, who shrugged her shoulders.

"I don't know," Walter said.

Pastor Perry met Walter's eyes again. Tears now streamed down his face.

"I think I did," he said. "I think we all did. Walter, I think something terrible happened. I'm sorry."

"Me too."

Walter stood and offered his hand to help Pastor Perry up.

"What do we do now?" he asked.

"We need to help the others," Perry said. "We couldn't have been the only ones."

"You're right," Walter said.

He turned toward the devastation behind them. The blockade, the bodies, the billowing smoke from a long dead fire, this was their work. They had done this. They were responsible for so many deaths. Walter felt nauseous again. His knees went weak, and he collapsed once again, hard on the road.

He cupped his face in his hands and cried. Betsy was quick to react. She hurried to his side and wrapped her arms around him and held him close. She was warm. Walter buried his head in her shoulder. Some time passed before he was able to compose himself.

We need to help. But where do we begin?

Next to them was a police cruiser. Walter had an idea.

Chapter Fifty-One

John

JOHN RAISED the rifle to his shoulder and stared down the barrel. The shadow before him took a step forward. Its features remained hidden in the dark. John felt his index finger on the trigger.

His head was heavy, and it was hard to focus. He just wanted to close his eyes.

The figure took another step forward, this time into the shadow of the prison building. Upon doing so, his features became clearer, all but his face, which remained blinding white in the sun. John saw the metallic bodysuit. It was silver, with interlocking layers that worked like scales, one on top of the other. It wasn't perfect, though; it had been damaged. Rust colored blood was crusted over bullet holes.

"No closer," John said.

"John," the shadow said as it took another step.

John squeezed the trigger. *CRACK!* His ears rang from the echo of the blast. The shadow fell instantly. Using the gun as a crutch once more, John stepped away from the wall and toward the creature on the ground.

Harry spat blood. The shot had entered the base of his neck, just above the center of his collar bone, where there was a slight divot in the skin. Blood poured from the wound.

John watched the creature struggle to move. It would die soon. He wanted to see it's face.

He limped through the shadows until he was near enough to finally see the creature clearly. It was haggard. Its eyes were tired. The cheeks were sunken and shallow beneath a coarse beard. Despite his distorted features, John recognized him immediately. He was a shell of the friend he once knew.

"Harry, what have you done?" he asked. "How are you alive?"

"I could ask the same of you," Harry replied. His eyes were daggers staring up at John.

"You were dead. I saw you," John said.

"For all the world knows, I am dead," he answered. "You might as well be too. Look at you. Where have you been all these years?"

"Here and there," John said simply.

"I almost thought you died, it took so long to find you."

"I left everything behind. I found a place where no one bothered me, and I started to forget who I really was. It was nice for a change," John said. "Why did you need to look for me?"

"I was going to kill you; John. I killed Mark. You were the only other person that could trace the armbands back to me. You were too big a risk."

"I see."

"John, I was reminded everyday of who I was and what you did to me," Harry said. He glanced down at the suit, John followed his gaze.

"It keeps you alive?" he asked.

"It allows me to move."

"Why?" John asked.

"Because I can't just move on from what happened. I realized my purpose when they took my body."

"Is that so?"

"Yes. I realized soon after that night; it had never been about what we created. We were naïve."

Harry's breathing became weaker. John saw it took all his strength to speak.

"So, you gave up," John said. "We were going to change the world. It was all right there."

"It didn't matter, John," Harry started. "You and Mark went behind my back. We would have gotten rich but at the cost of how many lives? Didn't that bother you?"

"Harry, if I had known then. . ."

"You did know John. I told you," Harry coughed. "It doesn't matter now. Actually. I want to thank you. You opened my eyes."

There was a moment of silence between the men as Harry caught his breath.

"You and Mark helped me see the world how it really is," Harry said. "I thought I was creating the bracelet to help people. My mother. Really, I wasn't better than anyone else. I just wanted to keep her alive because I didn't want to live without her."

"And that's wrong?" John asked. He watched the sweat trickle down Harry's forehead. His skin was pale. He was dying fast.

"If I were the best example of humanity, and still my actions were dictated by self-interest, how much worse would someone lesser be?" Harry asked.

"You wouldn't have said this ten years ago. You had a purpose then. Whatever this is, whatever you have created here, there was no purpose behind it. There is nothing left of you," John said.

"John, you don't see the world like I do," Harry said. He struggled to catch his breath before going on. "It is beautiful. We aren't. We are ugly, vicious. We are the worst of God's creatures. I realized this. I was made to destroy humanity."

"Oh?" John laughed. "This! This was your grand fucking purpose? You piece of shit."

"I was driven by rage and an understanding you cannot grasp."

"No," John shook his head. "You are bitter and angry. That's all. You are not a servant of God."

"I never wanted this, John. . . It came to me. You created me. . . I'm just doing what had to be done," Harry groaned.

John shook his head and looked up at the light blue sky above.

"It's weird, ya know?"

Harry didn't say anything. John let his thoughts come together before he finally spoke.

"I had a dream the other night. I guess I have them a lot. But I had a dream about Elly. Only she was real. I could reach out and touch her. I held her in my arms. And for the first time in ten years, it felt like she was right there with me," John said.

Harry closed his eyes. He recalled their faces. They had faded with time, but they were there, like an old dusty photograph at the bottom of a drawer.

"John," Harry began, but the words caught in his throat. He couldn't speak.

"I thought of Abby and Helena every single day," John said.

"Jo. . ." Harry spat blood.

"I couldn't drown the memories anymore," he continued. His eyes slid closed.

"She was right there, and do you know what she said?"

There was only a moment's pause before he continued.

"She said, '*Don't die, daddy. Don't die.*'"

When he opened his eyes, tears were welling in the corners.

"John," Harry spat as blood filled his mouth.

John turned away from Harry. Behind him, he heard the garbled sound of someone choking.

He was lightheaded and just wanted to close his eyes.

There was a police cruiser parked nearby.

John shuffled to the car and collapsed inside the passenger seat. A computer monitor and radio system was next to him. He closed his eyes and sank into the seat. He could rest here. Just for a moment, he thought.

PSSSHHHH! "Hello? Hello? Is there anyone out there?"

John jumped awake. His eyes wide open focused on the radio next to him. He waited. No one said anything more. He couldn't even be sure he heard anything. He lifted the receiver and clicked the button on the side. What was he supposed to say?

"Hello?" he said.

There was no reply. He hadn't heard anything. He closed his eyes again.

PSSSHHHH! "Are there survivors? Are there any survivors?"

The voice was frantic. John opened his eyes again and lifted the receiver to his mouth.

"I'm a survivor," he said. "Who is this?"

PSSSHHHH! "Are you wearing an armband?"

"No."

PSSSHHHH! "Were you wearing an armband?"

"No. Who is this?"

John asked again. He was too light headed to keep talking. He just wanted to hang the receiver up, but something inside, some last remaining strength told him to hold on.

PSSSHHHH! "Are there others with you?"

John looked over at the metallic figure lying on the pavement.

"No, just me," he said, then almost as an afterthought, he added, "He's dead."

PSSSHHHH! "Repeat. Who is dead?"

Harry Davis, John thought. They don't know his name, though. He closed his eyes.

PSSSHHHH! "I repeat who is dead? Was it him? Was it him!?"

"Yes," John sighed.

"Did he say yes?" Walter asked Betsy, who stood beside him. Tears were rolling down her cheeks.

"Yes," she cried. Walter lifted the receiver to his mouth.

"Are you still there? Hello?"

There was no reply. Betsy wrapped her arms around Walter and wept into his chest.

"It's over," she cried. Walter held her close. It was okay now he wanted to say. He wanted to say something strong, something that gave finality to their struggle, but there was nothing. Instead, he felt hot tears run down his cheeks. He buried his face in Betsy's hair, and together they wept tears of joy and tears of pain.

THE RECEIVER FELL from John's hand. Behind his eyelids, a dim light began to shine. As it emerged from a cold darkness, the light was small and insignificant. The deeper John fell into the darkness, the brighter and larger the light grew. It was warm and inviting, like the sweet, soft glow of the sun rising behind a fog in the early morning.

LIKE A MIST, she walked out of the light, slowly taking shape as she moved closer. She was tall and slender as John remembered her. Her hair floated gently, golden brown waves cascaded around her shoulders. At her hand was Helena.

John ran to them. He no longer hurt; he felt young and full of life. Their arms were spread wide, and John fell into their embrace. He had never forgotten what this was like; he only ever tried to numb the pain of not being able to feel it.

Thank You For Reading!!

If you liked this title, why not take the time to let the author know by leaving a review on Goodreads and all your favorite retailers!

About the Author

Josh Magnotta is the author and publisher of the science fiction anthology Odd Dreams and an award-winning reporter for a small newspaper in rural Pennsylvania. His debut novel, A Sweet, Soft Glow was released in 2020. He continues to write and find inspiration in everyday life.

Find out more about Josh on his website and on Social Media:

Also by Josh Magnotta

Odd Dreams: A Science Fiction Anthology

Consider visiting the FyreSyde's website and sign up for the newsletter, where you can get early cover reveals, exclusive discounts, etc. on Josh's upcoming books and many more!

Other Titles By FyreSyde Authors

An exiled prince must return to his former home to retrieve his sister. Together they must overcome a ruthless ruler if they wish to save their homeland.

CPSIA information can be obtained
at www.ICGtesting.com
Printed in the USA
LVHW011050151220
674215LV00003B/142